"It was an accident, that's all it was."

Poppy's eyes filled with tears. There was no fighting them anymore. They were going to come, and they were going to stream down her cheeks, and they'd drip off her chin onto her collarbone, and she was relieved that she didn't have to swallow them back a second longer.

But before they could blur her vision, he suddenly took her face in his hands.

He looked at her mouth, and her heart beat against her rib cage so wildly that she thought she could feel its vibration in her toes. He leaned closer and she could see the flecks of gold in his eyes. The individual points of stubble on his jaw. Justin... How many times had she imagined a moment just like this when she was a girl? Too many times to count. But he was supposed to hate her. He was supposed to be cursing her, even now.

He wasn't cursing her, though. His hands were cradling her face. His thumbs were moving in soft arcs over her cheekbones, where the tears had spilled. He brushed them away with the ease of someone she'd known forever.

And then he kissed her.

Dear Reader,

What a joy it was to write this book, the very first in my Hearts on Main Street series! Within these pages, you'll meet the Sawyer cousins, who've inherited their grandfather's antiques shop in Christmas Bay. They all have their own reasons for staying away from the small coastal town where they grew up— pasts full of pain, trauma, regret. And old loves that they might not want to run into right around the corner...

But run into them they do, and what follows is the beginning of healing for them all. Back in Christmas Bay, in the little antiques shop on historic Main Street, the Sawyers' broken hearts will finally begin to heal. And open up to love again.

So curl up, get cozy and get ready to meet Poppy Sawyer and Justin Frost. I so hope that their story of overcoming a tragic past touches you, and makes you believe in the possibility and wonder of second chances.

Happy reading!

Kaylie Newell

FLIRTING WITH THE PAST

KAYLIE NEWELL

SPECIAL EDITION

SPECIAL EDITION™

Recycling programs
for this product may
not exist in your area.

ISBN-13: 978-1-335-40202-8

Flirting with the Past

Copyright © 2024 by Kaylie Newell

Harlequin Enterprises ULC
22 Adelaide St. West, 41st Floor
Toronto, Ontario M5H 4E3, Canada
www.Harlequin.com

Printed in U.S.A.

For **Kaylie Newell**, storytelling is in the blood. Growing up the daughter of two writers, she knew eventually she'd want to follow in their footsteps. She's now the proud author of over twenty books, including the RITA® Award finalists *Christmas at the Graff* and *Tanner's Promise*.

Kaylie lives in Southern Oregon with her husband, two daughters, a blind Doberman and two indifferent cats. Visit Kaylie at Facebook.com/kaylienewell.

Books by Kaylie Newell

Montana Mavericks: The Anniversary Gift

The Maverick's Marriage Deal

Harlequin Special Edition

Hearts on Main Street

Flirting with the Past

Sisters of Christmas Bay

Their Sweet Coastal Reunion
Their All-Star Summer
Their Christmas Resolution

Visit the Author Profile page
at Harlequin.com for more titles.

For my girls, Lucy and Clara.
The brightest stars in my universe.

Prologue

Justin Frost stood at the window of his hardware store on historic Main Street, and looked out the window. The ocean churned in the distance, the morning fog cloaking the shops in silvery mist. It would burn off by noon, leaving the little town warmer today than it had been yesterday. But that wasn't saying much—spring on the Oregon Coast was nothing less than frigid.

Roo, the scruffy black dog he had temporary custody of, walked over, her claws tapping on the hardwood floor, and butted her head into his hand. He looked down at her and rubbed her soft ears, feeling a strange sensation inside his chest. It wasn't quite sadness—Earl Sawyer had lived a full life, after all. But he was still gone, leaving an undeniable void in his wake. Justin hadn't intended to like him so much. But he had, and now there were promises that needed to be kept. Responsibilities that he couldn't walk away from, no matter how tempted he might be.

He looked at his watch as the dog sat and leaned into his leg in that way big dogs do. She'd be here any minute. She'd pull up to the curb in some kind of fancy car, because he was sure she wouldn't be driving anything practical. She was a celebrity. Or, at least, Christmas Bay's answer to a celebrity, which didn't amount to being very famous at all. She was on TV two nights a week, and that was all it took.

He felt himself slipping back to a place he hadn't let himself go in a long time. Back to when he was eighteen years old, grieving the loss of his little brother, and so angry that some days he thought that anger might eat him alive.

But it hadn't always been like that. Before the accident, before the anger, there had been other emotions. Feelings for a girl who hadn't been his, but whom he could've loved if things had been different. But they hadn't been different, and it was hard to believe he'd ever felt anything but bitterness toward her, and the life she'd gone on to live.

Right about the time the dog lay down on his foot with a groan, a sleek black car pulled up across the street in front of the antique shop that had been his friend Earl's pride and joy.

Justin watched as the driver's-side door opened, and a tall blonde stepped out. She was wearing off-white slacks, dark sunglasses and a long coat that was probably worth more than his entire wardrobe. She closed the door and locked it with her key fob. The car chirped like a giant bird.

Then she turned and gave a quick, uncomfortable glance toward the hardware store. He was sure she wouldn't be able to see him standing there, since he hadn't turned the lights on yet. It was impossible to tell what she might be feeling behind those sunglasses, but he could guess well enough.

She was back. And that was going to have serious implications for everyone.

Especially him.

Chapter One

Poppy Sawyer squared her shoulders. She was home. At least in the literal sense of the word. She still couldn't wrap her brain around the general sense—which brought to mind family, friends, neighbors. Most of whom probably hated her.

She looked around her grandfather's dusty antique shop and took a deep breath. The space smelled leathery, bookish, musty. And it smelled comforting, too, bringing back childhood memories from before the accident, before she'd gotten her license—when she'd walk to the shop on Saturday mornings to help her grandpa behind the counter. There were always tourists coming in and out, but the most interesting part of working here had always been the locals. Having them wander in and tell stories about how Christmas Bay used to be—who had lived here, who had moved on. The neighborhood chatter had always fascinated her. She guessed that's why she'd gone into the television business. She could never get enough *chatter*.

Turning, she looked out the ancient, double-paned windows to Main Street beyond. It was still early, but the shopkeepers were starting to come outside to water plants, shake out rugs and turn around their signs that read, Yes! We're open! in that cheerful Christmas Bay way they had.

Even the signs wanted you to stay a while. It had been a
long time since Poppy had felt like she could get comfortable anywhere. Let alone here. Too many memories. A
good deal of them so painful that she found she was having a hard time catching her breath, even now.

"Miss Sawyer," said a voice behind her, "are you ready?"

She turned around to see her grandfather's attorney, a
portly, balding gentleman named John Anderson, smiling
at her. She licked her lips, and smiled back. Not a genuine
smile—she was too numb for that. Her weekend-anchor
smile. The one that conveyed smooth, steady confidence,
even if the weather guy had just said a hurricane was form-
ing in the Atlantic.

"Ready," she said.

"Cora and Beau are waiting in the back office. Shall
we?"

Poppy felt like she was being led into a courtroom.
Actually, that wasn't too far off. She'd have to endure the
reading of her grandpa's will—he'd been a man whom
she'd loved with her whole heart, and whose death was
still as sharp as a knife in her stomach—all while sitting next to her cousins. Two people she'd once been so
close to, but who were now like polite strangers, if she
was being completely honest. After high school, her entire family had fractured apart like a piece of ice under
the blow of a mallet.

She followed John through the antique shop. Past old
typewriters with small, fluttery price tags attached. Past
creaky saddles and cracked bridles in the Western sec-
tion. Past miscellaneous clothing—dresses from the fifties, aprons from the twenties, baptismal gowns from

who-knew-when. Toward her grandfather's office, where she saw her cousins waiting.

Cora sat close to her young daughter, Mary. Beau stood in the corner, his arms crossed over his chest, his handsome face drawn and tired-looking. He'd never been one to show much emotion. They'd teased him when he was little. Tried to get him to laugh by holding him down and tickling him until he broke. Those had been the best days of Poppy's life.

Swallowing hard, she walked into the office, and smiled down at her niece as she passed. At almost eleven, Mary had the trademark Sawyer blond hair, and freckles scattered across her slightly upturned nose. She also had big green eyes that looked impossibly sad. Which made sense, since she was still struggling with the loss of her father. Or, her stepfather, to be more precise. That was another side effect of Poppy's career. Relaying accurate information was paramount above everything else.

Poppy pulled out a chair and murmured a hello to Beau, who nodded back somberly. Sitting, she smoothed out her slacks. There'd been a lump in her throat since Tuesday. Since John had called requesting her presence at the reading of the will. No parents present for this part, he'd said. This was only for the grandkids. The grandkids who'd been the light of his life, who'd always felt a special connection with the antique shop.

She missed her grandpa more than she could express. He was the one who'd helped her through the accident and the weeks following it, that even now she couldn't remember clearly. Her parents had fought constantly in the aftermath. Blaming each other, blaming God, blaming fate. Never blaming Poppy outright, but she'd felt it in her bones, anyway. It was her grandpa who'd been a beacon for her, as steady and true as the lighthouse on the edge of town.

Swallowing the lump, she let her gaze settle on John, who'd sat down at the desk to open a letter. Handwritten, of course. Her grandpa had never learned to use a computer very well, preferring a pen and paper for as long as she could remember.

Behind her, Beau cleared his throat. Maybe struggling with the same lump she was. Not that he'd show it, of course.

Beside her, Cora dabbed at her eyes with a tissue, Mary's skinny arm around her shoulders. John eyed all of them over his reading glasses, his face etched with emotion. Their grandpa hadn't just been a client, he'd also been a friend.

"Earl would be so happy to have you kids in the same room after all these years," John said. "As you know, the healing of this family was what he wanted most in his life. And it's that final wish that brings us here today."

Cora glanced over at Poppy, her eyes red-rimmed, her nose shiny. She'd always been a pretty girl, but she'd grown into a beautiful woman. She gave a small smile, and there was that familiar dimple at the corner of her mouth. And all of a sudden, Poppy was overcome with grief. With regret for how it had all turned out. They were finally in the same room, but they'd lost so much time together. She'd missed her cousins desperately.

John looked back down at the letter in his weathered hands. "Alrighty, then. Without further ado. 'Dear kids…'"

Poppy felt tears prickle the backs of her eyes. She could almost hear the letter being read in her grandfather's voice. *Come on, Poppyseed!* he'd say when he picked her up from her orthodontist appointments. *Let's get a donut!* Those mornings had been some of Poppy's favorites. Some of her most precious memories. She knew her cousins had the same kinds of memories. Their sweet grandpa. And now he was gone.

"'I know that my asking you here today probably came as a bit of a surprise,'" John went on, "'but I knew you wouldn't be able to deny me this last request.'"

Poppy looked over at Beau. His eyes, like Cora's, were glassy. He looked as close to breaking as she'd ever seen him. He'd been away from Christmas Bay for a long time. He was a sport fisherman who made a good living winning tournaments all over the country. But a recent accident had left him with a badly dislocated shoulder in need of surgery, and his fishing career had come to a screeching halt.

"'You're all aware that I have an estate,'" John continued, "'and that I plan on dividing it evenly between you and your parents. I'm not a rich man, but I know how to save money, and I've been lucky with a few investments over the years. So there's a decent amount. Enough to help change your lives, if that's what you want. Enough to help you get back on your feet.'"

Cora looked up at that. Tears were running down her cheeks now. She was a stay-at-home mom. She was also a new widow, with a daughter she'd have to send to college on very little savings and life insurance from her late husband. Poppy knew this inheritance, although heartbreaking, was probably coming at a helpful time for her cousin. A gift from their grandfather from beyond.

"'But I'll get to that in a minute,'" John said. "'Other than my family, I really only have two things that mean anything to me. Roo and the shop. It's my hope that Poppy might be able to take Roo, since she was the animal lover growing up.'"

Poppy stared at John, who glanced up over his glasses. "It's okay," he said. "He knew your work schedule might not allow for it." Looking back down at the letter, he went on. "'You haven't met her yet, but she's a good dog. Loves her walks, loves people. If you can't take her, I'd like her to go to a home of your choosing. Someone who will love her as much as I do. I've asked Justin Frost to take care of her until you get here, Poppy. I know that might come as a surprise to you, but he's become a good friend.'"

Cora leaned over and put a hand on Poppy's arm. "Are you okay?"

All the color must have drained from her face. Her feet were tingling, like they weren't properly attached, but she forced a smile just the same. "Fine. Just...processing."

"Are you sure Grandpa was in his right state of mind when he wrote this?" Beau asked.

It was a fair question, and one that prompted John to lower the letter for a second. "I can assure you he was. I think you'll find there were reasons behind his requests. Ones that might not seem clear to you at the moment, but will hopefully make sense as time goes on."

Poppy folded her hands in her lap and dug her nails into her palms. Hard. Her grandpa's reasoning behind this was already clear. He'd wanted her to heal. And he thought that Justin was vital to that healing. She'd need to talk to him when she took Roo, and that was more than she'd done in the last ten years. She'd be forced to face him again, and in the process, face what she'd done. Maybe come to terms with it, maybe not. Either way, it was a brilliant play by a man who'd spent the last years of his life trying to bring his family back together by any means necessary.

But, Justin? It just seemed like an impossible ask. So impossible, that her stomach felt sour. Her heart lumbered inside her chest, struggling for a normal rhythm. *Justin Frost.* She knew he and her grandfather had grown close. Justin owned Brothers' Hardware just across the street, and checked in on him often. But nothing could have prepared her for this. Absolutely nothing. And as she raised a hand to her temple, rubbing it at the sudden throbbing there, she wondered if Justin had had any idea it was coming, either.

"'The second thing,'" John went on, "'is the shop.'"

Cora released an audible breath, and Beau scrubbed a hand through his blond hair. Poppy leaned back in her chair and watched John set aside the first page of the letter, and pick up the second.

"'I know it means as much to you kids as it does to me,'" he said. "'I've thought about this long and hard, and selling it outright would be wrong. Not before you have time to really decide what you want to do with it. It's a cornerstone in this town. But, most importantly, it's your history. It's our family's history. You all have your own lives now, away from Christmas Bay. But I'm asking you to come home for one year, to run it together.'"

There was a gasp, and it took Poppy a second before she realized it had come from her. Her cousins were staring at John as if an alien had just crawled out of his skull.

"That's…there's no way that could work," Beau said. "Surely, he knew that."

John held up a hand, and continued reading. "'Before you decide not to do this—and it's absolutely your choice— I'd like you to think about it. It's not impossible. As I write this, you're all in a position to come home again. At least for a period of time. Poppy, you might have to make some concessions at work, get creative, but it wouldn't be the first time.'"

It felt like all the oxygen had been sucked out of the room. Poppy's head, which had been throbbing a minute ago, was now swimming. How could he ask this of them? But the answer was clear. He'd seen this as a way to bring them back together. The family breaking apart had been the biggest tragedy of his life. That was no secret. This request actually made perfect sense, when thinking about it from her grandfather's perspective. He'd had such a simplistic way of looking at life. *Not seeing enough of your family? No problem! Work together for a year, and it'll fix everything!*

Cora cleared her throat. "Um, Mr. Anderson—"

"John, please."

"John. I don't understand. Grandpa had to have known we'd need to move back to Christmas Bay in order to do this."

John nodded, his glasses slipping down his nose. "Yes, he knew that."

"And he knew how difficult that would be?"

"He knew it would be difficult emotionally. And he knew it was a big request. But he felt like it might be the last chance for you kids to form meaningful relationships again."

"We get along fine," Beau said.

Cora looked over at him. "You know what he meant."

"Yeah, I know what he meant. He wanted us to be inseparable, like when we were kids. But we aren't kids anymore. Things happen. Life happens. We all grew up." He shook his head, clearly frustrated. "Grandpa was the best man I ever knew…but I don't think I can do this. I'm trying to get back to fishing. How am I supposed to do that running an antique shop, for God's sake?"

Poppy couldn't believe she was about to open her mouth, because she felt the same way Beau did. She couldn't do it, either. How was she supposed to anchor a Portland news desk from Christmas Bay? Never mind that she'd been thinking of quitting for a while now. On the worst days, when she was the most unhappy, and feeling the most lost.

"The rivers here are incredible," she said. "You grew up fishing them. You could fish them again. At least for a year."

"But the tournaments aren't here, Poppy. And what about money? We're *all* supposed to live off the revenue from a tiny antique shop in Christmas Bay? Where are we supposed to live?" His face was getting red now. It was a lot to process.

"Your grandfather thought of that," John said.

They all looked over at him.

He began reading again. "'You'll each get a portion of your inheritance now, and the rest after the year is up. After that, if you want to sell the shop, that's okay. It's not for everyone, and you won't be letting me down by letting it go. But at least you'll be making a sound decision, not one made out of necessity or emotion. I love you all very much. Please try to understand why I'm doing this. Remember, family is everything. Much love, Grandpa.'"

John put down the letter and took off his glasses. "Well," he said. "There you have it."

The clock ticked on the wall above his head. Poppy glanced up at it. It was a plastic rainbow trout mounted on a piece of driftwood. Fairly cheesy, but it had been a Christmas present from Beau when he was twelve, and it had hung in their grandpa's office ever since, proudly displayed over his desk. Right then, the soft ticking sounded like sonic booms.

"I know you'll want to discuss this," John continued. "Take all the time you need. I have keys to the shop for each of you, as well as the apartment above it. I'm not sure how long it's been since you've seen it, but it's comfortably furnished. Two bedrooms and a sofa sleeper. Your grandpa had been renting it out, but it's been vacant since last summer."

Mary frowned. "Mom, are we moving here?"

"No," Cora said. "Well, I don't think so. I don't know. I need to talk to Aunt Poppy and Uncle Beau about it, okay? Why don't you go poke around in the shop for a while? There's lots of interesting stuff in there."

Mary stood there for another few seconds, her brow furrowed, before she finally wandered out the door.

John pushed back his chair and stood, his knees popping. "I'll leave you kids alone for a bit. I'm going to meet a few friends down at the donut shop for some coffee. I'll leave my card—just give me a jingle when you've had a chance to talk it over. I'm sure you'll have plenty of questions, so don't be afraid to call with them. I have Elks tonight, but I'll be available before and after."

He opened his battered leather briefcase, tucked the letter inside and snapped it shut again. Poppy thought that snap sounded very final. Suddenly, she felt like a little kid being dropped off at school for the first time. She had no idea what to do with herself.

John patted her on the shoulder. Nodded at Cora. Shook Beau's hand. And then he was gone.

Pinching the bridge of his nose, Beau walked over to the window and sat with a groan. "Oh, Grandpa. What the hell were you thinking?"

"He wanted us to be happy again," Cora said.

"I know. The money isn't important to me. I just loved him. But no matter what he said, I feel like *not* doing this would be letting him down."

"We all loved him," Poppy said. "But I think we have to be honest here…"

They both looked over at her with strained expressions on their faces.

"We could also use the financial help right about now."

Beau raised his eyebrows and glanced out the window. Her Mercedes was parked at the curb, clearly visible from where they sat.

Her cheeks warmed. "Leased. And the payments are killing me."

"You must be making good money at KTVL," Cora said.

"I'm making okay money. Not as much as you'd think. And I've got student loans up the wazoo. And the truth is…" She paused to collect herself. Other than her grandfather, she hadn't told a single soul what she was about to tell her cousins. She'd been too afraid to. And besides, it had seemed like an abstract idea at best. Nothing that would ever come to fruition. Until now. She thought of the words in her grandpa's letter… *Enough to help you change your lives…*

The room was so quiet, she thought she could hear the swoosh of blood in her ears. Her cousins were looking at her expectantly.

"The truth is," she said, her voice hoarse, "I've been thinking about leaving the station."

Cora's mouth hung open. Beau stared at her, clearly confused.

"What?" he said. "Why?"

She looked down at her hands. There was a chip in her new manicure. She was always supposed to look perfect on camera. But she wasn't perfect. She'd never been perfect, and she was tired of pretending she was.

"I've been unhappy for a while. Depressed, I guess, because of things I've never dealt with properly."

She knew she didn't have to go into any more detail than that. They knew what she meant. It was true, she was unhappy. And she didn't know if being back in Christmas Bay, back where she'd run into Justin every day, was going to help, but she had to try. What she'd *been* doing obviously wasn't working.

Cora reached out and put her hand on Poppy's knee. "I should've done a better job of keeping in touch. I'm sorry I haven't been there for you."

"You've had a lot going on, too."

"Recently. But I meant for all these years. I've been awful at keeping in touch with anyone."

"We all have," Beau said.

Poppy nodded. "I guess that's why we're here."

They were quiet then, the ticking of the fish clock the only thing filling the uncomfortable silence.

After a minute, Beau sighed. "Well, obviously we're going to need some time with this. I wasn't planning on going back to Eugene until tomorrow, anyway. Do you guys want to meet for dinner tonight to talk about it?"

Cora worried her bottom lip with her teeth. "Sure, we

can do that. Mary would love to stay overnight. We can walk on the beach, go to the lighthouse. We haven't been back in so long, what with Travis being sick. I meant to come see Grandpa last fall…" Her eyes welled with tears.

Travis, her late husband, had had a cruel, aggressive form of cancer. The time between his diagnosis and his passing had only been a few months. Not only was Cora still grappling with the loss, but she was also dealing with the shock of it. There were dark shadows underneath her eyes and fine lines around her mouth. Honestly, Poppy thought a little time in Christmas Bay might do her some good.

When Poppy had come home to see her grandfather in the past, the visits had always been short and cautious, because she hadn't wanted to run into Justin. But the first place she'd go—besides the donut shop for a maple bar, of course—was the beach. She'd never been able to get enough of the ocean, and its endless turquoise beauty. It had been a comfort when nothing else had.

She watched Cora now, full of empathy. She couldn't say she understood exactly how she felt, because she'd never lost a spouse before. But she'd experienced loss. Traumatic loss that she was still trying to get her mind around to this day. She knew how it could change someone's life. Take it in directions no one ever thought possible. Just look at her—she was sitting in her grandpa's antique shop, contemplating coming home again.

"Aunt Poppy?"

She turned to see Mary standing in the doorway, her baby fine hair tucked behind her ears.

"Yes, honey?"

"There's a man here to see you."

Poppy's stomach dropped. It was strange, but she knew who it was. She knew the same way she could tell a storm was coming. She could just feel it in the air.

Chapter Two

Justin stood just inside the antique shop's front door, not wanting to come any farther inside. This wasn't going to be easy. Baby steps would have to be enough for now. If he could stand to be in the same room with her again, he'd call that progress.

He waited while the girl walked toward the back office. Cute. She looked just like a Sawyer with that hair and the freckles. She had Cora's eyes. Once upon a time, he'd known Cora, too. He'd known all the Sawyers. He and Beau had been on Christmas Bay High's football team together. Those had been good times, simple times. And then his world had come crashing down, in the form of two uniformed police officers on his front step.

He dug his fists deeper into his pockets and felt the muscles in his shoulders tighten.

"Aunt Poppy?" He heard the girl's voice. "There's a man here to see you."

After a minute, she appeared in the doorway.

She stood there staring at him in her expensive pantsuit, with her freshly blown-out hair. She *looked* like she belonged on television. Poppy had been born for this. Always stunning, always popular. But she looked different than she had as a teenager, with her bouncy ponytail and mischievous smile. This Poppy was guarded. Her body language and the set of her mouth told him that all her defenses were up. As they should be.

Slowly, she began walking toward him. Her heels clicked on the hardwood floor. He could smell the faint scent of her perfume from where he stood. Something that made him think of summertime. Of flowers and honey. Of sitting outside and feeling the warmth of the sun on his bare skin.

She came to a stop a few feet away and swallowed visibly. He could see her pulse tapping at the base of her throat, where a simple strand of pearls lay. She was scared to death. But he wasn't in the mood to put her at ease. Somewhere deep down, where his pain was the sharpest, he wanted to watch her struggle.

After all, she'd been able to grow up. To wear pantsuits and drive fast cars, and make men heady with the scent of her perfume. His little brother hadn't been able to grow into anything. He'd died in an overturned hatchback with its muddy tires in the air. Justin could still picture it, sprawled out underneath the full moon, with the ocean waves thundering in the distance.

"It's been a long time," she said.

He thought her voice might've broken then, but he couldn't be sure. She might be hating this moment with all of her being, but she was also a professional. Trained not to show emotion under stress.

"It has," he said.

She stared up at him. Maybe waiting for accusations to start flying. Because they'd never really spoken again after that night. He'd left for college after graduation. And she'd left as soon as she'd been able to as well.

She turned and gestured toward the office. "We just... John just read us Grandpa's letter. I know he wanted me to take his dog."

Justin nodded. Roo was why he'd come over. He knew he'd have to deal with Poppy sooner or later, and he wanted to get it over with. But there would have to be introductions first, time for Roo to acclimate. Since Earl had passed, she'd grown wary of people, scared of things that hadn't bothered her before. Justin thought she simply missed her human. She was sad, just like the rest of them.

"I'll be honest," she said. "I don't know if I can have a dog right now. If I go back to Portland..."

He raised his eyebrows. *"If?"*

She looked away for a second. When she looked back, her face was a perfect mask again.

"I don't know if Grandpa told you what he was going to write in that letter?"

"He only told me about Roo," he said.

"Oh. Well...there's more. A lot more. And Beau, Cora and I need to figure out what we're going to do with Grandpa's estate."

"What about your parents?" he asked before he could think better of it. It was none of his business.

She made a dismissive motion with her hand. "My parents, Beau's, Cora's...they're scattered all over the country now. They barely talk. We've all kind of grown apart. But Grandpa wanted the cousins to be in charge of this part of his estate. We're really the only ones who ever came back after the... After the...uh..." Her voice trailed off. She clearly hadn't meant to get into this territory so soon. If ever.

"After the accident?"

"Yes. After the accident."

She couldn't look him in the eyes when she said it, and instead focused on a spot over his shoulder.

He stood there, his hands buried in his jeans pockets, his emotions churning. He used to hate her. He used to be in awe of her. He didn't know what he was now. He might never know, because she'd be leaving soon, and he'd probably never see her again. Earl was the only reason she'd come back to Christmas Bay. The last of the Sawyers would fade away, just as surely as the ocean mist would disappear before lunchtime.

"She's a good dog," he said, making sure his voice revealed nothing. "Comes when she's called, doesn't have accidents. But she'll need some time. I can't just hand her over to you. Since your grandpa passed, she's gotten fearful. She was left alone in the house after he had his heart attack and it was traumatic for her. If you decide you can't take her, I'll help find her a home. I owe Earl that."

"Thank you. I didn't even know he'd gotten a dog. He'd been talking about it for a while, but he never said anything. I've been so busy though…"

She frowned. There was guilt there—he recognized it immediately. She'd probably have a hard time with that. But he couldn't bring himself to feel sorry for her. She should've come home more often. Especially when Earl started not feeling well. Of course, there was the possibility she didn't know he hadn't been feeling well, but still. She should've been here. They all should've been here.

"Anyway," she said. "I'm sure she's a lovely dog."

He thought of the way Roo had looked up at him this morning, so adoringly. He'd take her himself, but he didn't have a yard, and he worked too much. Besides, Earl had wanted her with Poppy.

"I wanted to tell you," he said. "I'm sorry about Earl. He was a good man, a good friend to me. And I'll miss him."

"Thank you. I appreciate that."

A heavy silence settled between them. He'd already said more than he'd been planning to. Being in her general vicinity wasn't very comfortable, so he took a step backward, toward the door.

"Well," he said, "I should go. I have to open the store in a few minutes."

"Of course. Thanks for coming by."

"Let me know when you're ready to talk about Roo. We'll make it work, if that's what you want."

"Okay," she said. "I appreciate you keeping her for now."

These polite formalities were ridiculous. What he wanted to do was yell at her. Break something. Demand an answer. Why had she been speeding that night? *Why?*

But he didn't do any of those things. He just gave her one last look, with his chest so tight, it was hard to breathe.

And walked out the door.

Poppy stood at the window, watching him cross the street. Tall, broad-shouldered, impossibly handsome. Dark brown hair, warm hazel eyes. A stubbly jaw that was already going a little gray. It looked good on him. He'd grown into a man who'd make most women look twice. She hadn't seen a wedding ring. She wondered what Justin Frost's story was. What she knew about him wasn't much. Unlike her parents, his had stayed in Christmas Bay. They were well-liked, and had a lot of support here, so that made sense.

But her family? After the accident, they'd become pariahs. Her cousins had fiercely defended her, until the Sawyer name had become synonymous with heartache and drama. Whether people hated them as much as she'd felt like they had, she didn't really know. Poppy had finished high school, but only barely. She'd gone from a carefree, happy, cross-country standout, to a girl nobody recognized. She'd started hanging out with the wrong kinds of kids, had gotten into trouble that she almost hadn't been able to get out of. Her parents, fighting constantly about the accident, and dealing with the horrible, endless repercussions, had divorced. Nastily.

But by some kind of miracle, or more likely because her grandfather had refused to have it any other way, she'd applied with his urging to the University of Oregon, gotten accepted and had gone on to study journalism. It hadn't taken her long to realize that reporting the news made her feel like less of a story herself. As the years went on, she'd climbed the ladder, dealt with slimy bosses and unending harassment, and had eventually landed a weekend-anchor position. Sure, she had to fill in for other anchors and write copy during the week, but at the time it had felt like a real step up, and another step closer to realizing her dream of becoming the next Katie Couric.

But over the last year or so, it had become more and more apparent that running away from the trauma of that night wasn't going to solve anything. In fact, she seemed to be digging a bigger hole with all the denial. She'd been allowing herself to live in a fantasy world where she hadn't killed her boyfriend, and her family hadn't fallen apart afterward.

Poppy Sawyer was damaged goods. That's how she'd come to see herself. Damaged, broken, worthless. So when she'd told her cousins that she was depressed, she'd meant it. And she wasn't quite sure where to go from here.

She licked her lips with a tongue that felt as dry as a cotton ball, and watched as Justin walked back inside his hardware store and flipped on the lights. Like the antique shop, his storefront was part of Christmas Bay's historic Main Street. The building itself had been around since the late 1800s. Redbrick and two-story, it had cheerful black-and-white awnings over the windows. Coastal Sweets, Poppy's favorite candy shop as a kid, was right down the street, and Mario's, the best pizza place in town, was only a stone's throw from that. The small police department was a block down in the opposite direction, along with the fire department, which looked like it belonged on a Christmas card. The chief even parked an antique fire truck out front over the holidays. The only thing missing was the Dalmatian in the front seat.

If a person stood just right, they could catch a glimpse of the rocky beach in between the buildings, the ocean choppy and blue-gray this morning. Seagulls dipped and bobbed on the misty breeze, their squawking reminding her of home. Reminding her of simpler times, when she'd been a simpler person.

Justin turned the sign around in his window, and propped the door open, probably for a bit of fresh, sea air. Crossing her arms over her chest, Poppy shivered slightly, thinking about what had just happened. She'd talked to him. They hadn't said anything significant, but they'd stood a few feet apart, and exchanged actual words. Before this morning, she wouldn't have been able to imagine that kind of scenario. But before this morning, she couldn't have imagined a lot of things. Much less the possibility of actually staying here. Where things had begun for her. And where they'd ended.

"Who was that, Aunt Poppy?"

She startled at the sound of Mary's voice behind her. She turned and pulled the girl into her side. Mary was tall for her age, with long, gangly arms and legs. She'd probably go through an awkward phase as a preteen. But if she took after her mother, she'd grow into those legs and then some. And then she'd have to fight off the boys with a stick, as her grandpa used to say.

"Just someone I used to know," Poppy said. "Someone I haven't seen in a long time."

"I heard Uncle Beau say he hates us. Why would he hate us?"

So Cora hadn't told her. It was an upsetting story, and one that Mary probably wouldn't understand at only ten years old.

Sharing the tragic details wasn't something Poppy wanted to tackle right now. Her head was so foggy, her heart so bruised. She just needed a cup of coffee.

"He doesn't hate us," Poppy lied. "But it's complicated."

"I asked Mom. She won't tell me anything. I don't know why—I'm not a baby."

"I know you're not. And she doesn't think you are. But protecting you is her job. She's just doing her job."

"She didn't even tell me that Dad was sick until—until…" Her voice broke.

Poppy hugged her. Technically, they were cousins, but she had a long-distance-aunt relationship with Mary. She sent cards with money in them for her birthday. She'd call on Thanksgiving and Christmas. But when it came to truly knowing her niece, and what she'd been through recently, Poppy realized she didn't know anything.

"I'm sorry, honey," she said. "All I can tell you is that your mom loves you very much. And she's doing her best."

After a few seconds, Mary pulled away and wiped her eyes. "Yeah…"

"You know, I think Grandpa kept some hard candy behind the cash register. Would you like a piece?"

She nodded. "Yes, please… Do you think I can meet his dog?"

Poppy's stomach sank. She kept forgetting about Roo. What in the world was she going to do about that? Her grandpa was right—she'd been the animal lover growing up. But she hadn't had a pet, not even a fish, since high school. She wasn't equipped for a dog, emotionally, or otherwise. But this wasn't just any dog. Besides the antique shop, Roo was the last link she had to her grandfather.

"Oh, you know, Mary, I'm not sure how long we're going to be here…"

Mary looked down at her shoes, one of which was untied, and Poppy's heart melted. Justin had been civil. Maybe he'd be okay with a visit later this afternoon. All of a sudden, she just wanted to see a smile on her niece's freckled face. There was such sadness hanging in the air. Some puppy love might go a long way.

She touched Mary's chin. "I'll see what I can do, okay?"

Justin finished ringing up a customer, a young woman who was in the middle of painting her toddler's ceiling. She had paint in her hair, under her fingernails. Even some speckles of it on her eyelashes.

He handed over the half gallon of robin's-egg blue. "Just

call if you need any more, and I can have it mixed by the time you get here."

She smiled. "How late are you open?"

"Until six."

"Okay, thanks so much."

Then she was out the door with a wave of her paint-speckled hand, and the store was empty again. Which wasn't great, because that only gave him more time to think about Poppy. And extra time thinking about Poppy wasn't what he needed.

He looked at Roo in her crate. She was lying down, her big head on her paws, looking back at him. She'd been so quiet this morning that he was tempted to let her out.

He scanned the shop. It was only the two of them in the store at the moment, so what could it hurt? He walked over and unlatched the wire door to the crate. Her tail thumped against the side, and she lifted her head, watching him with those big, caramel eyes.

"Hey, baby," he said. "Want to come out for a few minutes?"

She got to her feet and shook, sending her tags into a cacophony of jingles.

"I'll take that as a yes."

She stepped out and trotted around the store, sniffing every corner.

"Uh-oh. Do you have to go potty?"

Stopping at that question, she cocked her head and pricked her ears. One stood straight up, and the other collapsed over one eye. She was pretty damn cute. Earl had been planning on doing a doggy DNA test on her, but had never gotten around to it. She was an Irish-wolfhound mix of some sort. Maybe some Lab thrown in for good measure. She was black, and had wiry fur, tinged with gray at the ends. Her legs were roughly a mile long, and she had to weigh close to a hundred pounds. Too much dog for a lot of people, but she'd always been well-behaved. Earl had never had a problem with her pulling on the leash or running off.

He wondered if Poppy was even in a place that allowed dogs. He had no idea if she rented or owned, or if she was home enough to realistically consider this. The fact that he'd need to find all this out was unsettling. Just being around her for five minutes this morning had been stressful enough. How was he supposed to work out the handover of the dog without losing his mind in the process?

At that thought, the front door opened with a blast of salty air. Grabbing Roo's collar, he looked up to see his mother walk in.

"Justin?"

She glanced around and untied a bright red scarf from around her hair. She had natural curls, so the use of the scarf on misty mornings was a common occurrence.

"Back here, Mom," he said. "Behind the plumbing supplies."

Frowning, she craned her neck toward the sound of his voice. "What are you doing back there?"

"Roo is out. I had to grab her when you came in."

"Oh," she said tightly.

Evelyn Frost didn't used to be as chilly as her last name implied. She'd once been the quintessential stay-at-home mom to Justin and his little brother, Danny. She'd baked cookies after school, taken them to their sporting events and back-to-school nights. And she'd done it all with a smile on her beautiful face.

She was the kind of parent his friends had been jealous of. She was always around, always supportive of her kids. Which was a good thing, because their dad hadn't been home much. A well-known attorney in town, with his sights set on one day becoming a judge, he hadn't had much time for after-school events. He'd left most of those details to his wife.

But then, all that had changed. And life as Justin knew it had come to an end, and a new life began. One where his mother stopped coming to his games, or having much of anything to do with him at all, really. He'd stopped being Justin, and had started becoming the son who'd lived. The problem was, most of the time he didn't feel like he deserved to be here when Danny wasn't.

She set her keys on the counter. "Roo," she said evenly. "Earl's dog?"

Justin walked back over to the crate and opened the door. "Sorry, girl," he said under his breath. "She hates dogs."

He tugged on Roo's collar, and she responded by stiffening her legs. Justin tugged harder, and after a few seconds she went reluctantly inside. Which was a good thing, since he had no idea how he would've forced her.

He latched the door, then turned to his mother, who was watching him with a disapproving look on her face.

"What?"

"Nothing," she said. "I just can't believe you agreed to this. Wasn't there someone else who could do it?"

"Earl didn't want someone else to do it, he wanted me. And I don't mind. She's a good dog." He looked down at Roo. "Aren't you?"

She thumped her tail against the crate.

His mother huffed, refusing to acknowledge his words.

Instead, she held on to the purse that was slung over her shoulder with an iron grip.

"I was on my way to the gym," she said. "And I wanted to stop by to see if you're free for dinner tonight."

"That depends."

"On what?"

"On if you're trying to set me up again."

"Honestly, Justin. I don't know what you're talking about."

"You forget how small this town is. People talk."

She inspected her nails. "I'm not trying to set you up. But if I *were* trying to set you up, I don't see anything wrong with that. You're almost thirty and I want grandkids."

"Mom. Please."

He'd had exactly one serious relationship since college that he'd basically sabotaged because marriage had been off the table for him. Sasha had wanted a family, and he'd had no interest. He'd seen what could happen to kids on a regular, run-of-the-mill evening. No, he liked his life the way it was. Unattached and uncomplicated.

His mom shrugged. It didn't matter how often he asked her not to, she was going to keep pushing. And he guessed he couldn't blame her for that. He had a feeling this obsession with grandkids was more about trying to fill some of the emptiness that Danny had left behind. And there wasn't going to be any filling that. Even with fifty grandkids.

His mother looked out the window, to where Poppy's car was parked, and her expression changed. It hardened, her lips growing thin.

He thought about what he'd said a minute ago—people did talk in a town this small. So odds were that she knew exactly whose car that was. And that the reason for this visit might not have anything to do with inviting him to dinner. It might have more to do with a morbid curiosity that she couldn't help.

He took a step toward her with his hands in his pockets. "Are you okay?"

"Of course," she said. "Why wouldn't I be?"

He watched her for a few seconds.

"Because I thought you might know that Poppy Sawyer is in town. For the reading of Earl's will."

She continued looking out the window, deathly still. "How nice for her. She gets an inheritance. Why doesn't *she* take the dog?"

Her voice was so bitter. *Stop already!* he wanted to shout. *Just. Stop.*

But that would make him a damn hypocrite, wouldn't it? Because he hadn't been able to stop blaming Poppy, either.

"She's thinking about taking her," he said. "She just needs time to figure things out first."

His mother turned. Her hazel eyes were cold. She'd always been such a pretty woman, but anger had aged her. She looked much older than she actually was.

"You talked to her?" she asked.

"This morning."

This made her mad, he could tell. But the fact was, he was going to have to talk to Poppy about Roo. He'd have to interact with her on some level. Maybe, deep down, he felt like that was the only way forward out of this place where they'd all been mired for so long, and where his mother seemed to be stuck, struggling and miserable.

"I can't believe you," she whispered.

"Earl asked me to take care of Roo until Poppy can

take her. I have to communicate with her. I can't do it by osmosis."

Her lips, which had been thin before, practically disappeared.

"I'm sorry, Mom. I know this is hard for you."

She crossed her arms over her chest. "All this time, I never said anything about your friendship with Earl Sawyer..."

Justin bristled. "Because my friendship with him didn't have anything to do with Poppy."

"I never *said* anything because it wasn't his fault. But how can you speak two words to her? I don't care about the dog. I don't care about any of that."

Justin had spent a lot of time watching his mother hate the Sawyer family. Years. To the point where she and his dad had drifted apart, her fury coming between them like a brick wall. They'd stayed married, but they barely spoke anymore. And he couldn't say he'd dealt with the tragedy any better. But watching her now, with such disdain on her face...it did something to him. It broke his heart.

What was he supposed to say? She thought he'd broken the cardinal rule. Betrayed Danny by acknowledging Poppy's existence. He knew there was nothing he really *could* say.

But he took a deep breath, anyway. "Mom..." he began quietly.

She looked over. She'd been gazing at the car again. As if the ghost of her youngest son might be hovering near it.

"Have you thought about how young they were?"

She stared at him. "What do you mean?"

"I mean, they were just seventeen."

Her cheeks flushed. "I know how old they were, Justin. What are you getting at?"

"I'm saying, they were kids. Poppy was just a kid. And I get it—I haven't been able to reconcile it, either. But maybe—maybe..."

"Maybe *what*?"

He recognized her posture, the way she was holding herself, so stiff and unyielding. In those first few years after the accident, she'd stood like this and stared out the kitchen window for hours at a time. Justin would walk into the room and say something to her, and it had been as if she was in a trance. She hadn't heard him. Or hadn't wanted to hear him.

Because he was the one who'd lived.

"Maybe it's time," he continued, "to let some of this go."

"Let some of this *go*? Did I hear that right?"

He couldn't believe he'd said it, either. He rubbed the back of his neck, and tried again.

"You know, this morning when I saw her, I wanted to lash out at something, anything. I've been thinking about it ever since, that feeling. Don't you think there's something wrong with feeling like that? That I don't feel any different after all this time?"

"So what are you saying?" she snapped. "That we should run over there and make friends? Tell her it's okay that Danny isn't here anymore, but she is? She might've been seventeen, Justin, but don't forget she was speeding."

"I know. But it was also raining."

"The police said speed might've been a factor. Just because they never charged her doesn't mean—"

"But it does, though. It was an accident. The tire blew."

"*Enough*. Enough with the excuses."

"These aren't excuses, Mom. They're facts. And sometimes I feel like—"

He stopped short, because he didn't really know what he wanted to say. He felt like what? That losing his brother at such a young age had left him empty, and guilt had threatened to turn him inside out ever since.

"You want to move on." Her voice was like ice. Or more like an ice pick. She wasn't making this any easier.

"I want to heal."

"By forgiving her?"

"I didn't say that." But, of course, that's what made the most sense. He knew that. He'd known that all along. But what he didn't know was if it was truly possible. He had no idea where to start, no idea how to unburden himself of this weight that had rested on his shoulders for so long.

She narrowed her eyes at him. "Well, you go ahead. Let me know how that goes for you."

"Mom…"

"No, no." She held up a hand. "I'm late for the gym. I'm going to meet Jessie for yoga. Call and let me know if you can make it tonight."

"Don't be mad," he said.

"I'm not mad."

That was the thing. They'd all been so mad for so long, it was simply part of the fabric of their lives. Wrapping them up, cloaking them in its scratchy fibers.

As he watched his mother walk out the door, he wondered if letting the anger go might make his world a little softer.

Maybe it would. He really didn't know.

Chapter Three

Poppy walked through the apartment above the antique shop, her heels thudding hollowly on the hardwood floor. It was rustic, like she remembered, but her grandpa had it cleaned up nicely. It actually sparkled now.

Like John had said, there were two bedrooms and a pullout couch. Plenty of room for the three of them to live together, if that's what they chose to do. Well, the three of them and Mary, who was exploring all of the rooms, her eyes as big as saucers.

Poppy couldn't blame her. The antique shop alone was an endless source of entertainment. She remembered losing herself for entire weekends at a time, looking through the things on the shelves, the things in the back room that her grandpa hadn't had time to sort through yet. It was like a museum, only everything was for sale.

When she was little, the apartment above the shop had been rented out a good portion of the time. There were a few college students over the years, a couple who were building a house, and her favorite tenant ever, a sweet retiree named Rose, who had a chihuahua named Bean.

But there were times in between when it was vacant, and she'd been able to spend time up here with her cousins. Reading, watching TV, playing board games. What she remembered most was the orange shag carpet from the seventies, and the wood paneling on the walls. The wood paneling was still there, but the carpet was gone. The wood floors had recently been refinished, and they practically glowed in the morning light.

There was a simple kitchen, with a window over the sink that overlooked the harbor in the distance. No dishwasher, of course. A standard-size fridge, that was probably too big for the space, but that would come in handy if there was more than one person living here. The entire place was furnished in old, mismatched pieces from the fifties and sixties. Poppy had a great eye for furniture, and could usually tell with pinpoint accuracy which era it was from and how much it was worth. A by-product of having a grandfather in the antique business.

There was a green-and-yellow crocheted blanket draped over the couch that looked like it had come from one of the Christmas bazaars at the Methodist church. It was a sweet, cozy space. But she still couldn't wrap her mind around the thought of living here with her cousins. How could they make it work, when they'd have to turn their lives upside down to do it?

But then she remembered the words in her grandpa's letter. She guessed turning their lives upside down was the whole point.

Mary leaned over the sink and peered out the window. "There's a fire escape outside!" she said. "And you can see the boats from here!"

Poppy smiled and walked over to where her niece stood on the tiptoes of her Skechers.

"Yup. On Christmas Eve, this is a perfect place to watch the Flotilla of Lights. When all the fishing boats are lit up with lanterns. You don't even have to get out of your PJs to do it."

"Did you live here when you were little?"

"No, Grandpa usually had it rented out. But there were a few Christmases when it was empty, and your mom, Uncle Beau and I would have sleepovers up here."

"That must've been fun," Mary said wistfully.

Poppy looked down at her, remembering Cora saying once that Mary had terrible anxiety, even going through a period of time when she'd pulled her eyelashes out. She'd been seeing a counselor, but the urge waxed and waned with the stresses in her life. Poppy couldn't imagine how the trauma of losing a parent would affect any child, much less one with such acute anxiety.

She reached down and brushed Mary's hair away from her face. "It *was* fun," she said. "But it wasn't always perfect."

Mary frowned, gazing out the window. "But you had each other. You probably got to hang out and play all the time."

"Yes, but we fought a lot, too. Has your mom told you that?"

"A little."

"Well, we did. And your Uncle Beau cheated at cards." That made Mary smile.

"He did," Poppy said. "*Shameful* cheater."

Mary pushed away from the counter. "What are you going to do about the dog?" she asked. "About Roo?"

"Oh… I'm not sure, honey. I'm going to have to think about it. I'm not really prepared for a dog right now."

"But she was great-grandpa's dog."

The words made Poppy's heart twist. At ten, things were

clearer than when someone was almost thirty. Especially when you were almost thirty and lugging around major baggage. "That's true, she was."

"And that man is keeping her? The one across the street?"

Poppy nodded.

"Can we go see her?"

"Oh, honey. I don't—"

"Please?"

Poppy looked at her watch. Although, she had no idea why. She had nowhere to go, nowhere to be.

"I…" she began. But couldn't for the life of her think of a good excuse.

Mary waited, gazing up at her with those moss-green eyes. She thought about how hard her niece had had it.

Poppy exhaled as Cora walked into the room.

"It's just like I remembered," her cousin said. "Isn't it?"

It was better. Because the memory of their grandpa was here, and that made everything better.

"Cora," she said, "Mary wants to say hello to Roo. Do you mind if I take her across the street for a few minutes?"

Cora raised her eyebrows. She'd probably expected Poppy to hide from Justin for as long as possible, and she'd expected to hide from him, too. But she simply couldn't say no to Mary, and that's what it all came down to.

"I don't mind," Cora said, then lowered her voice and asked, "But are you sure you're up for this?"

"Honestly? No."

"So we can go?" Mary asked, clearly beside herself.

"Meet you downstairs, kiddo."

Beaming, Mary made a beeline for the door.

"What are we going to do about the shop, Poppy?" Cora asked, watching her daughter go.

"I don't have the faintest clue."

"Aunt Poppy!" Mary called from downstairs. "Come on!"

"Thank you for taking her. She's been so quiet lately. I'm surprised she asked you."

"I'm glad she did."

"Even though it means having to see Justin again?"

Poppy thought about that for a minute. Let the words settle into her consciousness. "Maybe it's a sort of punishment," she said. "For what I did."

Cora frowned. "Poppy…"

"Aunt Poppy!" Mary called again.

"I'll let you know how it goes. Pray for me," she added dryly.

When she got downstairs, Mary took her by the hand and tugged her toward the front door, where light was streaming in through the smudged glass.

They stepped out onto the sidewalk, and Poppy looked over at the hardware store with a bundle of nerves in her belly. She held a hand up to shield her eyes from the sun, the warmth of which felt good after the chill of the morning.

Mary stepped off the curb, but Poppy quickly pulled her back.

"You have to look both ways!" she said. "That's dangerous."

Mary bit her lip, her cheeks flooding with color.

"I'm sorry, honey. But I don't want you to get hurt."

That was the understatement of the century. Ever since the accident, Poppy had been acutely aware of all the bad things that could happen on a seemingly normal day.

"Let's go down to the crosswalk, okay?" she said, trying to lighten her tone.

Mary nodded, and they walked down the sidewalk hand in hand, passing tourists clutching their morning coffees and shopping bags full of treasures. The sea air was tangy and cool, and she pulled it into her lungs, trying to forget where they were heading, so she could enjoy the moment.

And then she looked up, and all of a sudden, they were almost there. The hardware store looked much sharper and more ominous up-close than it had from across the street, where distance had dulled it some. Even the name implied something deeper and more meaningful than just a place to pick up some gardening supplies on a Sunday afternoon.

She remembered Justin and Danny were already talking about opening a hardware store when they were teens. An ordinary dream for two boys to have, but they'd been sweetly adamant about it when their friends had laughed. Justin would do the books, and Danny would take care of the customers. And now, there was only one brother left to do both. But Justin had honored Danny's memory with the name posted above the awning. Brothers' Hardware.

Mary looked up, sensing her hesitation. "What?"

Poppy could feel her pulse tapping in her neck, reminding her that despite feeling frozen, she actually wasn't. She was a living, breathing person who was temporarily paralyzed out here on the sidewalk, underneath the hanging baskets still dripping from their morning watering. She'd finally come back to Christmas Bay. And she was going to have to deal with what she'd done.

She forced a smile at her niece. One of her numb ones. She was so good at those. "Just thinking, that's all."

"About what?"

"A lot of things. Justin, for one."

"We don't have to go if you don't want to," Mary said.

It was the sweetest thing, because she could tell Mary was dying to go in. They were *thi-i-is* close to Roo, and the excitement in her eyes was almost palpable.

"No, I want to," she said. "I'm just…"

Preparing myself? She'd already seen him once this morning, and she'd survived. He hadn't hurled insults at her, or told her what a horrible person she was. He'd been perfectly polite, if a little chilly. And who could blame him?

So, really, there was no amount of preparation that would help here. She was just going to have to get used to being uncomfortable. She was going to have to get used to having her defenses up, and keeping them there. But for how long, exactly? Was she going to stay in Christmas Bay long enough to fulfill her grandpa's wish of running the antique shop with Beau and Cora? Or would she go back to Portland, back to a job that she wasn't altogether sure she wanted anymore? One that had been a convenient way to distance herself from her own reality for a while. She just didn't know.

Mary squeezed her hand, and Poppy looked up to see a woman in workout clothes walking toward them. She had on sunglasses and a red scarf over her hair.

Poppy's heartbeat slowed, becoming a painful series of thumps against her ribcage. She was vaguely aware of a sharp ringing in her ears, of Mary's voice sounding far away. Her niece was asking again if she was okay. But this time, she wasn't. She wasn't okay at all.

Because the woman walking toward them was Evelyn Frost. Danny's mother. The same woman who used to call her *baby doll* and *sweetheart*, and who used to brush her hair away from her face and ask if she wanted more lemonade. At one point, Evelyn had been like a second mother to her. Poppy had been as comfortable at Danny and Justin's house as she'd been at her own. But then Danny had died, and Evelyn, who'd once said Poppy was like a ray of sunshine in their lives, had cut her out of them as precisely as if she'd done it with a razor blade.

She watched Evelyn approach, her strides long and purposeful, and realized that she was praying the other woman wouldn't recognize her. *Please, please, please...* She prayed to God she'd just keep walking past in a cloud of perfumed air and grim energy, that she wouldn't see Poppy at all.

But as fate would have it, God had better things to do.

Evelyn slowed, and swiped off her sunglasses. Her lovely eyes narrowed. She'd aged considerably since Poppy had seen her last, but she was still a striking woman.

Poppy stood there, unable to move, unable to blink. She felt like she might suffocate, and wondered briefly if someone could actually die from anxiety. She didn't think so. But she knew what a panic attack felt like. It *felt* like she might die. And that's the thought that kept running through her head as Mary squeezed her hand again. *This is it. I'm going to die...*

"*Well,*" Evelyn breathed.

People brushed by on the sidewalk, but Poppy barely noticed. Neither, it seemed, did Evelyn. For them, the world had come to a complete, jolting stop.

"Hello, Mrs. Frost," Poppy said. She didn't sound like herself. She sounded sick. Like her voice wasn't working right because she had a terrible, life-threatening illness. She thought she'd rather face an illness than this woman who was regarding her with such hostility.

"You look good," Evelyn said, her tone cutting. "You've

done well for yourself. I'm so happy your career worked out."

Poppy's throat ached. She fought for composure and tried swallowing, but couldn't get her muscles to cooperate.

"Danny never had a chance to have a career," Evelyn said. "Or anything else, for that matter. You remember he wanted to open the hardware store with Justin?"

She had to know Poppy remembered. The question was simply a weapon used to inflict pain.

"I think about what he would've been," the other woman continued. It looked like she might cry, and Poppy hoped that she wouldn't. If she started crying, Poppy's legs wouldn't be able to hold her up anymore. She pictured herself collapsing onto her knees in a fit of hysterics, begging Evelyn's forgiveness, while tourists stepped neatly around her.

"I think about him, too, Mrs. Frost," she said. "All the time."

"I hope so. I hope you think about him every day."

"I do."

"I just can't get past it."

"You can't…"

"I can't get past that you're here. And Danny—"

That did it. Evelyn's voice hitched. And Poppy's eyes filled with tears.

"Mom."

Poppy's gaze shifted to the blurry form of a man walking up behind Evelyn. Slowly, he came into focus. It was Justin.

"You forgot your keys," he said, touching his mother's arm. "What are you doing?"

She jerked away. "What are *you* doing, Justin? Why

aren't you angrier that she's here? Right in front of your store?"

Poppy felt like she'd overheard someone talking about her in the next room. Her face filled with heat, and her stomach turned.

Without another look at either of them, Evelyn snatched the keys from her son and stormed past.

Poppy watched her go. It was stupid to think that she could do this. Drop in on Justin like they were old pals or something, and she'd just been away a few years.

Justin stood there looking down at her. She felt his judgment all the way to her bones.

"I'm so sorry," she said quietly. She knew that if she lived to be a thousand years old, she'd never be able to say it enough.

Mary was still holding her hand. And if she hadn't had those soft little fingers grounding her right then, she might've just flown away. Up, up, into the atmosphere, past the curving blue horizon, and into the darkness of space. Maybe that's where Danny was. Maybe he was judging her from there, too.

She glanced down at Mary. "Let's go, honey, okay?"

"Okay," Mary said. She was clearly disappointed, but she was also clearly concerned about her. She could probably feel the trembling in Poppy's hand.

"I'm sorry about that," Justin said. "About my mother. She can't help it."

There were fine lines around his eyes. Around his mouth, which was set in a hard line.

"It's fine," she said.

They stood there looking at each other, as cars passed by on Main Street, as tourists walked by, unaware of the electricity crackling between them. Of the tension in the air that felt so thick, it could be sliced with a knife.

"Um," she said. Her voice was a dull croak, and she swallowed and tried again. "I was thinking about what you said about Roo. You're right. We should probably talk about that soon. Make a plan..."

She could feel Mary watching them, curious. As far as Poppy was concerned, the sooner they could talk about it, the sooner they could get down to ignoring each other. But even as she thought it, she wondered how she could ever ignore a man like Justin. Sexy, dark, brooding Justin. It seemed impossible.

"When were you planning on going home?" he asked.

Home. Obviously, he was talking about Portland. But for a second, she was confused, wondering what he meant. She *was* home.

It wasn't until right then that she realized how much she'd missed Christmas Bay, because she simply hadn't allowed herself to miss it. But now that she was here, now that she was breathing in the salty air, and feeling the dampness of it on her skin, she realized what a hole it had left in her life.

"I'm not sure," she said. "I'm taking some bereavement leave... I could meet you for coffee tomorrow morning?"

He nodded solemnly. He wasn't going to pretend to look forward to that. Which was fine. She'd look forward to it about as much as getting a tooth pulled. But it was what it was. He was right, they needed to talk about Roo, and get that sorted out. And that might end up with Poppy having to take her to a shelter. She didn't want to be indebted to Justin any more than she already was, and she didn't have an endless amount of time to try to find Roo another home.

She knew Christmas Bay's shelter was no-kill, and she'd be taken good care of there until she found another family. Poppy wouldn't allow herself to think about what her grandpa would say. She'd just have to turn that part of her brain off in order to get through the next couple of days, and deal with the guilt later.

"I can do that," he said. "Before nine? That's when I open the store."

"Sure."

"How about Donut Country? They have pretty good coffee."

Most people referred to the only donut shop in town as just that—the donut shop. Justin was bucking tradition by using its proper name. It had good coffee, but its maple bars were the best around. Poppy wondered if Justin remembered how much she loved donuts. They were her kryptonite.

"Sounds good," she said, giving Mary's hand a squeeze. She'd have to explain all of this later, but for now, she just wanted more space between her and Justin Frost. Being this close wasn't doing her nerves any good. She needed to take a deep breath, and it seemed like she hadn't been able to breathe at all since he'd appeared.

"Okay," he said. "I'll see you about eight thirty then?"

"Eight thirty."

He gave her a curt nod, smiled down at Mary and then walked away. Poppy stared after him.

"You're going to talk about Roo?" Mary asked.

It took Poppy a second to realize she was talking to her. "Yes, honey."

"Do you think you'll take her?"

"I'm not sure."

"Maybe we can take her."

Poppy knew Cora was even less prepared for a dog than she was. But she wasn't going to tell Mary that. She just gazed down at her niece, hoping that someday she'd understand all of this.

"Have you ever been to Coastal Sweets?"

Mary shook her head.

"Well, it's just about *the* best candy shop on the West Coast."

Mary smiled, the gap in her front teeth on full display. Poppy exhaled, relieved that the subject of Roo was behind them for the time being.

"What do you say we go check it out? It's only a few shops down, and we can even bring your mom and Uncle Beau something back. The lady who owns it is really nice. I used to go there when I was your age."

"Okay."

And with that, they headed down the sidewalk again, hand in hand, with Mary talking about her favorite kind of candy, and Poppy thinking about the man who still had the power to stop her heart.

Chapter Four

Poppy sat in one of the worn-out booths inside Mario's pizza parlor, and looked out the window to the ocean beyond. The sun was just making its fiery descent toward the water, touching it and turning it a sparkling orange-gold. There were a few tired-looking fishing boats in the distance, chugging their way back toward the harbor, their jobs done for the day.

Poppy looked at her watch. She was early, but she hadn't known what to do with herself back at the motel. Her room had felt lonesome and cold, and she'd been tired of pacing a hole in the flower-print carpet. So she'd pulled up to Mario's a half hour before she was supposed to meet Cora and Beau, the memories of coming here as a kid thick in her mind. It had been her favorite pizza place. Then again, it had been everyone's favorite pizza place. There'd been vintage video games in the corner, and every booth faced the water. Families had come here after soccer games, her friends had had their birthday parties here and she could almost hear their long-ago laughter ringing in her ears, like small ghosts dancing around her consciousness.

Mario's was one of those rare places in Christmas Bay she could still visit without hesitation, because nothing sad had ever happened to her here. Nothing difficult. When she'd eaten at Mario's as a teen and preteen, her family had still been intact, her life had been untouched by tragedy. So she not only liked the pizza, but she also liked the energy. Beau and Cora might wonder why she'd picked it over some of the nicer restaurants in town, but she could just say she thought Mary would like the video games. No need to go any deeper than that.

The door opened with a cool blast of sea air. Beau walked in, broad shoulders hunched, his blond hair blown all over the place. After taking off his sunglasses, he looked around, and when he saw Poppy sitting there, he smiled. It was a small smile, but it was more than she'd seen from him all day. It was comforting, that smile. Like Mario's, it brought back memories of better times.

She watched him walk over and slide into the booth across from her with a sigh.

"I knew you'd be here early," he said.

"I've been a little edgy this afternoon. I can't sit still."

"Me too."

"Have you heard from Cora?"

"She'll be here in a few minutes. Pizza was a good call. I guess Mary is a bit of a picky eater." He scrubbed a hand through his hair and looked around. "Hasn't changed much, has it?"

"It hasn't changed at all."

His gaze settled on her again, and he leaned back in the booth. "I keep going over it and over it. I still can't believe Grandpa did this."

Poppy knew exactly what he meant. Ever since this morning, since John had read their grandfather's letter, she'd felt like she'd been walking around in a dream. The only thing that had jolted her temporarily out of it was the run-in with Evelyn Frost outside the hardware store. And what a jolt that was.

She tucked her hands in her lap, her fingers suddenly cold. She wished she'd brought a sweater. She'd forgotten how chilly Christmas Bay could be in the spring. But her sudden case of the chills might have had nothing to do with the temperature, and everything to do with her nerves.

"What are you thinking?" Beau asked, watching her steadily.

The front door opened, and a family of four walked in. The kids made an excited beeline toward the ancient video games, their pockets jingling with quarters.

"Honestly?"

He nodded.

"I don't know. The thought of selling the shop breaks my heart."

"Yeah. But running it for a year?"

The tone of his voice said it all. Beau couldn't see himself in the antiques business. Poppy couldn't exactly see herself in it, either, but the thought of going back to Portland, and KTVL... She wasn't sure when it had started filling her with such dread. The truth was, she'd been trying to imagine herself starting over for a while now. She'd had no idea what she'd do if she wasn't a weekend anchor. No clue whatsoever. Until now, that is.

She swallowed hard. "Actually..."

"Actually, what?"

"I keep thinking about staying."

Beau stared at her, his mouth going slack. She wanted to squirm underneath that gaze.

"You can't be serious," he said.

"What?"

"Poppy. Nobody wants you here."

To anyone listening, that might've seemed like a stretch. *Nobody?* But Poppy knew what he meant, because she felt the same way. But sometime between the reading of her grandfather's letter and sitting across from Beau now, she'd begun to wonder what it would be like to stay. It was an option, but was it a viable option? She'd felt Evelyn's hatred in her bones today, and it had shaken what little confidence she'd had. What would staying be like, having to endure that kind of encounter regularly?

And then there was the question of Justin. She'd be right across the street from him. No more hiding, no more denial. It would be a trial by fire, there was no doubt. Could she do it? She really didn't know.

Beau's jaw was working back and forth.

"What about you?" she asked.

"What about me?"

"Your shoulder… Fishing. You need this inheritance, Beau."

"Like a hole in the head."

"Be serious."

"I am being serious. There's a reason I left, there's no future in Christmas Bay. And, yeah, the money would be nice, but my career isn't here. My life isn't here."

"Your career isn't anywhere if you can't fish," she said evenly. "You could stay here a year, get the surgery you need, heal up and then get your inheritance. It makes sense…"

He shook his head.

"Beau."

"What was he thinking?" he muttered under his breath.

He looked away, clearly emotional. Poppy wanted to

reach for his hand, but she knew he'd only pull away, so she didn't. Beau had always been a tough nut to crack. She just wished they could comfort each other, support each other, like they had when they were kids.

She waited for him to look back, and this time, his eyes were cooler.

"What about your job, Poppy?" he asked. "Are you serious about quitting? It's taken you years to get where you are, only to walk away now? On a whim?"

"It's hardly a whim. And, yeah, it's taken me a long time to get where I am. But it's been kind of soul-sucking, to be honest. I'm tired of the grind, tired of the cutthroat atmosphere. Tired of it all, really."

He watched her. "It's just hard to picture you quitting. It's what you wanted for so long."

"I know." That stubborn lump had lodged itself in her throat again, making it hard to talk. "But I need something…different. I'm not sure what yet, but I know it's not in Portland."

"And you think it's here."

"I don't know. I have to think about it. I'm not sure I'm strong enough to face the hostility here. At least not long-term. I mean, today…"

She hadn't meant to bring up Justin or Evelyn.

He leaned forward, obviously reading the look on her face for what it was. Pain.

"What happened?"

She grazed her bottom lip with her teeth before answering. "I saw Evelyn Frost. On the street outside the hardware store. It didn't go well."

"What did she say?"

"Oh, you know. Just that she hopes I think about Danny

every day. And she can't understand why I'm here and he isn't."

"Seriously?"

"No. She has every right to feel that way, Beau."

"It was an accident. An *accident.* You were just a kid, and our entire family fell apart afterward. We've all suffered, but you've suffered the most."

"But not more than they have. She's right. I'm here and Danny isn't, and that's the reality of it all."

His expression was grim. "You're never going to forgive yourself, are you?"

She was quiet. The answer was simple—how could she forgive herself when Danny's family couldn't? She felt like she was caught on a horrible ride that kept turning in circles, around and around.

The kids across the pizza parlor were laughing and chasing each other around the video games. The smell of warm bread and cheese filled Poppy's senses, comforting her.

"You'd be willing to endure that every day?" he asked. "Because that's what would happen, you know. This is a small town, and she'd find a way to make you feel like garbage every damn day if you stayed here. You know it as well as I do."

Poppy didn't want to say it out loud, because she knew she'd sound like some kind of masochist if she did. But somewhere deep down, she felt like she deserved that.

The door across the restaurant opened, and they both looked over to see Cora and Mary walk in. Mary was wearing a cute yellow raincoat, reminding Poppy of the girl on the Morton Salt box. She ran over to give her aunt and uncle a hug.

"Can I go play video games?" she asked, turning to Cora.

Cora opened her purse and dug out some loose change, depositing it in her daughter's hands. "Have fun."

"Thanks!"

"This place hasn't changed a bit," Cora said, sliding into the booth beside Poppy.

"We were just saying the same thing," Beau said.

"Remember when Grandpa used to bring us here to celebrate good report cards?" Cora asked.

"All-you-can-eat pizza buffet," Poppy said. "And the jojos. Remember those?"

"Oh, my God. The *jojos*."

Poppy remembered how she and her cousins used to fight over the last of the deep-fried potato wedges, and she hadn't realized how hungry she was until right then. She hadn't eaten all day, only sucking down coffee—cup after cup—to get her through to the evening. All of a sudden, she noticed her hands trembling. Her knees quaking under the table. Working in television for her entire adult life had given her some bad habits. It wasn't unusual for her to skip eating for hours at a time. And if she lost a little weight in the process? Even better, since the camera added at least ten pounds. And probably more like twenty. Truth be told, she didn't have a great track record of taking care of herself. At all. Right now, food sounded wonderful. She wondered how it would feel to eat an entire meal and not count every calorie, or every minute it took to get it down, because she was rushing from place to place, or from set to set.

"So Poppy's thinking about staying," Beau said matter-of-factly.

Cora looked at Poppy, her eyes wide. "Is that true?"

Poppy shifted in her seat. With both her cousins staring at her like this, it was difficult, if not impossible, to question her own sanity.

"I feel like I owe it to Grandpa."

"We all feel that way," Cora said. "But staying for a *year*?"

"It's a lot. I wouldn't expect you guys to stay with me."

"But that's not what he wanted," Cora said. "He wanted us to run the shop together."

"Yes, but he had to have known the odds of that were slim."

"But not impossible," Beau said.

Poppy had pretty much written off Beau staying at this point, but those words make her heart jump a little. She didn't want to hope for too much—she absolutely could do it alone if she had to. Would it be pleasant? Probably not. But she could do it. However, if her cousins chose to stay as well, that would make all the difference in the world.

"I might be stubborn, but I'm not stupid," Beau said. "Like you said, my shoulder is trash right now, and fishing is off the table until I get that surgery. I'd be dumb not to consider staying, too. I guess I'll think about it if you do, Cora."

Cora leaned back in the booth, and looked over to where Mary was playing *Pac-Man*, her thin shoulders hunched in concentration.

"Well…" Cora said. "I'd be lying if I said I was looking forward to going back to our house. Travis was so sick there, and the memories…"

Poppy reached out and squeezed her cousin's hand. She could feel the tension radiating from it. Cora had never told her the specifics of those last days, but Poppy knew they'd been horrible. Her cousin was shy and quiet by nature, and didn't have a huge support system in eastern Oregon, where she'd been living since getting married. Poppy should've been there for her, instead of being so consumed with her career.

"Mary's been having a hard time in school," Cora continued. "She's got so much anxiety. I don't know, maybe a change of scenery would do her good."

"It might do you some good, too," Poppy said gently. "And we'd be here with you. Beau and I. We could help with Mary, and we could all reconnect. That's what Grandpa wanted."

Beau shook his head. "I can't believe we're actually talking about this."

"I know," Cora said. "Me neither. But being here with you guys again… It's bringing back some good memories."

Poppy looked from Cora, to Beau, and back again. She felt a distinctive warmth in her chest at the sight of them sitting there. In the familiar atmosphere of Mario's, with the sparkling Pacific Ocean outside the smudged windows— so beautiful, so vast. It made Poppy feel small and insignificant. Like all her problems were so tiny in the grand scheme of things. And when she looked at it that way, it felt like she might be strong enough to stay.

"Is this what we're doing?" Beau asked.

Poppy licked her lips. "I think so."

"None of us knows how to run a business," Beau said. "So there's that."

"But we've all had experience working summers for Grandpa," Cora said. "We can learn as we go. And the antique shop is so established that it'll probably run itself. At least in the beginning. All we'll have to do is unlock the doors, and the tourists will come. The location is fantastic, and word of mouth has always been its biggest strength."

"There's the inventory," Beau said, rubbing the back of his neck. "Furniture suppliers that Grandpa worked with. I could take over that part."

"I could do the books," Cora said. "I was always pretty good at math."

"And I could be on the floor," Poppy said.

Beau nodded. "We could all help back each other up. And remember, Grandpa was doing this by himself. I know the days he had the shop open were limited recently, but still. With all three of us, we could extend business hours, and we might even be able to make a profit."

Poppy felt the beginnings of butterflies against her rib cage. This could work. Yes, she had plenty of doubts after running into Evelyn this morning, but now, sitting here with her cousins, she felt better. There was strength in numbers.

"I'll have to talk to Mary about it," Cora said. "See how she feels. She might not want to leave school in the middle of the semester. Even though she's been having a hard time, she'd still be leaving behind all she knows."

"Of course," Poppy said. "Talk to her tonight, and see what she thinks. This would have to be a team effort, and Mary's part of the team."

"That would just leave the living arrangements," Beau said. "Grandpa kept the apartment up nice. There's room for all of us. I'll take the pullout and you guys can have the bedrooms."

"That's chivalrous of you," Poppy said.

"It's only for a year. I can sleep on a pullout for a year. Bachelors can make pretty much anything work."

"You say that now…" Cora paused, watching him. "You're not seeing anyone, Beau?"

He shifted, his jaw working. As far as Poppy knew, he'd only ever loved one woman. His college sweetheart, Summer. But he'd broken up with her when he'd gotten his first sponsor and decided to drop out of college and fish full-time. Poppy hadn't understood it then, and she still didn't understand it. Beau had been over the moon for Summer— that had been obvious to anyone paying attention. But, like Poppy, when things got too serious, Beau Evers split. Poor Summer had found that out the hard way.

"No," he said. "Nobody special."

Cora nodded. She was probably thinking the same thing Poppy was. Wondering why he'd let Summer go all those years ago. But, wisely, she kept her mouth shut. Whenever anyone asked Beau about his love life, he got all surly and snappy. Maybe he was having a hard time with that long-ago decision, too.

"I'm starving," Beau said. "Who wants pizza?"

"Me," Cora said. "Mary likes pepperoni and pineapple."

"Sounds good." Poppy's stomach growled at the thought of Mario's famous pepperoni pizza. Warm and spicy, with tons of melted cheese.

Beau nodded. "Sodas?"

"A Diet Sprite for me," Cora said.

"Me too. Thanks, Beau."

Poppy watched him slide out of the booth and walk up to the counter with his hands in his pockets. There were a few women sitting at a table nearby who were watching him with interest. He was that kind of guy. Beau walked into a room, and women noticed.

Mary ran up to him, and he draped an easy arm around her shoulders, life a father might. Or a good uncle.

"He's sweet with her," Cora said. "He's a natural with kids."

"Don't tell him that. It'll scare him away."

"He'd make a good dad."

"He would. But he'd have to settle down first, and I don't see him doing that anytime soon. Maybe ever."

Cora frowned. "You think?"

"Maybe that's too pessimistic. But Summer was just about perfect for him and you know where that went."

Cora shifted so she was facing Poppy. Her eyes were red-rimmed, like she might've been crying recently. Her grief was still so new and raw, that Poppy was surprised she was functioning as well as she was. They'd all been thrown a pretty major curveball with Grandpa's death and the letter, and Cora had already been reeling.

"I have to be honest," Cora said. "I'm not thinking clearly right now. Do you think this is a good idea? Staying here? Running the shop together?"

Poppy sighed. "I don't know. There's no doubt we could all use the inheritance. But I think we need each other more than the money, and I think Grandpa knew that. So any reservations I have are kind of overshadowed by that. I'm going back and forth. But right this minute? Yeah. I think it's a good idea. I think we can do it."

"I'm so relieved to hear you say that. I don't want to make a mistake with this. Taking Mary out of school and moving somewhere different would be a big deal. But I feel like we need to be with family right now. We need to be with you and Beau."

Poppy scooted over and wrapped her cousin in a hug.

The lump in her throat had returned with a vengeance, so she couldn't say anything without her voice cracking. So she didn't even try. She just hugged Cora, and hoped that she felt how much she loved her. How much she'd missed her.

"We're home," Cora said, so softly that Poppy barely heard. "Can you believe we're actually home?"

No, Poppy thought. It was hard to believe.

Chapter Five

Justin pulled up to his parents' 1960s split-level house—the one with the perfectly manicured yard and the spotless driveway—and cut the engine to his pickup. He had the windows rolled down for Roo, who was looking over at him.

"Sorry," he said. "We're here. That means you have to stay and be a good dog."

Her long, shaggy tail thumped against the seat. But her eyes looked sad. It was like she understood every word he said, and he wasn't sure how he felt about that. At the moment, it was easier talking to this dog over any human in his life, and that was unacceptable. He had to get out more.

Smiling, he rubbed her scruffy ears. "Don't look at me like that. This isn't the worst thing in the world. You could be at the pound, and *that* would be the worst thing in the world."

She licked his hand. A peace offering.

Justin glanced over at the house. Soft, yellow light spilled out the windows and onto the walkway where his mother's pink tea roses were just beginning to bloom. It was funny. Anyone passing by would assume the house was full of warmth, judging by its outward appearance. It looked cozy. Loved. But it was just about the coldest place

Justin knew. All the life had gone out of it the day Danny died. Now, it was just a place where his parents lived.

Justin opened the door and climbed out of his truck, narrowing his eyes at the little blue hatchback across the street. A car he'd never seen before. Which, in and of itself, was hardly earth-shattering. This was an older neighborhood, and not everyone had a garage, or room for friends and family to park in their narrow driveways. But something about the *way* this car was parked, directly across from his parents' house, like the driver might have business there, set him on edge.

When his mom had come into the hardware store and invited him to dinner, he hadn't been serious when he'd asked if she was setting him up. But now, as he eyed the car with a small stuffed animal hanging from its rearview mirror, he had a feeling that setting him up was exactly what she was up to. After all, it wouldn't be the first time. She'd done this before.

Once, a few years back, he'd come to Sunday dinner, only to be met at the dining-room table by a petite brunette. She'd been a new clerk in his father's law office, and she'd accepted the dinner invitation not knowing her boss's wife was trying to matchmake. It had been inappropriate on so many levels.

Rubbing his temple, he stepped up to the front door. He could say he was sick, that he couldn't stay. Or he could be honest, and come right out and tell his mother that he wasn't up for this. Or, better yet, that he wasn't going to have anything to do with it. But, of course, that would leave this poor mystery woman sitting at his parents' table, stood up by a date that she probably hadn't even agreed to.

Before he could raise a hand to knock, he saw the sheer

white curtains part in the living-room window. His mom peered out and wiggled her fingers at him. He watched her, irritated.

The front door opened in a whisper of perfumed air, and she stepped out onto the porch, shutting it behind her.

"Honey, don't be mad…"

He closed his eyes for a second, summoning all his patience. When he opened them again, she was clutching her hands in front of her chest.

"*Please* don't be mad," she repeated. "But she's the nicest girl…"

"I'm sure she's nice."

"She's a personal trainer at the gym, and we got to talking the other day, and I invited her for dinner, because you know how much I love my gym family."

"I know you do, Mom."

"She's newly single, and you're single, and I thought, what could it hurt?"

His frustration rose. "I can't believe you did this. *Again.* After I asked you not to just *today.*"

"There was only that one other time." She glanced over to his truck parked at the curb, and frowned. "You brought the dog?"

Roo had her head sticking out the half-open window. She whimpered softly.

"Yeah, I brought her. If you can fix me up with a complete stranger without even asking, then I can bring the dog."

"Not inside, though."

Justin cocked his brow. "How bad do you want me to stay?"

"You know I don't like dogs," she said tightly.

"You used to like dogs."

"No."

"When we were kids, we had a dog."

"We did not."

"Yes, we did. Underfoot."

"That wasn't our dog," she said. "That was a neighbor's dog, and we were just keeping him for a few weeks while they were out of the country."

"You loved that dog. You fed him Nilla wafers and let him sleep under the covers."

"I don't remember that."

"Liar," Justin said. "Yes, you do."

"That was a long time ago."

"So? What does that have to do with anything? The question is whether or not you like dogs, and Underfoot is Exhibit A."

"*Okay*, she can come inside," she said. "But you have to stay through dessert. Promise?"

"Does she get a cookie?"

"Don't push it."

Justin smiled, and leaned down to kiss his mother on the cheek. For the first time in a long time, the tension between them eased a little. Maybe it was because he'd promised to stay, so she was getting what she wanted. Maybe it was because she had a dinner guest, and was in a better mood than usual because she had someone to cook and get dressed up for. He had no idea why, it was just nice.

"What's her name?" he asked.

"Hmm?" She'd been looking over at the truck again, her ruby-red lips pursed. And just like that, the tension was back.

"What's her name? My date for the evening."

"Oh. Kristy. Her name is Kristy. You actually went to high school with her, honey. She was in Danny's class."

Justin stared at her. A stranger was one thing. Someone he could talk to for an hour or so, exchange socials with and never see again. But someone he knew? That was different. That was completely different, and by the sudden flush of her cheeks, his mother knew it, too.

"Kristy Isaacs?" he asked.

"You remember her!"

"Of course, I remember her," Justin whispered. "Our school was the size of a postage stamp, Mom."

She glanced over at the living-room window, as if Kristy Isaacs was standing there looking back. Justin's head was throbbing. What a cluster.

"Just dinner and dessert," his mother said primly. "That's all I'm asking."

"You do realize this isn't normal, right, Mom? This isn't a normal thing to do. Setting your grown-ass son up on blind dates at your house?"

"Justin, don't be crude."

He pinched the bridge of his nose. "Can I ask one question?"

"Of course."

"Why are you doing this?"

"I told you. I want grandkids."

"I think there might be more to it than that."

"Like what? Honestly, we need to get back inside. I left Kristy with your father, and he was about to get his stamp collection out."

"Does any of this have to do with Poppy?"

His mother's gaze grew cool. All the light had gone out of her eyes, just like that. "Excuse me?"

"The timing of this *date*."

"I have absolutely no idea what you're talking about."

He didn't believe that for a second. All the puzzle pieces had slid neatly into place in the last few minutes. Of course, this had everything to do with Poppy. This dinner was her way of trying to distract him. Clumsy as it was.

The knowledge settled into Justin's bones like Novocain. Numbing him. Just in time, apparently, because right then the front door opened. His father stood there on the stoop looking at them curiously.

"What's going on out here?" he asked. "This young lady is bored to death, and I can't say I blame her. *I'm* bored, and I like stamps."

His dad looked dapper in a pair of khaki slacks and a blue collared shirt. In his mid-sixties, he was handsome and fit, and was very close to realizing his dream of becoming a circuit court judge. It showed. He exuded a smooth, unflappable confidence that could often be mistaken for a lack of warmth. He was actually a very sensitive person, but Justin knew he kept that part of himself locked away for a reason. Sensitive people opened themselves up to a lot more pain than people with a tough outer shell.

"We were just coming inside," his mother said, smoothing her hair away from her face. She'd blown it out tonight, and her curls had transformed into dark, silky waves that caught the light of the setting sun. Danny's hair had been the same color.

"Yeah," Justin said. "But first, I'm gonna get Roo real quick."

His mother shot him a look, but didn't argue. His dad shrugged, looking like he didn't care either way.

He watched his parents step back inside the house, neat

as a pin, nothing out of place, and frowned. This was going to be a long night. He felt bad for Kristy, who had no idea what she'd agreed to.

And he felt bad for himself, because he knew *exactly* what he'd agreed to.

Evelyn watched her son from across the table. He reached for the potatoes, helping himself to a spoonful before offering them to Kristy, who was looking at him appreciatively. He'd always been such a handsome boy. Tall and dark, with a smile that could light up a room.

Well, that's how he'd been as a boy. As a man, that smile was much more guarded. She guessed there were good reasons for that. He'd had a hard time with his brother's death. Of course, they all had. But Justin had struggled in a different way. And she'd always had a feeling that had to do with Poppy. There'd been something there. She'd seen it in Justin's eyes when Poppy had come over to their house for movies or pizza. And she'd seen it in Poppy's eyes, too. There had been a spark between them.

Evelyn hadn't thought much about it back then. Kids were kids, and their crushes, like their friendships, could be fickle. But after Danny had been killed, Justin seemed to have felt a different kind of grief. Evelyn had never known if that was because he was dealing with guilt for how he felt about his little brother's girlfriend, or if he was grieving the loss of Poppy in his life as well. As far as she knew, they'd never spoken again. But any time her name came up—and her name had come up plenty in the years following the accident—he'd been strangely defensive. Yes, he was furious, that was obvious. But he was also protective of her in a way that Evelyn hadn't been able to get past.

She was livid with Poppy Sawyer. The fact that her oldest son apparently saw something redeemable in her was too much to bear. What in the world would Danny think?

The whole thing felt like a slap in the face, and when Justin had brought up forgiveness this morning, well… Evelyn had literally seen red.

Sitting here now, biting into a warm, buttered roll, she was surprised she'd recovered enough to host dinner at all. But here she was. Here they all were, dining with a lovely young woman who'd known Danny, Justin…and Poppy, too. Not that it mattered. The only thing that mattered, was that Justin was talking to her now, and she was smiling wide.

"Don't you think so, honey?"

She looked at Paul, who was watching her closely. He was probably a little annoyed. He'd been carrying most of the conversation while she'd been lost in her own little world. She had a tendency to do that. Drift off, leaving everyone behind. It was like losing time. After the accident it had come in very handy. She didn't know what she would've done without being able to get lost in her mind sometimes.

"Hmm?"

"Don't you think it's warm for spring on the coast?"

Oh, dear. So this was what it had come down to. Weather. Poor Kristy would be wondering why she'd said yes to this dinner in the first place.

Evelyn dabbed at her mouth with her napkin. "Oh. Yes. Warm."

Justin cleared his throat. "So, Kristy. What have you been up to since high school? Mom said you work at the gym?"

Kristy smiled. She really was a pretty girl. Dark hair and eyes. A healthy, dewy glow. Evelyn couldn't help but imagine what a baby from her and Justin would look like. Maybe it would have Kristy's eyes and Justin's smile. She stopped herself before she could go any further with that train of thought. Maybe this *was* weird.

"That's my side job," Kristy said. "I work at the credit union. I've been there for about five years."

"Oh," Justin said a little stiffly. "That's cool."

Evelyn wished he'd just sit back and relax, but nobody asked her. And it was also kind of her fault for putting him on the spot like this in the first place.

From underneath the table, she felt something brush against her leg. She lifted the tablecloth and saw Roo looking up at her with her caramel-colored eyes. Evelyn was surprised she even fit under there, she was so big. The last time she'd checked, she was lying at Justin's feet, looking every bit the loyal companion.

But now, she was staring a hole right into Evelyn's soul, pushing into her leg with her warm, fluffy body. Probably wanting table scraps. She wondered if Earl had fed her people food. Dogs were such sensitive beings, and Justin said she'd been having a hard time since her master's death. She was grieving, and that was something Evelyn could relate to.

Her heart squeezed before she could properly rein it in. Whether or not this dog was missing Earl was none of her concern. What *was* her concern, was that she was drooling on her slacks, which were silk.

"Justin."

"Yeah?"

"The dog."

She jabbed a finger toward Roo, knowing a look of disgust had settled over her face that she didn't exactly feel. What she wanted to do was reach down and rub those soft-looking ears. Take that face in her hands and lean close to that wet nose. She hadn't had a dog since she was a girl. Despite what she'd told Justin earlier, she remembered the neighbor's dog, Underfoot, very well. She'd been sad when they'd come back from Europe and collected the nondescript brown mutt that had taken to sleeping under the covers with Evelyn. Paul had teased her endlessly about that.

She remembered Justin and Danny asking for a dog when they'd been young, but Evelyn had had her hands full with two little boys, and a marriage that honestly had been a little rocky at times. Having an attorney husband who ate, breathed and slept his work wasn't always the easiest thing in the world. A dog had simply seemed like too much at the time. But she'd always regretted that decision. Regretted that Danny never had that experience.

"Oh," Justin said. "Sorry."

He snapped his fingers, and the dog turned and went to him.

"I think she likes you," he said, patting the floor until she lay down at his feet again.

"I doubt that. She was just begging for food."

"She doesn't eat from the table. She just wanted attention."

Evelyn nodded curtly, hating how cold she'd become. When had that happened? She never used to be a cold person. Actually, she'd always been the exact opposite. Warm and loving and carefree. But losing a child had changed her. So that must be when it had happened. The night Danny had been taken from her.

"When is Poppy going to come get her?" she asked. And then wished she could suck the words back in. She hadn't meant to mention Poppy tonight, or anything else about the Sawyer family. Not with Kristy here.

"We're going to meet tomorrow morning," Justin said. "To talk about it."

"Poppy Sawyer?" This from Kristy, who raised her dark eyebrows. Evelyn could kick herself.

Justin nodded, looking like he didn't want to talk about her, either.

"She's back in town?"

"Yeah."

"Oh. When did that happen? I thought she was some big-shot news anchor in Portland or something."

Evelyn thought she caught a tone there. It was possible Kristy didn't like Poppy, either.

"She is," Justin said. "Her grandpa passed away, and she came back for the reading of his will. Roo is actually his…now hers, I guess. I'm just keeping her until she decides if she can take her."

Kristy smoothed her napkin in her lap, absorbing this. "Well. I'm surprised she came back at all."

"Why's that?" Justin asked.

He knows exactly why, Evelyn thought.

"I don't know. She can't feel very welcome here after…" Kristy glanced over at Paul, color flooding her cheeks. "After what happened."

Justin smiled, but it was tight-looking. Evelyn had seen that smile dozens of times, and it was never a good sign. He was getting ready to play devil's advocate, she could tell. *Wonderful.*

"It was a long time ago," he said. "And, of course, she's going to come home to help settle Earl's estate."

"I'm just saying." Kristy shrugged. "She's home now, but from what I've heard, she hasn't made a habit of it over the years."

"Why would she? If she doesn't feel welcome?"

Kristy didn't seem to have a good answer for that. Evelyn was no fan of Poppy's, but it was true that the woman was damned if she did, damned if she didn't. If she came home more often, she was the bitch who dared show her face here. If she didn't, she was the bitch who never visited her elderly grandfather. The fact that this was something Evelyn could sympathize with wasn't a welcome realization. She didn't want to sympathize with Poppy. And she didn't want her dog drooling on her slacks and tugging on her heartstrings, either. What had she been thinking when she'd hatched this asinine dinner plan? She hadn't been thinking at all. That was pretty clear.

She clapped her hands together a little too enthusiastically. "Who's ready for dessert?"

Kristy smiled, but then looked at Justin again, like she wasn't quite finished with this conversation. Paul cleared his throat, probably wanting to get dinner over with already, so he could watch a baseball game on TV. His go-to whenever things got remotely uncomfortable. Evelyn hated baseball by association.

"You remember what she was like in high school," Kristy said. "Right?"

Justin stiffened, the tension between them becoming visible.

"I remember," Justin said. "You didn't like her in high school?"

"Not really."

"Why?"

"I think she was self-absorbed. She thought the world revolved around her."

"Oh. I didn't get that from her at all."

"Huh," Kristy said flatly. "Interesting."

Evelyn shifted in her chair again. "So…dessert?"

"She was fearless," Justin said. "I think that was a turn-off for some people."

"She was reckless. There's a difference."

Evelyn looked from Justin, to Kristy, and back again. It was like the tennis match from hell. Neither one of them seemed to have heard her. In fact, the only ones paying attention to her were Paul and the dog, who'd raised her head from her giant paws, and was watching Evelyn with those melty eyes again.

"Reckless?" Justin said. "I'm not sure that's fair."

Kristy looked perturbed. Evelyn couldn't blame her. It was like he was picking at her just to pick. It was highly possible that having Kristy here, a girl he'd gone to school with so many years ago, was bringing out the kid in him. And not in a good way.

"Considering what she did, I think it's *very* fair."

Kristy said this softly, under her breath, but Evelyn heard her just the same. So had Justin, whose gaze settled on his mother apologetically. But what did he think would happen? This was how people reacted when he chose to defend the indefensible. Why in the world was Poppy Sawyer the hill he'd chosen to die on? Suddenly, she had a pounding headache.

"Dessert?" she asked hopefully. She sounded like a broken record.

Kristy looked over. But judging by the expression on her face, Evelyn knew there was no coming back from this. The subject of Poppy serving as a strange wedge between them. The truth was, she shouldn't matter one way or the other. But she did, Evelyn thought wearily. She always did.

Chapter Six

Justin walked down the sidewalk with Roo plodding along beside him. He had her on a short leash, but honestly, she probably didn't need one at all. She was glued to his side. Her big body bumped into his leg every now and then, as if she wanted to make sure he wasn't going anywhere.

Reaching down, he patted her on the head. He didn't have to reach far. It practically came to his hip. Tonight had been a total disaster. But every time he started feeling bad about that, he reminded himself that his mother had orchestrated the entire thing. She had to have known it would be uncomfortable at best. But that was the thing with his mother—she didn't stop to think about anyone's comfort but her own. If she was numb to everything, everyone else should be, too. It had been like that for years. In a lot of ways, she'd been operating like some kind of robot, never considering the consequences or repercussions of anything she did.

He continued walking, his pace slow, the ocean breeze chilly against his bare arms. The tide would be going out about now. He could hear the waves crashing in the distance, throwing themselves at the beach like a lover trying to get their arms around something that was always eluding them.

He looked up and saw that he was almost at the hardware store. Earl's Antiques stood right across from it, its windows dark in the dusky evening light.

Slowing, he glanced up at the second-story apartment. It looked empty. He wondered where Poppy, Beau and Cora were staying tonight. Probably in one of the small motels at the edge of town. He thought about Poppy unpacking a sleek travel bag. Pictured her taking her clothes off to get in the shower, and his blood warmed before he could help it. He wondered if she was lonely or if she'd reconnected with her cousins. Maybe they were presenting a united front in the face of losing their grandfather. Justin knew that despite not coming back to Christmas Bay much over the years, they'd all loved Earl very much. Loss was loss, no matter who you were.

Roo nudged his hand, and he looked down and smiled. She'd gravitated toward his mom. She'd gotten up more than once during dinner, and once had snuck underneath the table to put her head in her lap. That had been a surprise. His mother had tried to act annoyed, but he could tell she'd liked it. But for whatever reason, she'd kept up that ridiculous facade. Which was so stupid. Just because Roo had a connection with Poppy? But that's how much her bitterness had spiraled out of control.

Rubbing Roo's ears, Justin looked back up at the apartment, as the last of the day's tourists passed him on the sidewalk. He could smell the pizza from Mario's down the street, and it stirred something inside him. He remembered going there after football games, his hair still wet from the showers. He remembered Danny there, too. The quintessential brothers, never too far apart. And he remembered Poppy. The cross-country star, the homecoming queen, the young, magnetic beauty. Everyone had been a little bit in love with her back then.

There'd been a night after one of those games where he and Danny had gotten into it. *You like her*, his little brother had hissed. *I can tell you do.*

I have no idea what you're talking about. Justin had turned away, but Danny had grabbed his arm. His brother had been smaller, but he'd been strong. And he'd had anger on his side, which had made him quick.

Stay away from my girlfriend!

I don't want *your girlfriend.*

Justin felt his lungs constrict now, tightening uncomfortably like they did whenever he thought about Danny like this. Not framed by love and loyalty, but by jealousy and suspicion. He hated that Danny had been right. And Justin had never admitted to it—just denied it until he literally couldn't deny it anymore, because his brother wasn't there to deny it to.

He gritted his teeth until his jaw cramped. He'd walked Kristy to her car after the disastrous dinner and dessert. He'd said good-night awkwardly, and she'd given him an even more awkward hug, and that had been that. He knew he wouldn't see her again, and that was okay. Despite his mother hoping there'd be something between them, there wasn't a damn thing, and that wasn't anything that could be forced. Ever.

He stood on the sidewalk, cars passing every now and then, their headlights cutting into the evening like laser beams. He should head back to his house. Roo was probably starving by now, and he had laundry to do. Exciting stuff. Some people—including his mother—might think he was lonely, but he wasn't. He preferred his life this way.

Uncomplicated. Uncluttered by people and emotions. He went to work, he came home, he went to sleep. He did it all over again the next day, and that routine was something he could count on. Day in. Day out.

After a few seconds, he forced his gaze away from the empty apartment above the antique shop. Away from thoughts of Poppy, away from memories of Danny that were as tangled as fishing line around his heart. He wasn't going to let himself linger on the fact that he'd see Poppy again tomorrow morning. Sitting across from her and having coffee like two old friends connecting after all this time.

Turning, he tugged on Roo's leash, and she turned with him, pressed close to his side like she was his. He wouldn't let himself think about that, either. She wasn't his dog. She would go with Poppy, or if she didn't go with Poppy, she'd go with someone else. Someone who would love her and have time for her. Justin liked his life the way it was.

Alone. Definitely not lonely.

Poppy eased her car up the narrow gravel road leading to the pioneer cemetery at the top of the hill. It rocked over potholes, and skidded once or twice as the expensive tires tried to find purchase in the soft patches of loose dirt.

It was almost dark. A few twinkling stars had just appeared overhead, and the sky was easing from a dark, velvety purple to a deep, grainy blue. Wispy clouds lay at the foot of the horizon, like the hem of a gauzy dress, and the ocean churned there, its dark water roiling underneath the light of the half moon.

It was a beautiful evening, but most people probably wouldn't want to spend it in an old cemetery that was supposed to be haunted. At least, according to superstitious Christmas Bay locals.

The thought of ghosts had never bothered Poppy. When she was younger, she used to have dreams about Danny. He'd be sitting there when she turned around, or standing behind her in the mirror when she was brushing her teeth. She'd never woken up scared. The dreams were a strange comfort, a feeling that he was still with her in some form or another. And she took her comfort wherever she could get it.

As the years went on, she'd thought more and more about life after death. In her heart, she was sure there was something—something good and beautiful—on the other side. And maybe spirits lingered on earth. All she knew was that she'd never pictured Danny as anything but at peace. At rest. And perhaps that had been a survival mechanism— a way for her to live with what she'd done. But she felt the way she felt, nevertheless.

She pulled the car over and cut the engine. The windows were open, and the salty sea air permeated her senses. She could hear the crickets outside, serenading her with their delicate music, and she took a deep breath.

She used to come here a lot in the beginning. When the pain and shock had been the fiercest. She'd sit at the edge of Danny's grave and stare out over the cemetery to the mountains in the distance. Somehow, it had helped, being here. It was good to have a place to go, a place to think and feel close to him. She wished her grandpa had chosen to be laid to rest up here, but he'd wanted his ashes scattered in the ocean. That was something she, Beau and Cora would need to do this summer, but it was too hard to think about now, so she pushed that particular thought to the edge of her mind, where it wasn't as sharp. She was good at that. Pushing things aside.

She stepped out into the chilly evening air, then shivered, pulled her sweater around her shoulders and shut the door. She didn't bother locking it. It was funny how fast her city habits vanished whenever she came home. How fast she fell back into that comfortable small-town routine where nobody locked their doors, but absolutely should in this day and age. She'd only been home a day now, but she found that she'd been lulled into a false sense of security. She was home. Despite everything, she felt safe here. A leftover piece of her childhood that refused to abandon her when she needed it most.

Crossing her arms over her chest, she began walking up the hill toward the small headstone that was bathed in the silvery light of the moon. She'd needed to come here tonight to feel close to Danny. To apologize again. Every time she came home, she came up here to apologize. She had no idea if he heard her, of if he forgave her, but she hoped he did. It was all she could do.

More than once, she'd come to the top of the hill, only to see Evelyn there. Sitting next to a bouquet of fresh flowers and staring off into space. Poppy didn't think the woman had ever noticed her there, thank God. She wasn't quite sure what Danny's mother would've done if she *had* noticed. Screamed at her, maybe? Thrown rocks? There was no telling.

She looked up, half-expecting to see Evelyn there now. Keeping guard over her son, tonight and always. But there was nobody. Only the shadows and the trees, and the memories.

Poppy slowed as she approached the gravestone, her

heart beating heavily. From somewhere to her left an owl hooted. The waves crashed on the nearby beach, a low thunder that rolled in her chest. She could smell the heavy, sweet scent of the Scotch broom that surrounded the cemetery, along with wild roses, and flower arrangements from dozens of families and loved ones. The air was perfumed, making her sad. It reminded her of being up here in those early days.

She stopped at the small, bleached marker, and leaned down to run her fingertips over Danny's name. *Daniel James Frost. Son, brother, friend. Gone, but not forgotten.* The stone was cold and damp. Poppy felt her throat begin to tighten and ache. Her eyes filled with hot tears. It never got easier. And if it never got easier for her, how must it be for his family?

Poppy lowered herself to her knees, not caring that the grass would probably stain her slacks. Suddenly, her thinking was foggy, her brain slowing to keep time with the beat of her heart. She was falling back into her memories. Back to that night when the road had been so slick, and she thought nothing bad could ever happen to her. To other people, yes. But not to *her.*

She pressed her palm to the marble, and let herself feel the tidal wave of emotion that had been threatening since she'd driven across the city limits of Christmas Bay. She let it wash over her, let it steal her breath and all of her strength. She lowered her head and finally let the tears fall, giving herself over to the guilt and the grief and the sadness for this life taken, and for so many other lives changed forever in its wake.

"Do you forgive me?" she heard herself say. Her voice

was hoarse and thin. Almost a whisper. She didn't recognize it. She sounded old.

Of course, there was no answer, except for the sound of the crashing waves in the distance, and the curious owl above her. *Who?* it seemed to say. *Who are you asking for? You, or him?*

After a few minutes, she was able to catch her breath again. She swiped her knuckles across each cheek, catching the tears before any more fell onto her sweater. She was exhausted, spent. Trembling from the events of the last few days. Of the last ten years. Could she really live here again? After all this time? It seemed that she was on the verge of doing just that. She and her cousins had talked about it tonight, *really* talked about it. They'd come up with a tentative plan, one that would allow them to get through this next year as a family, supporting each other, helping each other forward, which was exactly what their sweet grandfather had wanted for them.

But there would be implications if she stayed. She would see Justin daily—he worked right across the street, after all. She would run into his mother again, and his father, too. And how would that go? Today might be a walk in the park compared to what lay ahead.

But at the same time, she felt a strange kind of serenity at the thought of staying. This was where she'd grown up. It was where her happiest years had been spent…before the accident. The antique shop had been her grandfather's favorite place on earth, and she had such wonderful memories there. Was it beyond the realm of possibility that she could be happy here again? At least temporarily—until she got her feet underneath her? Until she figured out what in the world she was going to do with her career? She thought it might be possible. If she could learn to coexist with all the people in town who didn't want her here, that is.

She looked up. It was dark now, the stars overhead twinkling in earnest. The cemetery was quiet except for the sound of the crickets and the owl, still questioning her motives. She thought she could hear her own heartbeat in her ears. It thumped steadily, rhythmically, reminding her that she was still alive, she was still here, she still mattered, even if it was only to her remaining family members, who didn't really know her at all anymore. Somewhere along the line, Poppy had become a stranger to them, and to herself. That young girl, the one who'd walked away from the accident with only a few cuts and bruises? That girl was long gone. She existed in the same place Danny did—in the cosmos. Somewhere in between what was, and what might have been.

Slowly, she stood, her legs tingling from being in one position for too long. She looked around at the darkened headstones, wondering why she wasn't uncomfortable here. At night, by herself. Part of her worried that she'd gotten so used to disassociating that she no longer recognized discomfort the way normal people would. She blinked and looked back down at Danny's stone.

"I'll be back soon, okay?"

The only answer was the crickets, singing through her pain.

She turned and made her way down the hill toward her glossy black car, which blended into the night, and all she could make out were the silver spokes of the wheels. She wondered what tomorrow morning would be like, sitting across from Justin and trying to make conversation. She wondered if she'd recognize anyone else at the donut shop, or if they'd recognize her.

Swallowing hard, she dug her keys out of her pocket, and hoped it would be quick and easy. As quick and easy as seeing Justin again could be, that is.

Justin sat in the corner booth by the window, steam rising from his coffee cup. He'd gotten Poppy a coffee, too. It sat across from him on the table, waiting for her.

He was early. He'd woken up around four, and couldn't get back to sleep. His head had been spinning, his stomach a little upside down. So he'd gotten out of bed and taken Roo for a walk before dawn, his neighborhood sleeping soundly underneath the grainy sky.

The door opened across the shop, and he looked over, but it was a woman and a girl, their hair tangled and windblown. It was one of those days. The sky was dark, with angry-looking clouds that seemed ready to burst at any moment. They probably would burst, and he'd walked here from the hardware store. He had no choice but to walk back in whatever Mother Nature decided to throw at him. It was fine. He didn't really care if he got soaked to the bone, so long as he didn't have to sit here with Poppy any longer than he had to. He was annoyed that his stomach was tight with anticipation.

The door opened across the shop again, and he looked over. This time, Poppy walked in. She was holding her hair back with one hand, a few silky blond strands falling in front of her face. She was wearing a pair of skinny jeans that hugged her curves, and a black turtleneck sweater. Still city-chic, but toned down some.

Letting her hair go and combing it out with her fingers,

she looked around the shop, her gaze growing serious when it came to rest on his. She smiled, but it was strained, and he knew she was dreading this, like he was.

She walked over and slid into the booth. The scent of her perfume made his gut tighten. This close, he could see her freckles, even under her expertly applied makeup. She was trying to hide them, no doubt. She'd always hated her freckles. He'd loved them.

"Good morning," she said.

"Morning."

She glanced down at the coffee, smiling. "Oh, thank you. I need the caffeine. I didn't sleep very well."

"Me neither."

Justin was finding it hard not to stare, now that they were so close to each other. He'd seen her on TV, of course. Most people in Christmas Bay had. But she looked different sitting across from him now. Younger. More vulnerable.

A couple of women passed by and looked over at her. They narrowed their eyes, and whispered something to each other before walking out the door. It was impossible to tell where they'd recognized her from—her job, or from the accident (because she was semi-famous here, she was also semi-famous here because of that. Or infamous, more accurately). She had to have noticed, but didn't let on.

Taking a visible breath, she looked up at him. Her eyes were like an arrow straight to his heart. Maybe this hadn't been such a good idea. He thought he could handle talking to her again, at least about Roo, but maybe he couldn't. Maybe ten years hadn't been long enough to heal whatever wound still throbbed inside him. It was depressing to think that she could still have this kind of effect on him, even now. Maybe he hadn't come nearly as far as he liked to think he had.

"I wanted to thank you again," she said. "For taking Roo like this."

He nodded.

"I don't know what I would've done without you."

"You would've figured it out." His voice was chilly, detached. He hadn't meant for it to come out like that, but it had, anyway.

"I'm not so sure," she said. "These last few days have thrown me for a loop, I'll be honest."

He raised his eyebrows. Did she want him to ask how she was doing? How her family was doing? It was none of his business. But wouldn't not asking make him an asshole? She'd just lost her grandfather, who'd also been Justin's friend. Good God. None of this was going to be easy. He wished he'd been drinking something stiffer than coffee.

He gritted his teeth, something that was becoming a habit lately, and put his elbows on the table. "I'm sure it's got to be hard," he said evenly.

So he was going to go there. Open that door. Act interested in what she had to say. What would his mother think of this? Scratch that. He *knew* what she'd think.

"It is," she said. Then paused, like she was trying to decide what to say. If she wanted to say anything at all. She took a deep breath and tapped her fingernail against the paper coffee cup. She kept staring at her hands like she expected them to speak for her.

"When are you going back?" he asked.

She sat there for a second, still as a stone. And then she looked up, and the expression on her face unnerved him.

"I'm not sure I *am* going back."

He frowned. She'd hinted at this yesterday, but he'd assumed she meant she was staying temporarily. This sure as hell sounded more permanent than that. Even though she couldn't possibly have anything keeping her in Christmas Bay long-term. At least not important enough to separate her from her career.

"And why's that?" Here he was again. Acting interested. But the thing was, he was interested. What would his existence look like if he had to see her on a daily basis? He couldn't even contemplate that. He didn't want to contemplate that, but at the same time, the thought of it filled him with a dangerous kind of excitement that he wouldn't have admitted to out loud.

She took a sip of her coffee, then licked her lips. "Grandpa left us the shop."

Justin watched her. That wasn't so unusual. In fact, it made sense. As far as he knew, Earl's kids came home even less than his grandkids did. And Poppy, Cora and Beau were the ones who'd loved the shop and had a connection to it. They'd practically grown up over there. Of course, he'd left it to them.

She must've read the look on his face, because she nodded. "That alone isn't why we'd stay. But the thing is, he made a stipulation."

"Oh?" Now, he was curious.

"He wanted us to run it. Together. For a year. Before we decide what to do with it."

Justin sat back slowly in the booth. *What?* Beau was a fisherman. And Cora... He didn't even know what she did. Poppy was a television personality. So the odds were pretty good none of them would know what they were doing.

Running a business wasn't rocket science, but it wasn't easy, either. He knew, because he'd been doing it for years.

"And you're going to do it?" he asked.

"Well, we've talked about it. It's not something we would've chosen, but there was a reason why Grandpa wanted this. He wanted us to form some kind of relationship again. A bond, like when we were little."

Justin shook his head. "That's one way to do it, I guess."

"He knew it would be hard for us to say no. We all loved him—we love the shop. And we're all at some kind of crossroads right now. The timing is right..."

He stopped himself before he could ask what kind of crossroads she was at, reminding himself that he didn't care. Despite what his mother thought, despite his conflicting emotions, he was still plenty angry at Poppy. So if she was going to be here, fine. If he was going to run into her, fine. But he didn't have to pretend to like it, and he definitely didn't have to pretend to care.

He shifted in the booth. All of a sudden, the little donut shop felt hot and claustrophobic.

"So you think you might stay," he said.

"I think so. Cora and Beau are thinking about it, too. Beau can't fish right now because of a shoulder injury that needs surgery. And Cora's husband just passed away. Cancer. She was a stay-at-home mom. She always planned on going back to school, but that kept getting pushed farther down the road, and it just hasn't happened yet. And as far as *I'm* concerned..."

He waited. He was aware of the pulse tapping in his neck—tapping, tapping, tapping. The muscles in his shoulders stretched taut underneath his T-shirt. He clasped his hands together on the table, like he was praying. *As far as you're concerned, what, Poppy?*

"I'm not sure I'm cut out for television," she said quietly.

"I'm sorry…what?"

The corner of her pretty mouth tilted. "Is that so hard to believe?"

He realized he was staring at her. It wasn't hard to stare at Poppy, but for once, it wasn't because of how she looked. He was trying to digest what she'd just said. She actually thought she wasn't cut out for television? Her. Someone who looked like they'd been born for it, who was so smooth and confident on camera that he had to remind himself this was someone he'd known once upon a time. Someone who'd been raised in his hometown. He thought she'd be on TV forever. He'd assumed that Portland affiliate was just the first stop on her way to the stratosphere.

"I'm just surprised," he said. "That's all."

"Why?"

"Why wouldn't I be? You're good at what you do, that's obvious."

"I guess. But I'm not happy, and it's taken me a long time to figure out that's what's really important."

"And you'll be happy in Christmas Bay?"

There was insinuation behind that question. And they both knew what it was. *How on earth could you be happy here?* He might as well have come out and said exactly that.

"I don't know," she said. "But I think this is where I need to be right now. I need to come to terms with losing Grandpa. And I need to come to terms with what happened to Danny."

He barely heard his little brother's name, her voice was

so hoarse. The way she said it sounded like it physically hurt. And it probably did. It hurt him to hear it.

"I left Christmas Bay for college," she continued, "and I never looked back. It wasn't right, how I left. I should've stayed. I should've…"

"You should've what?"

She shook her head, and her brow furrowed. "I should've stayed to face what I'd done. It's as simple as that."

He watched her. If it *was* as simple as that, he would've tracked her down a long time ago. To confront her. To force the matter. To give Danny justice, and to make himself feel better.

But it wasn't as simple as that. It never had been. To say she needed to face what she'd done implied that what she'd done had been on purpose. And as mad as Justin had been, he knew that wasn't the case. Obviously, she hadn't meant to have the accident. She hadn't meant for Danny to be hurt. Even his mother knew that, deep down. And the sooner they all accepted it, the better.

The problem was, *how* did they go about accepting it? It was a question that haunted him daily.

He took a sip of coffee, absorbing the information. People kept walking in and out of the donut shop with their waxy bags of warm, baked goodness, and the sugary smell wafting through the small space made his stomach growl.

"So," he said, setting down his cup again. "Where will you live?"

"The apartment above the shop is in great shape. There's room for all of us. It'll be a little cramped with Mary, but she sees this as an adventure, anyway. So I think it'll work out okay."

"And Roo?"

She shifted in her seat. "I was hoping you'd be able to keep her for a little longer? Just to give me time to get acclimated. And then I can take her. But I haven't decided if I'm going to keep her yet. Honestly, it might be better if I found her a home. I'm not used to taking care of a pet."

"I'm sure you'd settle in just fine if you kept her. Which, you know, I'm not saying you should. I'm just saying it'd be easier than you think."

"I don't know." She shrugged. "There are other reasons…"

"Like?"

"Like…getting attached, for one."

"And that's a problem?"

"For someone who's spent the better part of a decade making emotional distance an art form, it is."

He smiled. Only because he could relate to that more than she probably knew.

She stiffened visibly. Defensively. He could relate to that, too.

"What?" she asked.

"Nothing."

"Why are you smiling?"

"I can't smile?"

She didn't have an answer for that, but he knew exactly what she was thinking. *You're having coffee with me. What's there to smile about?*

"I can keep her for as long as you need," he said.

"It's not a problem?"

"She's a good dog. I've been bringing her to work with me, and she stays in her crate. She'd probably be fine with the customers, though. I think Earl let her have free rein in the antique shop. But she's more fearful now, so I'd rather be safe than sorry."

"Okay," she said. "That's a huge help. Thank you."

"You should come over to meet her a few times before you take her, though. Just so she knows you. She's a big girl, and if she decided to bolt or something, she'd probably drag you right down the street."

"Oh. Well. That's good to know."

He laughed at the expression on her face, unable to help it. She just looked so uncomfortable. The Poppy he'd known had had a gift with animals. She'd loved them all—dogs, cats, rabbits, horses, you name it. She'd been good with them, and they'd instinctively loved her back. There were some things about Poppy that he'd chosen to block out, but he remembered that part of her personality well. It was because it had always impressed him, how gentle and intuitive she'd been, even at a young age.

"*What's* so funny, Justin?"

"You just seem nervous. And that's not how I remember you at all."

There was the smallest spark behind her eyes. "How do you remember me?"

"You?" That was a loaded question. Because if he answered honestly, he'd unleash hell, and he wasn't about to do that. Instead, he took an even breath and held her gaze.

"I remember you being gutsy," he said. Really, that was all he needed to say.

"I remember that about me, too. But somewhere along the line, I changed."

Of course, she had. Anyone would've, after what she'd been through. But it sounded like she was disappointed with herself. Or like she didn't know herself anymore, and that was also something he could identify with. He'd changed, too.

They were quiet for a minute, the donut shop humming around them.

"I should've asked if you wanted something to eat," he finally said. "I remember you liking maple bars... Is that right?"

She smiled. "That's right."

He looked over at the counter, where there was a short line. "Do you want one?"

"No, that's okay. We went to Mario's last night and I'm still stuffed."

Again, they were quiet. But it seemed like an easier silence. Like some light had been shed on the narrow path that snaked between them, and he could see a little clearer now.

"Well," Poppy said, "I guess I should get back to the shop. We're meeting Grandpa's attorney there to finalize some things..."

"Of course."

She bit her cheek, looking like she wanted to say something more. Then took a deep breath.

"Justin..." she began.

He watched her.

"I know your feelings for me are complicated. I know you probably don't want to be near me any more than you have to be. But you and Grandpa were close. We're planning on spreading his ashes sometime this summer. I know it would've meant a lot to him if you came. If you could get past—"

"Poppy."

"Yes?"

"I'd be honored to."

She looked relieved. It was clear that she thought he despised her. Was this the kind of turmoil that she'd been living with over the last ten years? If she thought this was what the people of Christmas Bay thought of her, what must she think of herself?

All of a sudden, Justin could see what it was going to take for her to stay. That's what she'd meant by facing what she'd done. Did she feel like she needed to be punished? Like she deserved that? He wasn't sure, but he had a feeling that's exactly what it was all about.

"Thank you," she said. "That means a lot to me. I didn't want to start with that, obviously."

"Because you think I hate you."

She stared at him. Probably shocked that he'd opened the door to this kind of communication. Truthfully, he was shocked, too. He'd never meant to find himself sitting across from her, talking to her at all. Much less about his feelings for her. But there was something about the look in her eyes that he couldn't get up and walk away from. He couldn't leave it like this. It had been too long, with too much pain stretching between them. He needed some closure, and maybe this was the beginning of that.

"Well," she said evenly. "Yes."

"I don't."

Another shocker. He wasn't quite sure how he felt about Poppy. But hate didn't fit the bill.

She didn't look like she believed him, though. She watched him hesitantly. Like he was going to come up with a punchline at any moment. She was the joke, after all.

"I appreciate that," she said. "But you don't have to try to make me feel better, Justin. I don't expect anything from you. Especially kindness."

"Who says I'm being kind?"

"You were always kind."

"Because I was in l—"

He stopped short, but it was too late. Poppy probably knew what he'd been about to say because it was most likely written all over his face. *Because I was in love with you...*

She watched him, her lips slightly parted. His gaze dropped to them before he could help himself. And then he was imagining kissing her. Something he'd never done, obviously, because she'd been Danny's. And even though electricity had sparked between them as teenagers, they'd never explored that heat or intensity. They'd been off-limits to each other. And now, they were off-limits to each other because of the tragedy between them. Justin knew that even sitting here together would set tongues wagging in Christmas Bay. His friends would hear about it. His parents would sure as hell hear about it.

And then what would he say? *We were talking about the dog.* But it was a lot more than that, and he knew it.

Poppy sat back against the booth. Something in her expression shuttered. Her walls were back up. She didn't trust what he was saying, and he couldn't blame her. He barely trusted it himself. He didn't know where this softness toward her was coming from. This story had always needed a villain, and she was it.

"I really should go," she said.

He nodded.

"I'll call you?" she said, picking up her purse. "To come over and meet Roo?"

"Sure. No problem."

"Thank you, Justin."

He nodded again, and she was up and out the door. Guilt, heavy and cold, settled in his chest. He imagined what

Danny would say if he knew how Justin felt about Poppy, even now, years later. He liked to think his brother was beyond all that now. That these were earthly matters, concerning only earthly beings. But he couldn't help but wonder, just the same.

Taking another swallow of coffee, he looked out the window. The sun shone, bright and cheerful, unable to touch the chill inside his heart. So Poppy was staying. And just like that, things had gotten a hell of a lot more complicated. She was a reality that he was going to have to deal with once and for all.

He rubbed the stubble on his chin. The first thing he needed to do was get Roo accustomed to her new mistress. Because if there was one thing he knew for sure, it was that he didn't want to face any more emotional ups and downs. Having Roo was a link to Poppy that needed severing. He didn't trust himself around her. He didn't trust himself not to say or do something that he couldn't take back.

Something that would change everything if he let it.

Chapter Seven

Poppy stood behind the counter of the antique shop, watching Beau, who was getting ready to turn the sign around in the front window. The one that would announce that the shop was open for business again. The one that would cement this plan into place for the next year of their lives.

The Sawyer cousins were back. And they were here to stay.

Beside her, Cora took an audible breath. "This is it," she said. "I'm nervous. I feel like it's my first day of school or something."

"Don't be nervous, Mom," Mary said. "*Anything's* better than the first day of school. Those are gross."

Cora was going to homeschool Mary for the rest of the spring, but the plan was to enroll her at Christmas Bay Middle School in the fall. Poppy hoped she'd be more excited by then. She'd had a pretty rough road, so being home with her mom for a while probably wasn't such a bad thing. And she'd be helping in the shop, too. That would be good for her.

Poppy wiped a spot of imaginary dust off the counter. It had been nearly a week since their dinner at Mario's. They'd spent most of that time settling things back home, getting the apartment ready, and cleaning the shop from top to bottom until it sparkled. She knew she needed to call Justin to set up a time to meet Roo—he'd already had her for too long as it was. But their meeting at the donut shop had left her shaken. More than shaken—it had left her terrified that she wasn't as in control as she liked to think she was.

"Ready?" Beau asked from across the shop.

"Yes!" Mary said. "Open already, Uncle Beau!"

"Okay. Here goes."

He flipped the sign and unlocked the door. Then stood back as if he was about to be trampled by a herd of antique-loving tourists.

An elderly couple strolled up to the window to peer in half-heartedly, but then kept walking.

Poppy let out a breath she hadn't realized she'd been holding. She wondered, and not for the first time, what they'd do if business turned out to be so slow that they couldn't make a profit. Since they'd gotten a look at the books, they knew their grandfather hadn't made one in several years. He'd been living off his savings and investments. Beau kept reminding them that, unlike the last few years under their grandfather, they'd be open regular business hours, and that alone should turn things around. But Poppy worried, anyway. Because she was Poppy.

Cora looked at her watch. "Well, I guess we don't all have to be here today. Do you want Mary and me to go to the grocery store? We've been meaning to stock the fridge…"

"That'd be great," Poppy said. "And you're right, I don't think we're going to have a huge rush."

Cora frowned. "I know you've been waiting until everything is settled to figure out if you're going to take Roo. Have you decided yet?"

Mary slapped her hands together in mock prayer. "*Please* take her, Aunt Poppy. Please, please, please."

"Oh. Well… I'm not sure yet."

"We could take her if you can't, right, Mom?"

Cora gazed patiently down at her daughter. Mary had been talking about Roo nonstop since the reading of the will.

"We've got our hands full right now, sweetie," she said. "We all love dogs, but it might not be the best thing for her. She's used to a certain kind of life, and there are a lot of us in the apartment… It's just complicated."

Poppy watched Mary's expression fall, and her heart fell with it. She'd love to be that supercool aunt who would take Roo, and make Mary's entire year in the process. But she was so absorbed in her issues that she couldn't do anything but hedge whenever Mary mentioned the dog. But the truth was, she had to pick up Roo from Justin soon. And then she'd have to decide. No more hedging. No more anything.

The front door of the antique shop opened with a little tinkle of the bell hanging above it. They all looked over to see Frances O'Hara walk through. Frances was the sweet, sixty-something owner of Coastal Sweets down the street. A girl of about two or three skipped in beside her, clutching a small white paper bag. She was adorable. Towheaded and rosy-cheeked, she reminded Poppy of Mary when she was that age.

Poppy smiled, happy to see Frances. She didn't know her well, but the older woman had always been kind to her. Even after the accident, unlike a lot of people in town, she'd continued to be friendly and welcoming any time

Poppy came into her shop. Frances had aged some since Poppy left, but she was still beautiful. Luminous skin, poufy blond hair, perfectly applied makeup. She was wearing a Christmas Bay Middle School sweatshirt, and big, dangly earrings that sparkled in the morning light.

"Well, hello there!" Frances said with a smile. "We wanted to come by and welcome you to Main Street. And give our condolences on Earl, of course. He was such a dear man."

Poppy walked out from behind the counter, ready to extend her hand to Frances, but the other woman pulled her into a quick hug first. She smelled perfumy, like every grandmother Poppy had ever hugged before.

"So have I heard right?" she asked, patting Poppy's back before pulling away again. "You kids are going to be running the shop for a while? Word travels fast around here."

"We are," Cora said. "It was so nice of you to stop by."

Frances put a hand on the girl's shoulder beside her. "This is my granddaughter, Emily. We wanted to bring you some candy, didn't we, honey?"

Emily grinned up at Beau, clutching the bag in her chubby little hands. It was a little smooshed.

"Well, thank you," Beau said, clearly charmed.

"I picked 'em," she said proudly. "Gummy worms."

"Our gummy worms are very popular," Frances said, her gaze shifting to Mary. "I always have to order extra. And who's this?"

Cora put an arm around her daughter. "This is Mary."

"Hi, Mary. And how old are you, if you don't mind me asking?"

Mary didn't mind being asked, Poppy could tell.

"I'm ten, but I'll be eleven this summer."

"Well, now. That's almost babysitting age, isn't it, Emily?"

The toddler nodded and bounced a few times on the toes of her rainbow-colored sneakers.

"Have you ever babysat before?"

Mary shook her head.

"Maybe we can talk about it, if your mom says it's okay. Now, my memory is shot to bits. So don't be offended if I don't remember your name the next time we meet, okay, honey?"

"Okay."

"You just remind me. Say 'Frances, write it down!' That's what my kids always tell me. Write it down! But I never do."

Mary laughed.

"Try my worms!" Emily said. "They're *yum*."

"I will. I love gummy worms."

Frances's gaze shifted to Poppy, and her smile faded a little. "Now, remind me again…you're on the news, right?"

"That's right. But my station has given me some time off so I can be home for a while."

That was true, but it wasn't the whole truth. In order to stay for the entire year, she'd have to quit and hope they'd hire her back. That was if she decided to go back at all. It was something that she hadn't broached with her boss yet. She could just add that to the list of the things she was going to have to figure out sooner rather than later.

"Well, I just love that you three are going to be carrying on Earl's tradition here," Frances said. "He sure did love this shop. And he loved you kids. He talked about you all the time."

Beau looked over at Poppy. She could see the guilt in

his eyes. She understood how he felt, because she felt the same way. They should've come home more often. There were so many things she wished she could go back and fix. She wished she could be a better granddaughter, a better cousin. A better person all-around. But she couldn't go back and change any of those things. The only thing she could do now was try to move forward with those wishes in her heart.

The front door opened again, and Poppy looked over to see a couple of women walk in, sunglasses perched on top of their heads, coffees in their hands. They looked around with obvious interest, which made her feel better. Maybe they'd tell their friends about this place when they left. Maybe the shop would make some kind of profit after all. Maybe the people in town would treat her the way Frances was treating her now. Maybe it would all be okay. Maybe...

"Well," Frances said. "We should probably go. Don't be strangers, okay? Come down and see us."

"We will," Cora said. "And thank you for the gummy worms."

"There's more where that came from."

Frances reached down and grabbed on to Emily's hand and Poppy's heart lurched. It wasn't often that she let herself think about the fact that she was almost thirty and had no family of her own. Not even a prospect of a family of her own. But that was by design. If she didn't have a family, nothing bad could happen to them. She couldn't screw up in some catastrophic way and ruin someone's life. She was pretty sure she'd never have kids. It was too scary. But she could hear her biological clock ticking, just the same.

"Say bye-bye, Emily," Frances said.

"Bye-bye, Emily," the girl echoed in her tiny voice.

Poppy laughed.

And suddenly that biological clock was about as loud as she'd ever heard it.

Evelyn pushed her squeaky cart down aisle four of Christmas Bay's biggest market, which wasn't that big at all. Once a month, she drove into Eugene to stock up at the Costco there, but in between, she'd come to Cartwrights and get the groceries they'd run out of. They were constantly low on paper towels. And milk. For whatever reason, Paul could never get enough milk in his diet, even though she'd long suspected he was lactose-intolerant.

Slowing the cart, she reached over and grabbed some ketchup, not paying attention to the brand, and not really caring. She was more interested in the girl several yards ahead, who was pushing a cart that was twice as big as she was. She had a list in her hand that she kept looking down at with a frown. She looked too young to be here by herself, but who knew, maybe she was. She couldn't be more than ten or eleven, though. But what had Evelyn staring was the fact that she looked so familiar. She'd been trying to place her for the last minute or two, largely ignoring her own grocery list in the process.

She continued following behind her at a comfortable distance. The market was practically deserted this morning, and she didn't want to be too obvious about it. But it was bugging her. She knew almost everyone in Christmas Bay. Knew their kids. Their grandkids. And she couldn't place this girl, even though she *knew* she'd seen her recently. When was it?

For some reason, a strange feeling had settled in the pit of her stomach. Like she was nervous, but had no idea why.

The girl slowed in front of the pickles, and looked at her list again. She was cute. Gangly and thin, with freckles scattered across her slightly upturned nose. She reminded Evelyn of someone...

And then, like a lightning bolt out of a clear blue sky, it hit her. She knew exactly who this was. She'd been with Poppy a week ago on the sidewalk. The day Evelyn had stopped her. She'd barely noticed the girl because she'd only had eyes for Poppy. But this was definitely the girl who'd been with her. Those freckles alone should've clued her in. She looked like all the Sawyers with that blond hair and olive skin. They were a good-looking family. Even Earl, who'd been in his eighties, had been very handsome, fending off regular advances from all the widows down at the community center.

Evelyn slowed until her cart came to a squeaking stop. She was probably staring, but she was also lost in thought, and only half-aware—falling down a wormhole of thoughts and emotions. Thankfully, this didn't happen in public very often, but sometimes it did when she was especially stressed about something, and it was embarrassing when she came to. That's what Paul called it. *Coming to.* Like she'd passed out or something.

The girl looked at her list, then up at the pickles again. After a second of contemplation, she stood on her tiptoes and reached for a jar above her head. She was relatively tall, but the jar was taller, and she was having trouble getting her fingers around it. Evelyn watched as she pushed it to the edge of the shelf, and then, like it was happening in slow motion, it teetered there for what seemed like minutes. *It's going to fall*, Evelyn thought. It might even fall on the girl's feet, if she didn't jump back fast enough. But even as Evelyn made an aborted attempt to try and stop the inevitable, the jar went ahead and plummeted to the floor, shattering in an explosion of glass and pickles that went everywhere.

The girl stood there for a moment, shocked into complete stillness. It had missed her feet, thank God, but her jeans were spattered. Shards of glass were scattered all over the linoleum floor, like jagged little knives. She looked down at the mess, and her cheeks flooded with color, her eyes filling with quick tears.

Evelyn watched this, the sound of the shattering jar echoing in her mind and pulling her out of her strange, dreamlike state. She knew this wasn't healthy. She knew it wasn't fair to judge everyone she came into contact with by whether or not they were connected to Poppy. But she'd been living this way for so long, that it was second nature. It was how she went about her days. Keeping track. Keeping score. It was sad, really. She'd become someone she didn't really like that much.

Forcing that thought from her mind, along with all the others that had crowded there over the last few seconds, she stepped forward, careful to avoid the biggest pieces of glass.

The girl looked up, tears streaming down her face. She didn't say anything. She looked too mortified. Something about the look on her face, the way her long, dark eyelashes were spiked with tears, tore at Evelyn's heart. *Poor baby.* For kids that age *everything* was embarrassing. Your parents, your body, your social skills, or lack thereof. Breaking a jar of pickles at the grocery store? Beyond life-altering.

"Careful, honey," Evelyn said, holding out her hand. "Come here. I don't want you to step on the glass."

The girl did as she was told, and put her hand in Evelyn's. It was damp with perspiration and she was trembling like a leaf.

She stepped over the glass, looking down at the mess on the floor. Overhead, a nameless, faceless voice called for a cleanup on aisle four. Someone must've passed by without either one of them noticing.

Evelyn gave her hand a squeeze before letting it go, surprising herself. This wasn't like her at all, especially since this girl was related to Poppy Sawyer.

"Hey," she said.

The girl looked up, and there went the voice overhead again, impatient this time. *"Aisle four, please."*

"Don't worry. It was just an accident. We all have accidents, right?"

It was like the words were coming out of someone else's mouth. *We all have accidents...* Oh, the irony. It was true, everyone *did* have accidents. But broken pickle jars and fatal car wrecks weren't exactly the same thing.

"What's your name?" she asked.

The girl sniffed and swiped at the tears on her cheeks. "Mary."

"Are you here all by yourself, Mary?" Evelyn asked, looking around. She was aware of the protective tone of her voice. It had been a while since she'd used her mama-bear tone. But it had been a while since she'd needed to.

"My mom's next door mailing a present to her friend. She wanted me to get started on the shopping."

Evelyn smiled, relieved that Mary wasn't expected to grocery shop alone. Relieved that someone would be with her soon. And especially relieved that that someone wasn't going to be Poppy.

"This will probably be all cleaned up by the time she gets here," she said. "And she'll be so happy that you helped with the shopping. I wish I had someone to help with my grocery shopping. It's my least favorite thing in the whole world. I mean, yuck."

This got a little smile.

"I know you," Mary said after a second.

"You do?"

"You're the lady who doesn't like Aunt Poppy."

Evelyn's face warmed. When she'd left the house this morning, she never could've imagined she'd have this kind of encounter at the grocery store, of all places. She'd just needed paper towels and milk. She silently cursed Paul and his milk addiction.

"Well, I…"

"She won't tell me why."

"Oh."

"But I know it's bad, because most people like Aunt Poppy."

"They do?" Evelyn didn't mean to sound so surprised.

"She's really nice. She sends me birthday cards with money in them."

"Ah."

"I bet whatever you fought about, you could be friends again, if you tried."

Evelyn's ears throbbed. "You think?"

"My mom always makes me and my friends talk after we have a fight. She says it 'clears the air.' Do you think you could talk to her? To clear the air?"

Right about then, a man in a red apron rounded the corner with a mop and a bucket. He looked mildly annoyed. Evelyn put a hand on Mary's shoulder, ready to step in if he got salty. Despite Evelyn's wildly fluctuating emotions on the subject, accidents *did* in fact happen, and a broken jar of pickles was not the end of the world.

"So," the man said. "A little accident here?"

Evelyn nodded curtly. "Yes. I've dropped them before myself. They can be awfully slippery."

"Oh, it's no problem," he said with a smile, redeeming himself some.

"Well," Evelyn said. "I'd better get back to my shopping, Mary. Do you think your mom will be here soon?"

"I bet she's already here. She just hasn't found me yet."

"Okay. Well…have a good day."

"Ma'am?" Mary said. "What's your name?"

Evelyn couldn't help but smile. This child was so precocious. Before she could help it, she thought of Poppy again. How she'd been just like this when she'd been a girl. Full of personality and spark. She'd been a force to be reckoned with.

Evelyn had a fleeting image of Mary as a teenager. How she'd grow into her gangly limbs. How her hair would be shining blond, maybe pulled back from her pretty face, scrubbed free of makeup. Or not. Some teen girls wore an atrocious amount of makeup.

"I'm Evelyn," she said. Then held out her hand.

Mary shook it. A firm handshake. A grown-up handshake. But there was something behind her eyes that looked sad. Evelyn wondered what her story was. Everyone had a story.

"It's nice to meet you," Mary said.

"It's nice to meet you, too. Maybe we'll see each other again sometime."

"I bet we will. I'm going to be here for a whole year. My mom and I are going to help run my grandpa's antique shop. There's lots of stuff in there if you like old stuff. Some of it's dusty, but we cleaned it up and it looks pretty good now. You should come in. Do you like old stuff?"

Evelyn stared down at her, processing this. "You're staying?"

Mary nodded.

"You and your mom?"

"And my aunt and uncle. My grandpa asked them to run the shop together."

Evelyn's heartbeat slowed. Poppy was *staying*? How was that possible? She had a career in the city. She couldn't possibly stay here for a year. It didn't make any sense.

She realized that her mouth was hanging open, and she snapped it shut again. But her head was spinning, her stomach full of dread. *A year?* She had so many questions. *Are you absolutely sure? Your aunt is staying? Why, exactly? And why a year? What's that all about?*

She cleared her throat, trying to think of what to say. She felt like she might pass out, which was silly. But that's how she felt. So this was what happened when she was forced to face all the things she'd been pushing down for the last decade. It wasn't pretty.

"Mary? Honey?"

They both turned at the sound of a voice behind them. Standing there, looking very beautiful and very flustered, was Cora Sawyer. It had been years since Evelyn had seen her. She hadn't known her well, only running into her once or twice when Poppy and Danny had been dating. But she remembered her. She remembered all the Sawyers.

"Mom." Mary stepped around Evelyn to give her mother a hug.

"What happened?"

"I dropped the pickles."

The man with the mop looked over. He was almost done cleaning up. "It's no problem."

"It was *totally* embarrassing," Mary said.

"Oh, no. Are you okay?"

Evelyn shuffled quietly to the left, trying to make a clean getaway.

"I'm fine. Evelyn helped me."

Cora looked over, and her expression fell as she recognized her. She'd never been a direct target of Evelyn's rage all those years ago, but she was a Sawyer, so she'd felt some of it. Enough that there was a sudden, awkward tension between them now.

"Mrs. Frost," Cora said. "It's nice to see you again."

Evelyn wanted to laugh at that. A sudden cackle that would make her sound like the Wicked Witch of the West. *Nice?* She knew better than that. Cora had most likely been dreading this moment just as much as Poppy had, and was definitely counting down the seconds until it was over.

But Mary, the sweet girl with the clumsy hands, was a completely unexpected twist in this tired old story. Evelyn was finding herself wanting to be civil for her sake. Friendly, even. Or as friendly as she could manage under the circumstances.

She smiled. It was forced, but she didn't think it *looked* forced. Evelyn could be a good actress when she set her mind to it. "Hello, Cora," she said. "It's been a long time."

Cora nodded.

"I was sorry to hear about Earl," Evelyn said. "Everybody liked him."

"Thank you."

Evelyn paused, deciding whether or not to say anything more, or if she should just make her retreat already. On the speakers overhead, someone announced a special on sirloin steaks. *But you had to hurry, this sale would only last through the weekend!*

Cora shifted on her feet, clearly not caring about sirloin steaks, or what a great deal this was.

Evelyn watched her. And in the end, simple curiosity won out.

"Mary says that you're staying in Christmas Bay?" She managed to keep her voice even. A surprise, since she was falling apart on the inside. "For a year?"

Cora glanced down at her daughter. She looked like every mother in the world who wished their child wouldn't share private information with virtual strangers.

"Um...yeah. We're going to be helping with the shop."

"I see. And Poppy? She'll be staying, too?"

It was bold, but it wasn't bitchy. She thought it sounded perfectly normal, but, of course, there was meaning behind it. Just like there was meaning behind everything Evelyn uttered about Poppy.

Cora's shoulders stiffened a little. Nobody else would've noticed, but Evelyn did.

"She is."

"I'm surprised. Since she has the anchor job in Portland."

"Well, she hasn't worked that out yet. I'm not sure what her plans are for the long run, but for now, she'll be in Christmas Bay."

Evelyn nodded. *She'll be in Christmas Bay...*

"I asked Evelyn to come by the shop," Mary said. "I told her it looks really good."

Cora's eyes widened.

"I'd love to come by," Evelyn said, trying to put the other woman at ease. Knowing it was her fault for fostering this bitterness in the first place. But not letting herself linger on that fact for more than a second.

"Really?" Mary asked.

"Really."

"That's very kind of you," Cora said. She looked relieved that this particular run-in hadn't turned ugly. Like the one on the sidewalk, when Evelyn had accused Poppy of growing up and forgetting all about Danny. Or all the run-ins after the accident when she'd gone out of her way to confront Poppy, because it felt better to be mean to her than to face a future without her son.

She felt a stab of shame. It was cold and sharp, not pleasant at all. It was like getting a quick glimpse in the mirror and seeing that you weren't nearly as pretty as you thought you were.

Paul had been saying it for years—she needed to let this go. She needed to try to heal before the bitterness gobbled her up. She'd never listened, of course. Because how could he possibly know what was in her heart? And every time she'd hear a small inner voice say that he *did* know, because he'd lost a child, too, she silenced it as quickly as it had come.

"I'm not sure that I'm very kind," she said quietly.

Cora clearly hadn't heard her. She leaned forward and opened her mouth like she was going to ask what she'd said.

But before she could, Evelyn turned and walked away.

Leaving her cart where it was and not looking back. She just wanted to go home. Needed to get to her car before she did something stupid, like cry in the middle of the grocery store.

Chapter Eight

Poppy stood in front of Brothers' Hardware, her palms sweaty and her heart racing. She tried blaming that on her second cup of coffee this morning, but she knew it was about Justin, and didn't have anything to do with caffeine.

When she'd been about to look up the number to the hardware store a few minutes ago, Beau had wisely pointed out that that was silly. It was right across the street. She should just walk over there—she had to meet Roo, anyway.

So here she was. Trying very hard to be nonchalant about the whole thing, but feeling anything but. She was nervous about meeting the dog. And she was nervous about dropping in on Justin, even if she did have a good reason.

Rubbing her hands down her jeans, she took a deep breath. Then reached for the door, and opened it wide. She was hit with a rush of cool air that smelled like a mix of sawdust and rubber. There were a few people browsing in the narrow aisles. The floors were a scarred hardwood, and a few ceiling fans turned lazily overhead, making her feel like she'd stepped back in time to when Christmas Bay's Main Street had been even sleepier than it was now.

She looked around, smiling at a man in overalls walking past. He smiled back. The store had a good vibe. A homey, comforting feel. It was the kind of place where families shopped year after year. She wasn't sure when Justin had opened it, but he was obviously doing well. It suited him. He'd always been handy, she remembered that well. Whenever his parents' dishwasher broke, or the sprinkler heads weren't working, Justin had fixed them. They'd never had to call anyone, because he'd been able to fix just about anything. She remembered his mother telling her once that he was just like his grandfather in that way. He had a gift.

Her gaze settled on the front counter, where the cash register sat. Beside it, there was a large plastic jar asking for donations for the local animal shelter. So he was an animal lover. That was pretty obvious, since he'd taken in Roo. Justin had a big heart. She'd always known that about him. Part of the reason why she'd liked him so much, and why Danny had been so suspicious all those years ago.

Guilt, familiar and warm, heated her cheeks. If she'd been honest with Danny back then, if she'd accepted her feelings for Justin, would she feel so badly about it today? She wasn't sure. Sometimes it was impossible to untangle the guilt from the accident, from the guilt about Justin. It felt like the rest of her days would be flooded with guilt, and she'd eventually drown in it.

"Poppy?"

She turned to see Justin standing there, tall and handsome, in a red plaid shirt and jeans. Rugged-looking with more scruff today than he'd had when they'd had coffee. But what really stopped her heart were his eyes. They were honey-colored in the sun, but under the hardware-store lighting, they were darker. Richer and deeper. She knew she had no business appreciating his eyes though, or his scruff, or anything else about him. She was here for one thing and one thing only, and that was to meet Roo.

"Hey," she said.

"What are you doing here?"

"Well, we've got the shop up and running. Which means I've got time to meet Roo. I know you're working. Obviously." She smiled nervously. "But I thought I could meet her, and we could take it slow, since you said she's fearful since Grandpa died."

"Sure. Let me just…"

He stepped around her, making her want to lean away. But his arm brushed hers, anyway. So briefly that she barely felt it, but at the same time, that was *all* she felt. Suddenly, she was so aware of her pounding heartbeat that it was making her a little panicky. Was she about to have a heart attack? A stroke? She wouldn't be surprised—the last six or seven years of predawn mornings and ridiculously late nights, coupled with thousands of frozen dinners and no vacations, meant she was probably a perfect candidate for both.

"Let me just turn the sign around," he continued. "It's almost lunch, anyway, and I usually close from twelve to one."

She clasped her hands in front of her, wishing she wasn't so drawn to him. She wished she were calm and cool, and completely unbothered by this moment. She'd spent so much time in front of television cameras and under hot studio lights that something like this should've been a walk in the park. But it wasn't. It was one of the hardest things she'd ever done. And she'd done a lot of hard things.

"Are you sure?" she asked. "I don't want to inconvenience you."

"It's fine. We just need to wait until these last few customers clear out."

She watched him turn the sign around in the window, the muscles in his broad shoulders moving underneath his shirt. She looked away when she realized she was staring.

He walked back over to her, his hands in his jean pockets. They were faded Levi's, and looked so good on him that she wondered again why he was single. Justin was the kind of man who oozed sexuality and self-confidence. But he was also kind—in Poppy's opinion, his most important characteristic. But his looks were hard to ignore, even for her, someone who had every reason in the world to ignore them.

"So things are going okay over there?" he asked.

She nodded.

"That's good. It must be a relief."

"It is."

"And you've decided to stay? For sure?" His voice was even. Almost emotionless. But the look in his eyes betrayed his true feelings.

"I have."

He nodded, the muscles in his jaw bunching. She wondered what was going through his mind. Actually, no. She was glad she didn't know. She reminded herself that she was here for Roo, not Justin. Despite realizing that her old feelings for him hadn't disappeared with time. And the fact that he had a nice body, and an even nicer face, didn't matter in the least.

"Well, I've been doing this for a while," he said. "I know you're all new to running a business, so if you ever need anything, or have any questions, I'm here."

"Thank you."

"Sure."

She kept her hands clasped, squeezing her fingers almost painfully. "Frances O'Hara came in the other day."

"I know Frances. Nice lady."

"Very nice. She had her granddaughter with her. Emily, I think?"

"Yup."

"She brought us gummy worms. Mary was thrilled."

He smiled, but it was small. "She's got Alzheimer's. Frances, I mean. You should probably know that. She forgets names and dates, that's pretty common. But lately she's been getting confused about directions and bigger things like that. Her foster daughters are all here now—they moved back to be close to her, and they help in the shop. But we all keep an eye out for her, too."

Poppy's heart ached at the news. Frances was clearly a vital woman, and even though she'd alluded to the fact that she had memory issues, she'd only said it in passing. She hid it well. Poppy was glad to know, if only to do exactly what Justin had said—keep an eye out for her. She made a mental note to go down to Coastal Sweets more often. If her grandfather had been in that position, she hoped that someone would've done the same for him.

"I'm sorry to hear that," she said. "We were lucky with Grandpa. He never had to deal with any kind of dementia."

"No, he was sharp as a tack until the very end."

The very end... It was still hard for Poppy to think about her grandfather in the past tense.

The last of the customers walked out the door, leaving them alone in the shop that suddenly felt very quiet.

Justin walked over to the door and locked it, then turned to her again. The way he was looking at her could almost make her forget the sad, shared history between them. In another time, another place, if they'd met as adults, who knows what might've happened. How this story might've ended.

"So," he said. "Roo?"

"Oh...yes."

"She's over there in her crate."

Poppy nodded, and followed him behind the counter, where there was a massive crate in the corner. Inside was a big gray dog, lying down, her head on her paws. When she saw Justin, her tail thumped.

"Hey, girl," he said, leaning down to unlock the door.

She raised her head and licked his hands through the wire.

"She's really good in here," he said. "Doesn't make a sound. Sometimes I give her a bone with peanut butter in it. She likes that."

The dog stood and shook, jingling the tags on her collar. Poppy couldn't believe how big she was.

She stepped out of the crate, glancing hesitantly at Poppy. She went immediately into Justin's side. She leaned against him and licked his face as he kneeled down beside her.

"Well," he said, draping an arm around her and patting her fluffy shoulder. "Here she is. Poppy, meet Roo. Roo, this is Poppy."

Slowly, Poppy extended her hand for Roo to sniff. But the dog just watched her, not making any attempt to leave Justin's side. The look in her eyes was so intense that Poppy stepped back after a few seconds.

"I don't think she likes me."

"She just doesn't know you. It'll take some time. She's very sweet, I promise."

Poppy stared down at her. She was enormous. If she snapped at her, it wasn't like she'd leave a little bruise. She could do some real damage. Poppy loved animals, had especially loved dogs, but she also had a healthy respect for them, and didn't have any interest in getting bitten. She'd covered a story once about some sort of shepherd mix that had attacked its owner, and sent him to the emergency room to get his ear reattached. For some reason, that was all she could think about now, as Roo stared up at her, unblinking.

She touched her ear absentmindedly.

Justin smiled. "You look scared to death."

"I do?"

"Here." He stood and reached for a bag of treats sitting on the counter. "Let's try this."

He put a couple of them in her palm. His fingers brushed against hers, and it was hard to ignore the tingling heat left in their wake. She hadn't touched Justin since she was a teenager. And even then, those brief moments had been in passing. When he'd handed her something across the dinner table, or given her the remote as she and Danny sat on the couch watching TV. She'd been young, but she'd been aware of the effect he had on her. And she was aware now.

He took hold of Roo's collar, probably just to keep her from snarfing up all the treats at once, but to Poppy it felt like he was holding the dog back from possible attack.

"Poppy."

She looked up at him. "Hmm?"

"Relax."

She realized she was holding the treats so hard that her fingernails were biting into her palm.

"Why don't you hold one out?" he said. "She loves these things."

She nodded. Taking one between her fingers, she held it in front of Roo's quivering wet nose.

The dog sniffed it carefully, obviously tempted. But after a few seconds, she turned her head away, refusing it altogether.

Poppy's heart sank. Dogs were a good judge of character. So what did this say about her? The rational part of her brain answered right away. *It just means you're nervous, and she senses that.*

But the other part of her brain, the part that followed her heart, wanted to throw out all kinds of other possibilities. *What kind of person speeds on a dark, rainy night? On a road that her parents told her not to take in the first place?* A careless one. A stupid one. Maybe even a bad one...

Sudden tears filled her eyes. She turned away, pretending she had something in her eye. Not that Justin would believe that, but she couldn't admit to crying over a dog not taking a treat from her hand. Of course, that wasn't the real issue here. The real issues were her unresolved issues, her unresolved feelings. Trauma that she'd never unpacked. What kind of toll, exactly, did that take on a person year after year? She didn't have a psychology degree, but she knew it couldn't be good.

"Poppy? Are you okay?"

"My darn contact," she said. "Just one second."

She could feel him stepping closer. He must be wondering what he'd gotten himself into. He had no idea what kind of person she'd become. Haunted. Sad. A little strange. He must want her to leave already. To be out of his shop and his life for good.

"Hey."

He was waiting for her to turn around. But she couldn't. She couldn't face him. She wished he hadn't locked the front door. Maybe someone would've come into the shop and saved her from this moment. The incredibly awful realization that inside she was still the fractured, unhappy girl who believed she wasn't worthy of redemption. And that maybe she was going to hell. There were some people in Christmas Bay who probably believed that. Maybe even Justin's own mother.

"Poppy."

She forced a breath. Willed herself to calm down. She needed to get a grip. For his sake, as well as her own.

"Yeah?" she answered.

"Look at me."

"Justin…"

"Look at me, Poppy."

She turned then. The tears had receded, but her eyes were probably still glassy. There was nothing she could do about that, except fake it until she made it.

Justin gazed down at her, his mouth set in a hard line. He looked angry. Actually, he looked like he was holding on by a very thin thread, and that surprised her. She'd expected exasperation maybe. But not anger.

"Don't lie to me," he said.

She was vaguely aware of her pulse racing. Was this the moment she'd been dreading? Was this the end of the strange, gentle kindness he'd shown her so far?

At the tone of his voice, Roo nudged open the door to her crate, and retreated back inside. She lay down in a surprisingly small ball of dog fluff, and tucked her nose into her tail. She wasn't going to be a part of this nonsense. Poppy wished she could crawl in beside her.

"I'm not lying," she said quietly. Which was silly, because it was obvious she *was* lying.

He nodded curtly. "Uh-huh."

"I'm not."

"You know, you never talked to me. Never. Not once." Her eyes widened. "What do you mean?"

"You know damn well what I mean."

"I don't."

"I *mean*, after the accident. You never talked to me about any of it. Even before the accident, you wouldn't talk to me. You were never honest with me, and you're not being honest with me now. I don't deserve that, Poppy."

Her mouth hung open. *Talking?* It had been beyond the realm of possibility for her back then. Especially after the accident.

"I'm sorry...what?"

He didn't answer. Just continued standing there in a quiet smolder.

"You wanted me to open up to you?" she said. *"After Danny?"*

"You make it sound like it was impossible."

"It *was* impossible. I couldn't even look at you, Justin. I couldn't look at your family. I couldn't even look at myself in the mirror. How could you expect me to be honest with you about anything?"

"I know you couldn't look at me. What do you think that did to me? I'd just lost my brother. And then..."

"Don't say it," she said evenly. Tears were stinging her eyes again. It was a battle she was going to lose. She felt them pressing in on her with the pressure of a geyser.

"And then I lost you, too," he said, finishing.

She touched her temple. The room was spinning. "You hated me, Justin. You *hated* me."

"That's not true."

"After the accident, you hated me. I know you did."

"After the accident, I didn't know which way was up. I was grieving. I wanted somebody to blame. But before that…"

She shook her head. "No."

"You're going to deny it?"

"Deny what? There's nothing to deny."

"Damn it, Poppy. I just said don't lie to me."

He had her there, and she had to turn away before she said something that she couldn't suck back in. He was right. They'd never talked about any of this, and she hadn't thought they ever would.

"We felt something for each other," he said. "And we've never addressed it. Never dealt with it. And I guess that might be okay, except for one thing."

She waited. Her heart was beating so hard that she wondered how it was managing to function.

"Except for what?" she said. She didn't know why she asked. She didn't really want to know. Except she did. It was like that horrible curiosity people felt driving by an accident—you couldn't look away, even though you knew you should.

He touched her elbow and she closed her eyes for a second as the memories came rushing back. She remembered her gaze getting caught on his when nobody else was looking, like a hook catching on silk. She remembered the endless daydreams about him touching her, holding her. She'd felt so bad about those daydreams back then, because he was Danny's brother, and Danny was the sweetest guy.

Reluctantly, she turned back to him. As uncomfortable as it was, maybe if they finally dealt with this, if they finally got it out in the open, they'd be able to put it behind them. She was going to be in town for a year. There couldn't be any more hiding, no matter how much she wanted to do just that.

He dropped his hand from her arm, but it didn't matter. The damage was done. Her skin was pulsing.

"All that guilt from before is one thing," he continued, his voice gravelly. "I mean, I might learn to live with it. But I realized when I saw you for the first time last week, that getting over it isn't going to happen for me."

She looked up. Let her gaze settle on his. He was the accident that she couldn't look away from.

"Why?"

"Because," he said. "I still feel something for you. I can't let you go, and I have no idea what to do with that."

He'd said the words, but their meaning was eluding her. It was like they were fluttering around her like small birds, frantic and just out of reach.

She closed her eyes, trying to ground herself.

"Justin."

She realized she was about to argue. She was about to tell him that it simply wasn't possible for him to feel *anything* for her. Except maybe resentment. Or hatred, like she'd long suspected. But she couldn't say it, because she felt something for him, too. She always had. He'd known it. And so had Danny.

"I already felt like I was betraying my little brother before the accident happened," he said. "And then he was killed, and I couldn't even talk to him about it, say I was sorry. Ask for his forgiveness. I couldn't do a damn thing. And I guess I did hate you for that. But I hated myself, too."

The veins in his neck were protruding above his collar. His face was red. He was holding back, but at the same time, he was letting go. She wondered how much more there was to say. She didn't know if she could take much more.

"I can't do this right now," she said, shaking her head. "I'm sorry."

She tried to step around him, but he grabbed her elbow.

"You ran away from this before, Poppy. I'm not going to let you do it again."

Pulling her arm from his grip, she leaned back.

"You can't keep me from doing anything, Justin," she said. "I'm not some stupid teenager anymore. You don't get to decide what I run away from and what I don't."

"No, I don't, you're right. But I'm hoping you'll stay. That you'll talk this out. You owe us that much."

Us. She felt her throat closing up, like it always did when faced with memories of the accident and Danny. It felt like she couldn't breathe, like she was struggling for air. A therapist had told her that she suffered from panic attacks, something that she hadn't had a name for when she was seventeen. But now, she knew, and there was medication for it, thank God. Probably why she was able to keep from passing out now, even though it felt like the walls were starting to close in on her.

"What do you want me to say?" she asked.

Scrubbing a hand through his hair, he leaned against the counter. He looked tired all of a sudden. Older. The threads of silver in his dark hair looked more prominent than they had a few minutes ago. The creases around his eyes, deeper.

"I don't know," he said. "I don't know what I want you to say."

She watched him, her heart beginning to ache. *Justin.* She'd felt so many things for him back then. Then she'd moved away and pushed him to the back of her mind, where she kept everything else that had the power to hurt her.

Suddenly, she was tired of pushing him away. She wondered fleetingly what would happen if she just gave in. Would he hurt her if she did? Or would she only end up hurting herself if she didn't?

He took a deep breath. "It wasn't your fault, you know," he finally said. "The accident…"

Poppy had been told this before, of course. By friends and family. Her parents had said it over and over again, to no avail. She knew it was her fault—*of course*, it was her fault—and people saying that it wasn't only made it worse. Even when her therapists had tried to convince her that the accident was just that—a terrible, terrible *accident*—more often than not, she'd never go back to see them again.

And she knew why. People could say it wasn't her fault, and it didn't really mean anything, because it wasn't coming from Danny's family. The ones she'd been so desperate to hear it from all along.

Now, as she stood in front of Justin, she wondered if she'd heard him right.

"You don't believe me when I say that, do you?" he asked quietly. "That it wasn't your fault."

He'd read her mind. Which was scary.

She looked down at her shoes, at the cute little ballet

flats that she'd bought on sale last spring at Nordstrom Rack. They'd reminded her of the dance classes she'd taken as a girl, when she and her mother had been close, and dance classes and recitals were something they'd bonded over. Now, she and her mom only spoke periodically. Her parents had divorced not long after the accident, and her mother had remarried a man named Ted.

"No," she said. "I don't."

After a few long seconds, Justin reached out and touched her. She startled at the contact.

"I'm sorry," he said. "But will you look at me?"

She kept staring at her shoes. It was like she was frozen solid, physically unable to look up.

Gently, he touched her chin with the tips of his fingers. And then she finally let her gaze settle on him. Her breath was coming in short little gasps. But at least she was breathing.

"You want to know the truth?" he asked.

No.

"I'm glad you're home. I'm glad, because I feel like this is the only way we're both going to work through this. I've been burying my feelings a long time, Poppy. Seeing you is forcing me to face them again, and I'm grateful for that."

Grateful. She never thought she'd live to see the day where Justin Frost was grateful to her for anything.

"And what about your family?" she asked. "How do they feel about me being back?"

"They're going to have to work their way through it, too."

"I don't think your mom can ever see me as anything but a murderer, Justin."

"She's holding on to a lot of stuff. But she doesn't think you're a murderer."

She frowned. He had to know that wasn't true.

"My God," he said after a long moment. "*You* think you are, don't you?"

"I didn't say that."

"You don't have to. I can see it all over your face."

If he could see that on her face, then she was in trouble. Because there were a lot of other things that she might be betraying, too. Like how she still felt about him to this day, for example.

His gaze dropped to her mouth, and she felt her lips part slightly. Her heartbeat pick up a notch. He was standing so close that she could've touched him if she'd wanted to. And there was a part of her that did want to. She wanted to touch his face, his shoulders, run her hands down the muscular planes of his back. She wanted his arms wrapped around her, pulling her close. She wanted to feel the solidness of his body pressed against hers. And that made her a miserable person, because they were talking about Danny, weren't they? Worse, they were talking about what she'd done to Danny, and that was all it came down to in the end. What she'd done.

"You're not a murderer," he said, his voice low. "It was an accident, that's all."

Her eyes filled with tears. There was no fighting them anymore. They were going to come, and they were going to stream down her cheeks, and they'd drip off her chin onto her collarbone, and she was relieved that she didn't have to swallow them back a second longer.

But before they could blur her vision, he suddenly took her face in his hands.

She didn't know what to say. She didn't know what to do, except continue looking up at him, as if she was a child looking for guidance. *You need to lead*, she thought. *You need to lead me where you want to go, and I'll follow. It might not be the easiest road, but I promise you, I'll follow.*

He looked at her mouth, and her heart beat against her rib cage so wildly that she thought she could feel its vibration in her toes. He leaned closer and she could see the flecks of gold in his eyes. The individual points of stubble on his jaw. *Justin...* How many times had she imagined a moment just like this when she was a girl? Too many times to count. But he was supposed to hate her. He was supposed to be cursing her, even now.

He wasn't cursing her, though. His hands were cradling her face. His thumbs were moving in soft arcs over her cheekbones, where the tears had spilled. He brushed them away with the ease of someone she'd known forever.

And then, he kissed her.

Chapter Nine

Justin moved his lips over Poppy's slowly, gently. He knew deep down that really, this was a terrible idea. But the thing was, he was too far gone to be able to rationalize that to himself. All he could think of was *her*. How she smelled. How she felt. How she'd looked a minute ago with those tears in her eyes. He'd been able to see himself in them. His pain, his frustration and guilt. His desire. All of it was mirrored in her eyes.

A soft sound came from her throat. He wrapped an arm around her waist and pulled her closer, until he could feel the curves of her body pressed against him. He'd used to dream of kissing Poppy. He'd imagined how it would be to move his lips down her neck and kiss that hollow spot at the base of her throat. He'd imagined it so many times that it had simply become part of his consciousness. Part of the inner workings of his heart. And then the accident had happened, and they'd lost Danny, and all those imaginings had drifted away like dandelion seeds in the wind.

Only they hadn't gone far. He'd held on to them in secret. And now, here she was in the flesh. Just as lovely as she'd ever been, and more broken than ever. Somehow, the fact that she was broken made him love her even more. She understood what it was like to love and lose Danny, and they would always be bonded by that. He'd seen the suffering on her face that was so much like his own, and it had flipped some kind of switch inside of him. It was like he could finally see past the resentment. It was opening the door again to those other feelings. The ones that had him kissing her now.

And she was kissing him back. He'd been waiting, his stomach twisted in a knot of lust and anxiety, for her to put a stop to this. Because he was counting on her to be the sensible one, needing her to be sensible and realistic, because he sure as hell wasn't being either of those things. But she wasn't putting a stop to it. She was standing on her tiptoes, her arms wrapped hungrily around his neck. Like she'd been waiting for this just as long as he had.

He moved his hands over her hips and down the curve of her bottom, and heard her suck in a sharp breath.

Pushing her back against the counter, he traced her jawline with his lips. She tilted her head back as he moved his mouth down her throat, to that hollow place that he'd imagined kissing so many times before. It was soft and warm, and her pulse tapped there, underneath his lips. He could smell her perfume; he could taste it on his tongue.

His heart rammed in his chest as he found her mouth again. This time she kissed him back hard, wildly. He could feel her trembling against him—like her legs might give way if he didn't hold her up. *Poppy*... Her name reverberated inside his head, like a bell chiming the midnight hour. She'd thought he hated her, probably still believed that, no matter what he'd just said. But it was like her body was refusing to believe it. With every flick of her tongue, with every shiver and sigh, he felt like she might understand what lay in his heart at the deepest level.

From behind them came a sharp tap on the window.

Startled, he jumped. So did Poppy, and she pulled away, her eyes wide, like she was being roused from a dream.

He could relate. He put a hand on the back of his neck, where his skin was hot and clammy. His entire body was hot, and he turned to the window, ready to mouth to whoever it was that they were *closed.*

He heard Poppy pull in a swift breath.

And then he saw his mother, standing on the sidewalk, staring inside the shop. She looked like she'd just witnessed him murdering someone.

"Oh, shit," he said. "Oh no."

"Justin…" Poppy said his name, but nothing else. It was quite possible she was thinking about running toward the emergency exit right about then. If he knew the alarm wouldn't go off, he might just follow her out.

He turned to her. "One second?"

She nodded, looking too shocked to form any kind of coherent sentence.

Justin walked over to the door and unlocked it. His mother was standing there, still as stone. She was holding a sandwich bag at her side, and his stomach dropped. She did this sometimes. Brought him lunch as a surprise. It was very sweet, but she couldn't have picked a worse day to drop in on him if she'd tried.

"Mom."

Her face was beet-red. The hand clutching the lunch bag, shaking. He could hear the paper crinkling.

"I was bringing you a turkey on rye from that place on Sandpiper Street that you've been wanting to try," she said, her voice flat. "I should've called."

"I'm sorry, I…" He couldn't finish the sentence, because it was impossible to know what he was sorry for, exactly. As far as his mother was concerned, the list would be endless.

"No. Don't say anything, Justin. I don't want to hear it."

"I'm not trying to hurt you, Mom."

She held the sandwich bag out to him. "I'm going to go."

"Why can't we talk about this?"

Right then, it didn't matter that people were passing by on the sidewalk, watching them curiously. Suddenly, he didn't give a crap if the whole world knew his family business. That kiss had opened up a fissure inside him, and all he wanted to do was scoop out the poison that had settled there over the years. Now was as good a time as any.

His mom dropped the bag to her side again, the color beginning to fade from her cheeks. "What do you want me to say? That I knew this would happen? Okay, I'll say it. I *knew* it would happen. I knew the second she came back to town that it would happen. She has no right coming back here and turning our family upside down again."

"She's hurting, too. Just like we are."

"Don't you *dare* compare her pain with ours," she bit out. "Do you hear me?"

"I hear you."

"I don't think you do. I think you *say* you do, in order to get me to calm down or be quiet. In order not to have to deal with my outbursts or whatever. You and your father both do that, and it drives me nuts."

He frowned. She had a point. They'd gotten very good at tiptoeing around her.

"I'm sorry," he said. "I won't do that anymore."

She turned to go.

"Mom."

She stopped, and stood very still.

"All I'm asking is that we talk about this. Can we do that? Please?"

"I don't want to talk about it, Justin." She looked at him over her shoulder. Suddenly, he saw how much she'd aged. There were new lines and wrinkles around her mouth, between her eyebrows, on her forehead.

"You want me to forgive her," she said. "That's what you want."

"I want us to move forward."

"You want me to leave Danny behind."

"How can you say that?"

Her eyes grew glassy. "I don't know how to move forward without leaving him behind, Justin. I don't know how to forgive her without being disloyal to him."

"Forgiveness wouldn't mean being disloyal to him." He swallowed past the sudden tightness in his throat. Ironic that he was trying to convince his mother of this, when he'd felt the same way for so long. "Forgiveness would just mean...*forgiveness*. That's all. You don't have to choose between Danny and Poppy, Mom."

"Don't I?"

He watched her. He wanted to help her find the peace she deserved, but who was he to be trying to lead her anywhere, when he still had so far to go? All he knew was that he loved his mother. He'd loved Danny. And he was pretty sure he loved Poppy. And where the hell did that leave him?

Alone.

It left him feeling very, very alone.

Evelyn hated the heartbroken look on her son's face. She hated that he was caught in the middle of this, that he'd always been caught in the middle, but she honest to goodness had no idea how to fix it.

She turned to walk away before he could say anything else. It made her feel like she was in control. Of course, that was a bunch of baloney. None of them had a handle on this. They were all on some kind of roller-coaster ride from hell. She wondered if she'd ever be able to get off. She wanted more than anything to not feel so *angry* anymore. She thought she could deal with the sadness, if she just didn't have to deal with the anger, too.

She walked down the sidewalk with the sun warm on her shoulders. It felt good. The mornings were always so cold here. Maybe she should take a vacation, drag Paul to Hawaii or something. She had a cousin who lived on Oahu who was always trying to get them to visit. She'd meant to take the boys when they were little, but life always got in the way. Then, after Danny passed, she couldn't bring herself to take Justin by himself. So they'd never gone. She wondered if Justin knew the reason why. She supposed he did. She supposed he was hurt by that, along with the hundreds of other things she'd done over the years. She'd pushed away her surviving son, because she couldn't stand not having his brother, too.

She bit her bottom lip as she headed toward her little red car, thinking about the pain she'd inflicted on Justin without meaning to. But at the end of the day, she couldn't seem to change in the ways that mattered most. So she did things like dropping in on him with turkey-on-rye sandwiches, and fixing him up with athletic trainers who had nice smiles. She was forever trying to make up for her shortcomings.

"Evelyn!"

She turned.

A young girl was waving from down the sidewalk. Evelyn squinted at her, then realized it was the girl from the grocery store. Mary. She was coming out of Coastal Sweets, a candy bag swinging on her skinny arm.

"Wait up!"

She ran toward Evelyn, her blond hair flying. It looked like she'd gotten some sun recently, since her cheeks were flushed pink. Probably spending time at the beach, which would be good for just about anyone. Evelyn used to walk on the beach every day. That was before yoga. Now, she was a little pasty.

Mary came to a stop in front of her, out of breath. "Hey!"

"Hi, there," Evelyn said. "Mary, right?"

"That's right. I saw you from inside the candy shop, and I wanted to say hi."

Evelyn's heart squeezed. She couldn't remember the last time someone had actually run to catch up with her. She wasn't that popular.

"You got some candy?"

"Yup. Frances gave me some caramels on the house. That's what she said—'on the house.'" She used air quotes around *on the house*. "She's a nice lady. She can't remember my name, so she just calls me sugar lump. I like it."

Evelyn smiled. "I like it, too. Can't go wrong with a nickname like that."

"My mom says she's got Al-Al—"

"Alzheimer's?"

"Yeah. That. She's got that, and that's why she can't remember my name and some other stuff, but we're going to be checking on her this summer, since we're right down the street."

Mary said this proudly, like she was happy to have a grown-up job like checking in on someone.

"I'm sure she'll appreciate that."

"I might babysit Emily. But only when Marley is in the next room. Sometimes she helps out at the shop, and she has to bring Emily with her because her husband is a baseball coach in the summertime, and he's gone a lot. So I'd play with her in the back room. It's all set up with toys and a TV and stuff. It's pretty cool."

Evelyn nodded.

"Have you met Emily?" Mary asked, opening her bag of candy and rooting around in it.

"I haven't."

"She's *so* cute."

"She sounds cute."

"Here. Do you want a caramel?" Mary asked, holding one out in her hand. "It's on the house."

Evelyn laughed. "Wow. Well, thank you. I'd love one."

Mary beamed. Emily, whoever she was, had nothing on this girl with her gap-toothed smile and freckles that were scattered across her sunburned nose like brown sugar.

"What are you doing today?" Mary asked, her caramel jammed in her cheek. She looked like a squirrel hoarding nuts for the winter.

Evelyn unwrapped the candy and popped it in her mouth. She tried to stay away from too much sugar, and didn't allow herself treats very often. But this was delicious.

"I was just going over to visit my son," she said. "To take him some lunch."

Mary perked up at this. "Did you get to see Roo?"

Evelyn moved the caramel over to the other side of her

mouth, the sweetness exploding on her tongue. She might have to go over to Coastal Sweets and get herself a bag of these things. She'd share with Paul. He'd be thrilled.

"I didn't," she said. "I didn't go inside the shop. Justin came outside." She left out the part where she'd seen him and Poppy making out like two hormonal teenagers.

"My aunt went over there a little while ago. I might go over there, too. Maybe I can play with Roo or something."

"Oh!" Evelyn said quickly. "Uh, he closes up for lunch and I think he and your aunt are…talking right now. It might not be the best time." That was the understatement of the century.

"Oh." Mary deflated like a balloon.

Evelyn stood there looking down at her, suddenly over-come with emotion. She was so thin. Her skinny little shoulders were angular underneath her pink Taylor Swift T-shirt. And she looked so sad, so let down by the fact that she couldn't go visit that damn dog, that Evelyn reached out and touched her arm.

"Hey. Do you know what a Fiat is?"

Mary shook her head.

"It's a sports car and it's really cute. If you go ask your mom, you can come see it. It's parked right over there. I'll even let you sit in the driver's seat." When Evelyn was Mary's age, this would've been the saddest excuse for a distraction ever. If there weren't dolls involved, or at least a board game or two, you could forget about it. But Mary seemed more easily pleased than Evelyn ever was as a child. Or as an adult, for that matter.

"But you have to make sure it's okay with your mom," she said.

Mary grinned. "I will! I'll be right back!"

She turned and ran toward the antique shop, her hair flying.

"Just walk!" Evelyn called, to no avail.

She watched the girl run inside the shop, hoping she didn't choke on that caramel.

After a few seconds, Mary came tearing outside again and waved at Evelyn.

"She said it's okay!"

Evelyn waited as she ran back up to her, breathing hard. "She said it's okay, but I have to be back in ten minutes. And she said to tell you thank you."

"Anytime," Evelyn said. And then, before she could think better of it, she added, "Maybe when we get to know each other better—I can take you for a drive with the top down. That's pretty fun."

"Yeah!"

They began walking down the sidewalk toward the car, and Evelyn was aware how odd this was. She and Poppy's niece. Just walking together, shooting the breeze. As if nothing horrible had happened between their two families. Nothing at all.

Mary looked up at her, tucking her hair behind her ears. "My dad used to have a car with no top."

"A convertible?"

"Yeah, a convertible. I never got to ride in it because I was a baby, but I've seen pictures. It was blue. He named it Sally."

Evelyn smiled. "Ah. Was it a Mustang?"

"Not sure," Mary said with a shrug of her sharp little shoulders. "I don't know much about cars."

"I don't, either. I just like mine because it's cute. I know when to change the oil and that's about it. Is your dad going to come visit you over the summer?" she asked without thinking, and immediately wished she hadn't. Mary hadn't mentioned her dad before this. There was a good chance he and Cora were divorced.

Mary grew quiet, and Evelyn wanted to kick herself. It was the small-town nosiness in her. At least she came by it honestly.

"My dad died," Mary said. "He had cancer."

Evelyn stopped and turned to Mary with a frown. The girl stopped, too, and kicked at a pebble with the toe of her sneaker.

"I'm sorry."

Mary stared down at the sidewalk. "I miss him."

"Of course, you do."

"What do you think happens when we die?"

It was an innocent question, but so blunt that it felt like someone had hit Evelyn in the chest with a baseball bat. She'd asked it many times herself. And she still didn't have an answer. She knew what she wanted to believe— she wanted there to be a beautiful heaven, full of love and laugher and light. But the truth was, she just didn't know. She guessed that's what faith was all about—believing in something when you couldn't see it. And her faith was in short supply these days.

"You know," she said, "I'm not sure."

"I think there are dogs there."

"You do?"

"Yeah. And ice cream and roller-skating. Lots of roller-skating. I think angels just skate everywhere and they never fall down because they've got wings, and they always have an ice cream cone in their hand. And it never melts, either."

Mary had a faraway look in her eyes that made Evelyn smile. "I like that," she said. "Roller-skating angels."

Danny was a great athlete, but he'd also been uncoordinated to an almost comic degree when he was little. She and Paul had bought him skates for his ninth birthday, she remembered, because there had been a rink in Eugene that they used to take the boys to on the weekends during those cold, coastal winter months. He and Justin had liked skating, but Danny fell a lot. He had perpetually bruised knees and scraped palms. Evelyn's heart ached at the sweet memory of kissing those palms.

"I hope I'm right about the ice-cream part," Mary said. "My dad liked rocky road. It was his favorite. We got it a lot for him when he was sick…"

She let her voice trail off, and Evelyn watched her, wanting to pull her into a hug, but she didn't want to overstep. Maybe she didn't like to be touched, or was embarrassed by public displays of affection.

"You know what?" Evelyn asked.

"What?"

"I bet you're right. I bet there's so much ice cream. And I bet you can eat it really fast and not get brain freeze."

Mary giggled.

Evelyn smiled, happy she'd gotten a laugh out of her, but still wanting to give her a hug. They had something in common, after all. The loss of someone they loved.

They continued walking toward the Fiat, but slower this time. Mary talking about her old school, and how mean the kids had been to her there.

Evelyn shook her head. Kids could be so cruel. A lot of them didn't learn to be kind and empathetic until later on in life. Hard experiences taught a person hard lessons.

Evelyn had had hard experiences, but she was still waiting on the universal-kindness part of the lesson.

"Well," she said, stopping in front of her car. "This is it. My baby."

Mary grinned. "Pretty. You should name it."

"You think?"

"I could help you."

"I'd love that."

"You mean it?"

Evelyn nodded. "Sure."

"Any name I want?"

"Any name you want."

Mary reached for the passenger side door, and looked over at Evelyn. "Can I sit in it?"

"You can sit in the driver's side, remember?"

She moved around and climbed inside, and Evelyn got in beside her.

"What's this?" Mary asked, pointing to the gearshift.

"This is a manual transmission. That means you have to shift the gears yourself. I grew up calling these kinds of cars stick shifts."

"Is it hard?"

"Not once you get the hang of it."

Mary looked all around the car, seeming genuinely excited to be sitting in the driver seat. Evelyn was right—she was easily pleased.

"Did you teach your kids how to drive?"

"No. Their dad taught them."

Mary watched her, her blue eyes soft. "I heard about your son. My mom told me what happened. I'm really sorry."

"Oh. Well. I appreciate that."

"She told me that Aunt Poppy was driving the car."

Evelyn nodded, bracing herself, but feeling strangely open to this conversation at the same time. "Yes," she said. "She was."

"That's why you don't like her."

Nobody ever talked to her like this. For years, friends and family skirted the subject—careful not to bring Danny up, or Poppy, or any of the Sawyers, really, for fear of how she would react. It was true there had been some moments. Some bad days when she'd reply with a quick flash of anger, or worse, a flood of tears. But she felt like she'd gotten better, more emotionally stable where her son and his accident were concerned. But still, people avoided mentioning Danny. She realized with a sad little dip of her stomach that she'd been avoiding the subject, too. And she didn't want to avoid Danny.

"It's complicated," she said quietly.

Mary nodded, then bit her lip like she wanted to say something more, but was trying her hardest to be respectful.

Evelyn remembered what it was like to be Mary's age. Always feeling as if she'd said or done something wrong. Feeling endlessly curious about the things going on around her, but being shut out of conversations because she was too young.

She leaned back against the leather seat. She watched Mary, who had her hands on the steering wheel, her eyebrows knitted in thought.

"Is there anything you want to know?" Evelyn asked. "About the accident? I know you must be curious."

"I don't want to make you sad."

"You're not going to make me sad." That might not be altogether true, but she was willing to risk it.

Mary sat quiet for a minute, letting this settle. Clearly wanting to choose her next words carefully. Evelyn thought that was sweet. It showed a lot of maturity for her age.

"How old was he?" Mary asked. "Your son?"

"He was seventeen."

"The same age as Aunt Poppy?"

She nodded.

"Do you still miss him?"

"I do. I miss him every day."

Mary stared out the window to the sidewalk beyond. "Me too. With my dad. Do you think they miss us?"

"I'm sure they do. But I bet it's not the same kind of feeling. I bet it's easier somehow."

"You think?"

"I do."

"I hope so," Mary said. "That would make me feel better. If he weren't sad."

"I'm sure he's not."

"And your son isn't sad, either."

Evelyn loved how that sounded—she wanted to believe it. And sitting here now, it felt believable.

"How did you get over it?" Mary asked. "Him dying?"

It was one of those questions that went deeper than just the words. Mary was asking for herself, too. *How did you get over it? How am I going to get over it?* The answer was, she wasn't going to get *over* it. She would get *through* it.

"I didn't," Evelyn said. "But I learned how to live with it. It becomes a part of who you are, and that's okay. It does get easier."

That last part was hard to get past her vocal chords. *Did it get easier?* She supposed for a lot of people it did. She knew that for her, some things *had* gotten easier. She'd learned to live with the pain. It had lost its sharp teeth. It was now more of an ache. A low vibration that she walked around with daily. But the anger, the resentment, the bitterness… Those things had only grown. They had claws that had sharpened to a razor's edge. To the point where Evelyn cut herself on them often.

"Sometimes it doesn't feel like it'll get easier," Mary said. "Sometimes it feels worse. When I think about never getting to see him again. When I think about things I want to tell him, and can't."

"You can always tell him those things," Evelyn said. "I talk to Danny all the time."

"You do?"

"I do. About things that are going on in my life. Things that I know he'd want to hear about. I know he already knows, but it makes me feel better, closer to him, to say them out loud."

Mary nodded, running her hands over the steering wheel.

"Do you keep a journal?" Evelyn asked.

"I used to. But I lost it, and I never got another one."

"Well, I write in a journal every night. I write to Danny, like I'm writing him letters. That helps me, too."

"Maybe I'll try it."

"If you do, let me know how it goes, okay?"

"Okay."

They sat there for another minute or two, quiet. But it was an easy silence, and Evelyn realized that for the first time in a long time, that low vibration was more of a soft hum.

It was nice.

Chapter Ten

Poppy hadn't waited for Justin to come back inside the hardware store. She'd seen his mother standing outside the window, and when he'd headed over to unlock the door, she'd slipped out the back. The dog had watched her walk past, judging her with those beautiful eyes.

She'd been too upset to go back to the antique shop. What was she supposed to tell her cousins? That she'd just made out with *Justin Frost* and his mom had busted them like they were in high school again? That's exactly how she felt. Like they were in high school, and his mother had walked in on them kissing on the couch.

She'd gotten in her car and driven directly to her favorite lookout spot over Cape Longing. She stood there now, the occasional car passing by on the highway behind her, and stared out over the crashing waves below. From here she could see several miles each way, the rocky beach stretching out like a massive arm, reaching for the mountains in the distance. The wind whipped her hair around her face, and she reached up to hold it back with one hand. It was chilly, bordering on cold, but her ears were still burning. Her cheeks were hot from the embarrassment of what had happened.

She imagined going back to the antique shop and sitting

Cora and Beau down. *Sorry, guys. This really awful thing happened that I couldn't help. Well, I guess I could help it, but it felt like I couldn't at the time, and now I'm going to have to leave. Sorry. Good luck to you.*

What in the world was wrong with her, anyway? Was she so blinded by her attraction to Justin that she'd let all her common sense fly right out the window?

Her phone vibrated in her pocket, and she dug it out, her freed hair immediately snatched up by the wind. She saw Cora's name flash across the screen and she bit her cheek. Her cousin would be wondering what happened to her. She was supposed to have been back by now, and Cora was a mother through and through. *If you're going to be late, check in!* She could hear her cousin saying it now, with that disapproving little frown on her lips.

"Hello?"

"Poppy? Where are you?"

"I'm…" She looked out over the sparkling ocean, not wanting to go into details, but knowing that trying to keep this from her cousins was futile. This was Christmas Bay, after all. They'd know soon enough. "Something happened. At Justin's."

"I know."

"You know?" Now, that was fast, even for Christmas Bay.

"Well, I don't know exactly what, but I know something happened. Justin was here looking for you. He seemed upset."

"He did?"

"Did you two have an argument or something?"

Or something.

"No. Worse."

"Worse? What do you mean?"

Poppy swallowed.

"Welcome!" her cousin said. Then in a whisper, "Sorry—customers. I have to run. Are you okay?"

"I'm fine. I'll tell you about it when I get back. Ten minutes?"

"No rush. And I have something to tell you, too. You'll never guess who Mary's with."

"Who?"

Poppy heard the muffled sound of a woman's voice asking how much something was, and if she could put it on hold.

"Sorry, Poppy," Cora said. "Can I call you back?"

"No, that's okay. I'm on my way."

"See you soon."

The phone went dead, and Poppy stood there holding it, wondering who on earth her cousin could have meant. Mary didn't know anyone in Christmas Bay.

Taking a deep breath, she turned back to her sleek black car. She eyed the paint job that reminded her of a starless sky, and had a brief thought of getting something different. She already stuck out like a sore thumb around here, and this car didn't help. Maybe she'd get a Subaru, something with all-wheel drive for the winter.

She opened the door and sank down into the buttery leather seats. Something that would help her blend in. Suddenly, that's all she wanted to do.

Blend in and disappear.

Justin threw his line into the still, dark water of his favorite mountain lake, and managed to snag his hook on some twigs. Again. He yanked on his pole with a frustrated groan.

His friend Mike looked over, his Mariners baseball cap riding low over his eyes, protecting them from the early evening sun. "Need some help?"

"No."

"Okay. Just thought I'd ask, because you're casting like someone who needs some help."

"Thank you."

"You're welcome."

Mike smiled and looked back out over the water that was slapping lightly at the sides of the aluminum boat. Roo stood sentry over the bow, behaving perfectly, and looking like she was having the time of her life. Justin made a mental note to tell Poppy that she was a good fishing companion. The thought that he might have to help find a home for her made his gut tighten with guilt.

Reeling in his line, he ground his teeth together. He was just going to have to cross that bridge when he came to it. And the fact that he was getting attached to this dog wasn't going to enter into the equation. Okay. It might enter into the equation a little, but he wasn't going to let it affect him. He did not need a dog right now. Dogs required too much time, too much attention. The only thing he could do for her was try to make her life comfortable until she went to her new home. He thought he'd been doing a pretty good job of that so far.

As if reading his mind, Roo looked back at him and wagged her long, shaggy tail.

"I think she likes it out here," Mike said. Mike loved dogs. He had two golden retrievers named River and Lake. If there was any question as to what he liked to do in his free time, you didn't have to look further than the names of his dogs.

"I think so, too," he said. "Now, if I can just keep her from falling in, I'll call it a win for the day."

"You said this was Poppy's grandfather's dog?" Mike knew who Poppy was, but had never met her. It didn't matter. Her reputation preceded her. There was the relatively famous anchor-woman thing. And the accident, which probably would have been enough on its own.

"Yup."

"And when is she going to take her? Because it seems like you're enjoying having a dog."

"Not enjoying. Keeping my promise to Earl. There's a difference."

"Not much of one, from where I'm sitting."

"Shut up."

Mike ignored that, and reeled in his line, then cast it out again, effortlessly avoiding the twigs that kept snagging Justin's line. Mike was a good fisherman. Better than Justin on his best day, which annoyed him to no end. His friend would probably be interested to know that Beau Evers was back in town. *The* Beau Evers of the sportfishing world, and native son of Christmas Bay. But Justin hadn't mentioned it, and apparently Mike hadn't heard yet. Sometimes the grapevine around here got clogged with inconsequential things. Like who had been caught kissing whom, and where.

At that thought, Justin pulled his own hat lower over his eyes, as if Mike were about to start grilling him on the subject they'd just laid to rest a minute ago. His friend had heard there was someone Justin was interested in. Had maybe even kissed. Justin could thank his mother for this, as she'd no doubt hashed it out with her two closest friends, both of whom had mouths the size of the Grand Canyon.

"I'm not ready to discuss this with you," he'd told Mike.

Mike had just cast his line out again and nodded with a smirk on his lips. They'd been friends for a long time. He knew Justin better than to take that at face value.

"Anyhoo," Mike said now, his tone maddeningly casual. "Whenever you *are* ready to discuss it, you can tell me if this person is Poppy Sawyer."

Justin shot him a look.

"Bingo."

"Please."

"Look," Mike said. "You've been denying for years that you still have a thing for this Poppy chick, but it's like the more you deny it, the less I believe you."

"I don't have a thing for her." *Lie.* "We have history, that's all."

"Uh-huh."

"Where did you hear about Poppy and me, anyway?"

"I didn't. I was just guessing, but it looks like I was right."

Justin turned back to the water, scowling. This was what he got for kissing Poppy like some lovesick teenager. At the time, he'd known it was a bad idea. Of course, he had. But standing so close to her, breathing in her scent, seeing the pattern of those freckles across her nose... It had been too much. He'd given in to the desire he'd felt for her since he *was* a lovesick teenager. And then his mother had knocked on the window, and had nearly shocked the life clean out of him.

When he'd come back into the store, Poppy was gone. The only proof that she'd ever been there was the faintest scent of her perfume, and the soft whimpers from Roo, who'd been looking in the direction of the rear exit.

"Why don't you just talk to me about it, man?" Mike asked, glancing over at him. His friend was one of those guys who looked a lot younger than he actually was. He had a baby face that was clean-shaven and perpetually tanned. He had a quick smile and kind eyes, and most everyone loved him. He was a good friend, more like a brother than anything else. He'd never met Danny, but Justin knew they would've liked each other. They had the same sense of humor, the same lighthearted way of looking at life.

"What's to talk about?"

"Come on," Mike said. "That's exactly what I mean. I know you're full of it, and *you* know you're full of it. Why don't you just come clean about how you feel about this woman? I know you're sure as hell not talking to your family about her. And there's not a whole lot of people who like you well enough to listen to you wax poetic, except for me. So here I am. Ready to listen. Ready to give advice. Whether you want it or not."

Justin fumbled with his bait, putting it on the hook with clumsy fingers.

"I appreciate you wanting to give me advice, but I don't need any," he said flatly. "We kissed. We kissed, and that's the end of it. It's not like there's any chance of a future with her."

"Why not?"

Justin gave his friend a look.

"Okay," Mike said. "I'll admit, she's not the conventional choice."

"That's putting it mildly."

"But what if you could forgive her for the accident? What then?"

Justin cast his line out, and this time managed to avoid the worst of the weeds and twigs. The hook sank to the silty bottom of the lake, where the fish were waiting in the murky water. "There's nothing to forgive," he said. "It was an accident."

"Yes, it was. But I still think you've got a lot of things to work through. I would, if it was me."

Obviously, that was true. He struggled with it daily. But the real question was, *why* should he work through it? To forgive Poppy? Or to have a relationship with her? The former seemed doable. The latter seemed laughable. Even if she felt the same way, even if his family could get past it, she'd have to forgive *herself* first.

It didn't even matter. It was just a kiss. A momentary lapse in judgment. It wouldn't happen again.

"Have you talked to her since this happened?" Mike asked.

"No. It was awkward as hell. My mom saw us."

Mike's eyes widened.

"Yeah." Justin rubbed his jaw, suddenly feeling exhausted.

"Elaborate."

"Poppy came over to meet Roo. We started talking, one thing led to another, and we kissed. Then there was a knock on the window, I turned around…"

"Ouch."

"Yeah. *Ouch.*"

"And your mom hated her already."

"I'm not sure *hate* is a strong enough word."

"Then what happened?"

"I went outside to try to talk to her. That went about as well as you'd think. Then I came back in, and Poppy was gone."

"Did you go after her?"

"I tried. I couldn't find her anywhere. She hasn't called. She just split. Par for the course where this woman is concerned."

Mike frowned. "That's not quite fair, man."

Justin's ears burned. His friend was right, as usual. She probably needed time to figure out how she felt about this. But he was hurt that she'd run away. It seemed like she was always running away from him.

"She thinks you hate her, Justin," Mike said. "And now your mom has even more ammo against her. I'm not sure I'd stick around, either."

Justin reeled his line in. "True."

"Want my advice?"

"Do I have a choice?"

"Not really."

"Then fire away."

"Don't give up on her that easily," Mike said. "Go find her. Make her talk to you. Don't be a chickenshit."

"Eloquently put."

"I don't believe in beating around the bush."

"Clearly."

Mike lowered his pole and pushed his baseball cap up on his forehead so Justin could see his eyes.

"I'm serious," Mike said. "Don't make the same mistake I did."

Mike had been in love with the same woman for seven years. They'd dated on and off, but when it came down to it, commitment had scared him. She'd met a financial advisor a few years ago, gotten married and was now pregnant with their first baby. Mike was still in mourning.

"That's a little different. Tiffany was your girlfriend."

Mike shrugged. "Love is love, dude."

Rubbing the back of his sunburned neck, Justin looked out over the water. A couple of blue jays squawked overhead. The breeze blew against his skin, and brought with it the smell of lake water and pine trees. He frowned at nothing in particular. *Love is love.* Was that what this was? Love? He wasn't sure.

Sighing, he reached over to give his friend a hearty pat on the back. Roo shook, jingling the tags on her collar. The sun was getting lower in the sky, and all of a sudden, Justin felt his stomach growl.

"I could go for pizza and a beer right about now," he said. "Are you hungry?"

"I could eat."

"Good. I'm buying."

Poppy watched Cora count the till. They'd had a good day, lots of tourists coming in and out. Business was picking up—maybe they'd even make a go of this place. At least for the time being.

Even so, Poppy was preoccupied. She was having a hard time moving on from the subject of Evelyn. Or more specifically, Evelyn's visit with Mary a few days ago.

She leaned against one of the vintage pianos they had in the shop, and accidently hit an off-key note with the palm of her hand. It reverberated through the empty space, loud and hollow. "I still don't get it," she said. "Do you think she wanted to show off her car or something?"

Her cousin looked up from the wad of cash in her hand

and frowned. They'd been over it and over it, but were still trying to work out Evelyn's motivation. "I truly think she was just being nice. At least, that's the feeling I got from Mary."

"But this is a woman who wouldn't cross the street to put a Sawyer out if one of us were on fire."

Cora gave her a half smile. "Maybe that's not how she feels anymore."

"I doubt that. Especially after the other day."

"I *knew* Justin still had a thing for you. I just knew it."

It was hard arguing with her, since he *had* kissed her. But it was only a kiss. It didn't mean he felt anything more than a momentary pang of attraction. He'd said a lot of things right before that kiss, but she couldn't bring herself to believe any of them. She just couldn't let herself trust him. She couldn't let herself trust, period.

"Maybe she's not as bad as we thought," Cora said.

Poppy considered this. She never really thought Evelyn was anything other than a grieving mother, who had every right to treat Poppy the way she had. It was harder knowing that she'd let her resentment bleed over to the rest of the Sawyer family, but even that Poppy could understand at the end of the day. Her son had been killed. That would change someone fundamentally. Evelyn wouldn't necessarily stop to think about who deserved her ire, and who didn't.

"I just wish I knew what was going on in her head," Poppy said. "I've always wanted to know."

"You don't think she'll ever sit down and talk to you about this?"

Poppy laughed without meaning to. "Her? Never."

"But she's talking to Mary."

"Maybe that's her way of moving forward. Of making peace with it."

"It's a start," Cora said, closing the till and locking it. "But I think she's got a long way to go."

Beau walked in and cracked his knuckles. "Welp, I just got off the phone with my first furniture dealer."

"Awesome!" Cora said. "How'd that go?"

"Pretty well. He did business with Grandpa, so it wasn't like I was forging new territory. But it was good."

"I'm surprised at how interested people are in the bigger, more expensive things in the shop," Poppy said.

"I know. Beau sold an entire dining room set yesterday, first thing in the morning."

"And they wanted to know what else we had in the back." Beau grinned. Poppy knew he'd gone to the river last night at dusk. He couldn't do any serious fishing with his shoulder injury, but he'd dropped a line in and sat there for a long time. It had been close to ten when he'd climbed up the stairs to the apartment. She guessed it probably felt good to be on the water again, even if it wasn't in the way that he was used to.

"Uh, Poppy," he said, crossing his arms over his chest. "Don't look now, but I think there's someone here to see you."

She turned, not expecting to see Justin standing outside. But there he was—tall, tanned, muscular. He stood on the sidewalk, holding Roo's leash. Nobody would've known that she wasn't his dog. They looked like they belonged together.

At the sight of him, Poppy's stomach dropped.

"Wow," Cora breathed. "I forgot how handsome he is."

"Do I need to get the hose from out back?" Beau asked. "To cool you off?"

"There's nothing wrong with *looking*."

Poppy's face warmed. She'd done considerably more than look. In fact, her entire body burned with the memory.

Beau leaned against the counter and reached over to pluck a gummy worm out of Mary's bag from Coastal Sweets. There was usually a bag from Coastal Sweets next to the cash register now. "Are you gonna go out there, or are you going to leave him standing there all night?"

Poppy shot him a look. "Give me a second, bossy."

He winked at her. It felt like old times. His teasing tone, her and Cora bonding over a cute boy. Her heart thudding inside her chest, reminding her that she was alive and kicking. It had been a long time since she'd felt this way. A very long time.

Cora walked over and switched off the overhead lights to the shop. "Well, kids. I promised Mary I'd take her to a movie tonight. Beau, do you want to come?"

"What's playing?"

"Something with Zac Efron. She's got a massive crush on him, but don't tell her I told you."

"Mum's the word. Yeah, I'll come. Let me get my wallet."

"Poppy, want to meet us there?"

Poppy smiled and nodded. "Sure."

"It starts at seven thirty. I was thinking we could grab dinner before. But if you don't show up, I'll just assume..."

"I'll be there."

Beau walked by and elbowed her in the ribs. "Bye, cuz."

And then she was alone, watching Justin peer through the window, people weaving around him on the sidewalk.

Hesitantly, she walked toward the front door and unlocked it, her pulse tapping in her throat.

Surely he was here to talk about what happened. Or maybe not. Maybe he just wanted to hand off Roo, and be done with this once and for all. But she didn't think so. There was a drawn expression on his face that suggested this visit went deeper than just Roo, or even that kiss.

She pushed open the door, then stepped out onto the sidewalk and into the breezy spring evening. It was sunny, but there were dark clouds on the horizon. A storm was blowing in. Christmas Bay was famous for its storms. They were strongest in the fall and winter, when tourists would come from all over to watch the spectacular waves crash against the rocky beaches and the mossy cliffs of Cape Longing. But spring storms weren't unheard of, and more often than not, the entire town would lose power from the strong winds that would blow in off the sea.

Poppy pulled her sweater tighter around her shoulders, and then looked down at Roo, who was watching her quietly. She held out her hand, and the dog sniffed it, touching her cold wet nose to her knuckles, before stepping back to Justin's side.

"See?" he said. "We're making progress."

"I think you're being overly optimistic."

"I wouldn't know how. I'm a pessimist by nature."

"Good to know."

He gazed down at her, and she could smell his scent from where she stood. Woodsy, musky. It reminded her of being in his arms a few days ago, and her belly curled into a tight little ball. It almost felt like a dream, kissing him. Hazy and warm, and starting to fade a little in her mind. If it wasn't for the look on his face now, the tilt to his lips, she might've believed it had been a figment of her imagination.

"I tried to find you," he said, his voice low. "That day. But you were gone."

"I went to the lookout. Over the cape."

"Ahh. I remember you and Danny hanging out there. Mom was always afraid he'd fall off the cliff or something."

She looked down at her shoes. "I think she was probably more afraid of him being with me, than of falling off the cliff."

"That's possible," he said. "She knew how he felt about you, and my mother was always worried about losing us. And now...about losing me."

Poppy nodded solemnly. "I can't say I blame her."

"Here's the thing." He put his hands in his jean pockets, Roo's leash looped around his thick wrist. "I'm not saying kissing you was the best idea. But it happened, and I'm a grown man. I'm not a kid anymore, and neither are you. She doesn't have to approve of this, Poppy."

She looked up at him, into his darkly handsome face. His jaw was shadowed with stubble. His eyes were almost black in the fading light of the day. She could see herself in them, standing there with her arms around her torso, hugging herself. For comfort, maybe. Or warmth. She wasn't sure which.

"You make it sound like there's something between us," she said.

"I'm not saying there is. But if there *was*..."

The wind picked up, bringing with it the tangy smell of rain. Poppy's hair blew in front of her face, and she pushed it back again. It felt surreal that she was standing here with Justin, in Christmas Bay again. Talking about whether or not there was something between them. Talking about a kiss that had definitely happened, but felt soft and dreamlike now.

Justin looked up at the sky and took a visible breath. "I was going to walk Roo. Do you want to come?"

She glanced over at the darkened antique shop. She'd said she'd meet everyone later, but getting to know Roo was important, too. If she was ever going to take her, she needed to feel comfortable with her, and Roo needed to feel comfortable, as well. A walk was probably a good idea at this point. Even if it meant more time with Justin.

"Sure," she said. "Let me just run in and get a jacket."

She hurried inside as another gust of wind pushed her along, as if wanting her to get a move on already. She grabbed a windbreaker from behind the counter, and pulled out her phone to send Cora a quick text saying she might not make dinner and the movie. Then she grabbed her keys and headed back outside, locking the door behind her.

Smiling up at Justin, she stepped around the big gray dog. "Where to?"

"I thought we could go to the park on Fourth. It's by my place, so Roo's been there before and likes it. There are always other dogs to play with."

"Sounds good."

They began walking, listening to the muted sound of the waves crashing in the distance. Some clouds moved over the sun, which was making its way toward the horizon, and the air was instantly chillier. Poppy zipped up her windbreaker, glad she'd thought to grab it. She'd grown up by the ocean, but had forgotten how cold it could get. Portland's weather was much balmier in comparison. If mist and fog could be called balmy. But still.

The shopkeepers they passed were busy closing up for the day, bringing their standing signs inside before they could be blown over by the wind. The hanging baskets over the sidewalk swung back and forth, and tourists scrambled to their cars with their bags tucked underneath their arms.

"I hope it doesn't dump before we get there," Poppy said, tucking her chin into the collar of her jacket.

"It might. But a little rain won't hurt us."

That's where he was wrong. Poppy knew firsthand what rain could do. Especially driving over the speed limit. A storm lover when she'd been a kid, she'd never felt the same about them since the accident. When the sky got dark, so did her mood.

Swallowing hard, she gazed ahead, not wanting to think about the accident. But it was always there. Always lurking at the edge of her consciousness.

Justin reached down and gave Roo a pat. The dog seemed happy to be plodding along next to him, as if their partnership was meant to be.

"She likes you," Poppy said evenly.

"She's a good girl."

"Are you sure you don't want to keep her?"

She'd meant for that to be lighthearted, but it came out sounding tight and a little desperate. She wasn't looking forward to finding Roo a new home, if that's what it came down to. She felt like it would be letting down her grandfather, and no matter how much she tried to justify it in her mind, she knew that's exactly what she'd be doing. It was possible to keep Roo, of course, but that would require her to be responsible for another living thing, and she wasn't sure she was up to it. At the moment, it felt like she couldn't even be responsible for herself.

"I've thought about it," Justin said.

She looked over, surprised.

"But she should be with you."

A stab of guilt, cold and sharp, punctured her belly. "You'll think I'm an awful person if I don't keep her."

"I won't think you're an awful person."

"I *should* keep her, though. Right?"

"I'd understand if you didn't. It's a lot of responsibility."

"I wish Grandpa had understood that. But sometimes I feel like he didn't know me very well."

Justin watched her. She could feel his gaze as she stared at the sidewalk ahead.

"He knew you," he said.

"I'd love to believe that. But having us all come back to run a shop that we know nothing about? Asking us to stay here?" She shook her head. "I don't know."

"But you're making it work. He knew you would. He probably knew how good it would be for you to face this place again. All of you."

They kept walking. The wind whipped around Poppy's shoulders. Ominously. Like it knew something she didn't. In the distance, there was a low rumble of thunder. Roo whimpered. A few stinging drops of rain hit Poppy's cheeks as she looked up at the sky.

"Uh-oh," she said.

"Maybe we should take a detour. My house is right around the corner."

Just as he said it, a sharp clap of thunder made them jump.

"Your place sounds great," she said quickly. "I hate lightning."

He moved closer and put an arm around her shoulder.

She didn't want to feel comfort from Justin, but more than that, she didn't want to be in a position to need it from anyone. But it was such a kind gesture, so sweet and easy, that it made her heart squeeze.

"I don't like it, either," he said. "Let's go."

Chapter Eleven

Justin held the door open for Poppy, and waited as she walked past him into the foyer. His house was a small Craftsman that was on the list of historic places in Christmas Bay. He'd done some work to it over the years, but he'd always stayed true to its past, never straying too far from its original lines.

He was proud of his place, but other than inviting Mike over for a beer and baseball game every now and then, he rarely had people over. Normally he didn't think too much about his social life, or lack thereof, but having Poppy here, standing in his living room and shaking out her damp hair, was making him feel like he'd been living under a rock for the last few years. No real friendships other than Mike, no relationships of any kind. He dated, but that was more of a physical thing than anything else. Nothing that went deeper than a couple of weeks before he stopped it in its tracks. Saying something stupid like, *it's not you, it's me.*

The sudden realization made him feel restless and unsettled.

"Here," he said. "I'll get you a towel. One second."

The rain was coming harder now, streaming down the windows in miniature torrents. The wind pushed against the small house in insistent gusts, making the old wood creak and pop every now and then.

Justin grabbed a towel from the hall closet and came back to see Poppy looking out the window. Very still, very quiet. She had her arms wrapped around her waist, as if she was cold.

He walked up slowly behind her, knowing she was lost in her thoughts. He wondered what exactly those were, curious about her, in more ways than one.

"Here you go," he said, his voice low.

She turned and there was a distant, haunted look in her eyes. Something that made him sad.

"Thank you."

She rubbed the towel over her hair, and he could smell her shampoo from where he stood. It stirred something inside him. A longing, a desire that he wasn't sure what to do with. He'd kissed her the other day. And she'd kissed him back. But that's where it needed to end. He had nothing to offer someone like Poppy. Someone who had the world at her feet. And then, there was their history. There was no getting past that. It was thick and complicated, and would mire them both in place if he let it.

Thunder rumbled in the distance, rattling the house.

"I forgot how fast these storms come in," she said.

"I'm just sorry we didn't get to finish our walk."

At the word *walk*, Roo lifted her head from her paws. She looked up at Justin and cocked her head, her fur wet and spiky around her eyes.

Poppy watched her. "She's so smart."

"Really smart. It's almost like she knows what I'm about to say before I say it."

Poppy set down the towel on the end table, then lowered herself to one knee in front of the dog. She held her hand in front of Roo's nose, and was rewarded with a lick on her fingers.

She smiled. "Progress."

"I told you. It'll just take some time, that's all."

Poppy stroked Roo's head, and the dog closed her eyes, soaking it up. Except for another rumble of thunder, this one softer, the house was quiet. Justin watched the woman and the dog, his heart beating steadily inside his chest. What would his mother think of this? Of Poppy making herself at home here? Since she'd seen them kiss, she'd stayed away. Hadn't answered the phone when Justin called. Hadn't come by the shop or texted to see what he was doing. He figured she just needed space. Some time to sort this out. God knew, he needed the same thing.

After a minute, Poppy stood up. She ran her fingers through her hair, smoothing it down. Her mascara had smudged a little from the rain, but that didn't do anything but make her look sexier, as far as Justin was concerned. He had a feeling she spent a lot of time trying to look perfect, trying to *be* perfect. This moment of vulnerability was nice.

She looked up at him, pulling her bottom lip between her teeth. He wanted to kiss her again. Actually, he wanted to do more than kiss her. Much more, and his pulse quickened accordingly.

"You actually think time is all it's going to take?" she asked.

"Sure. She's friendly. She's already coming around."

Poppy frowned. "I'm not just talking about Roo."

The house felt even quieter than before. It was like time had ground to a stop, and everything was holding its breath. Waiting for him to answer.

"You're talking about my mother?"

She shook her head. "I'm talking about everyone. Her. Your dad. You…"

After a long moment, he stepped toward her. And to his surprise, she didn't move away. She just looked up at him with those eyes that had once been so full of fire, but were now only full of pain and regret. She was too young to be this damaged. But, then again, so was he.

"It'll take some time," he said. "But I think we'll all get there eventually."

He reached out and ran his knuckles along her cheekbone. Her skin was like warm satin. She'd been lovely as a teenager. But the woman she'd grown into was simply stunning. He wasn't sure if he'd ever looked too much beyond her beauty before, but he was looking now. There was so much more to Poppy than what she presented to the world. She'd been shattered by Danny's death. She was shattered still. He understood how she felt on the most primitive level, and all of a sudden he was overcome with sadness for how their lives had turned out. Poppy could have been someone he'd confided in after the accident. They could have leaned on each other, given each other comfort. But he knew that wouldn't have been possible back then.

He rubbed the pad of this thumb across her lips, and she closed her eyes. He'd told Mike that he had no future with Poppy. That there was no possibility of anything working between them. But in his heart, he questioned that. Could they get beyond this pain to find something else? Anything else?

"I'm just trying to figure out how you really feel," she said, opening her eyes and looking up at him. "About me. About all of it."

The words rang like a bell in his ears. He'd told her there was nothing to forgive her for. But that wasn't true. He'd blamed her for the accident—of course, he had. But forgiveness was a tricky thing. The thought of it had come and gone over the years, brushing by him like a stranger on a train. But now, it was more than just an idea, or a distant hope that had sparked a flame inside of him. It was becoming a proper fire, something that he wanted to step close to and warm himself against. He didn't want to turn away from it anymore. He didn't want to turn away from Poppy, either. He wanted to wrap his arms around her, explain how he felt—how he'd *always* felt about her. But he knew if he opened his mouth, the words would elude him, like they always had. No matter how hard he tried, he couldn't seem to express what was in his heart.

Shoving a frustrated hand through his hair, he stalked over to the window, where the rain was coming harder now.

"Justin?"

"Yeah."

"What's wrong?"

She walked up and put a hand on his shoulder. He stiffened. Her touch was something that could permeate his entire body. Could affect the way his heart beat, or the way air filled his lungs. He wasn't sure he could stand this much longer. They'd have to explore what was happening between them, or he'd have to walk away from her for good. Being in limbo like this was too hard.

"I don't know how to do this," he said, his voice gravelly.

"You don't know how to do what?"

"I don't know how to feel what I'm feeling for you. And

I sure as hell don't know how to get you to trust in it, when I can't even put it into words."

After a few seconds, he turned around. Her face was flushed. Her lips were full and pink, glistening in the fading evening light. She was so beautiful that his chest constricted just looking at her.

"What are we going to do?" she asked.

The question was simple enough. But the answer had never been simple. It had never been easy, even when Danny was alive. Maybe especially when Danny was alive.

He rubbed his jaw, feeling the stubble scrape against his fingertips. He hadn't had time to shave this morning, opting to give Roo a walk before heading to the shop instead. Ever since Earl had passed away, his life had been one big question mark after another.

And now, Poppy was standing here. Waiting for an answer that she had to know wasn't going to materialize. At least not as neatly as they both would have liked.

"Maybe we just start at the beginning," he said. "And go from there."

She watched him.

"I've always wanted to take you to dinner."

A smile played at the corners of her lips. "Dinner..."

They'd never had a chance to go on a date. To explore any kind of feelings growing between them.

But here, now, it felt like moving toward whatever this was might be possible. But not easy. It damn sure wouldn't be easy.

"Are you asking me out, Justin?" she asked.

"Depends."

"On?"

"On whether or not you'd say yes."

The rain continued tapping on the window. Roo scratched behind her ear, sending her tags jingling. And Justin waited. If she ended up letting him take her out, things between them were going to change. He was sure of that. Whether they'd change for the better, he didn't know. But they'd definitely change. It would be a turning point, a move in a direction other than backward, and as far as he was concerned, that was a good thing.

"Okay," she said.

"Okay, what?"

She smiled. "Let's go on a date."

Evelyn pulled her little red Fiat up to the curb in front of the antique shop and cut the engine. She looked over at the sign in the window that read, Yes, We're Open! and felt her stomach clench.

She hadn't planned on doing this. Hadn't planned on coming in this morning, or ever, for that matter. But for some reason, she'd found herself in the garage the other day, and had found Danny's skates. She hadn't been looking for them. She'd been looking for her raincoat, but there they'd been. Lying on top of an old box labeled *Goodwill*.

She let her gaze settle on them now, sitting beside her in the passenger's seat. After she'd found them, she'd brought them inside and gone over them with a soft rag dipped in leather oil. Paul had walked in and asked her what she was doing, and she didn't even have an answer for him. She'd looked over and shrugged, and he'd walked back out without saying another word. She guessed he'd learned to leave well enough alone.

Reaching over, she picked up the skates. They were boys' skates, but she thought they'd probably be the right size for Mary. Maybe a little big, but not by much. Mary had mentioned roller-skating to her. More specifically, she'd mentioned roller-skating angels, and Evelyn hadn't been able to stop thinking about the coincidence. What were the odds? Maybe it was a sign. Fate. Kismet. Whatever. But she hadn't been able to let it go, and before she'd known it, she was climbing into her car this morning, telling Paul that she'd be back soon.

She hadn't let herself think of the specifics—that stopping by the antique shop would probably mean seeing Poppy again. She'd pushed that thought out of her mind, where it had stayed until now.

She opened her door into the chilly morning air, and the breeze immediately whipped her curls around her face. They'd be a frizzy mess by the time she got inside, but for once she didn't care. Let them be frizzy. It was just hair, after all.

After stepping out of her car with the skates tucked underneath her arm, she closed the door behind her, then looked over at the antique shop again. Her nerves tingled. Maybe on some level, she was *hoping* to see Poppy. Maybe she wanted to confront her, like she had that first day. Or maybe she wanted to get a closer look at her to see what all the fuss was about. At least as far as Justin was concerned.

Or maybe she just wanted Danny's skates to go to someone who would enjoy them.

Liking that thought better than all the others, she stepped onto the sidewalk, and walked to the front door. The shop looked cute. There were a few rocking chairs out front, and baskets of colorful flowers in front of the window. As far as she could remember, Earl had never had flowers out front. That was a special touch that either

Poppy or Cora had added. It was homey. Very small-town antique shop.

Evelyn reached for the door and pushed it open. A little bell tinkled above her head, announcing her arrival. If she'd been having second thoughts, and wanted to walk out before anyone noticed her, it was too late now.

She looked around. Vintage lamps illuminated the shop in soft yellow lighting. It smelled a little musty, but in a pleasant, old-fashioned kind of way. She'd only been inside once before—years ago, when she'd been looking for a gift for a friend. The shop had been more hodgepodge back then, a little messy and unorganized. Those days were long gone. Everything was neat and clean, the aisles wide and sparkling. The old wood floor gleamed, and smelled like lemon cleaner. It was a warm and welcoming space. She imagined it being a cozy reprieve from the rain and fog in the winter months—somewhere the tourists could browse and sip their coffees, and let their hands and feet warm up before venturing outside again.

"Evelyn?"

She startled. She'd been in her own little world again. Lost somewhere between reality and imagination.

She turned to see Poppy standing there. Her pretty face was drained of color.

Evelyn looked down at the skates under her arm. All of a sudden, she couldn't believe she'd done this. It was like she was standing outside her own body, watching herself struggle with what to say. This was something a neighbor or an acquaintance would do—drop off an old pair of skates. *Here you go! Danny isn't using them anymore, so...* It wasn't something a bitter enemy would do. It wasn't something Evelyn Frost would do.

She licked her lips, which were dry as a bone. She'd forgotten to put on lipstick before she'd left the house, and she never forgot to put on lipstick. *A bitter enemy.* Was that what she was? Was that what she wanted to be?

"What…?" Poppy let her voice trail off.

Evelyn couldn't blame her. She probably thought she'd lost her mind.

Evelyn cleared her throat, and forced herself to look at the other woman. Properly look at her. And she could clearly see what all the fuss was about. She was gorgeous, even with her pale face and worried brow. She almost looked like a caricature of a real person. Nobody was *actually* this attractive. But Poppy Sawyer was. She always had been. Boys had always lined up for her. Including Danny.

"I don't know if Mary told you," Evelyn said. "But we spent a few minutes together the other day. She wanted to see my car…"

"Oh. Yes, she told me."

"Well, we talked a little. And she mentioned roller-skating." Evelyn decided that she didn't want to go into the specifics of their conversation. That Mary had asked her what she thought heaven would be like. That felt private. Like it was supposed to stay between the two of them.

She cleared her throat again. She couldn't have guessed how hard it would be to stand here and have a civilized conversation with Poppy. But she was doing it. So far, she was doing okay.

"She mentioned roller-skating," she repeated, "and I found these old skates of Danny's in the garage, and I thought she might want them. They weren't doing anything but gathering dust, and they're in pretty good shape. I put some leather oil on them. If they don't fit, she can give them away. But I thought she might be able to use them..."

Poppy watched her for a minute. Then smiled hesitantly. "That's very sweet of you. I think she'd love that."

They stood there, silence settling between them. There was nobody else in the shop, no customers, no Cora or Beau. And no Mary. Evelyn wondered what she was up to. She'd looked so sad about her father. So crushed over his passing. Evelyn understood how she felt. They'd shared that brief moment of melancholy.

"I'm glad you're here," Poppy said. "I've been wanting to apologize."

Evelyn stiffened. "For?"

"For the other day. For what you saw at the hardware store."

"Well. Justin is a grown man. It's none of my business." Easy to say. But did she actually believe that? Not really. Not when it came to Poppy.

The younger woman nodded. Evelyn was close enough to see there were faint lines at the edges of her mouth. A line between her knitted eyebrows. And for a second, she could see past Poppy's beauty, past the careful facade, to the person inside. Quiet, remorseful, introspective. Was this what Justin saw when he looked at her? Probably. Justin had always been able to see deeper than most people. It was a blessing, or a curse, depending on how you looked at it.

"I just..." Again, Poppy's voice trailed off.

If Evelyn had been in her normal mood, with her normal bitterness consuming her, she wouldn't have cared if Poppy didn't finish her sentence. She would've turned smartly on her heel and walked out the door. *Use the skates, don't use them, whatever.* Then again, if she'd been in her normal mood, she wouldn't be here in the first place.

But instead of turning to go, she took a step forward. And then another, and set the skates on the countertop next to the old cash register that looked like it had been around the block a few times.

"You just, what?" she asked.

Poppy took a visible breath. She was having a hard time with this, that was obvious. And why wouldn't she? Evelyn had made her a punching bag for a long time. That couldn't feel good.

Evelyn realized this was probably the first time that she'd attempted to understand how Poppy felt. Or wondered about it, even. After the accident, and over the years that followed, Poppy's feelings hadn't registered on Evelyn's radar at all. And if they had, she would have pushed them away, neat as you please. She had enough feelings of her own to deal with, thank you very much.

But something about this moment, about today, was different. It was leaving Evelyn unsure of herself for the first time in a while. Because if she was going to open the door to understanding how Poppy felt, what else was she going to open the door to?

Poppy clasped her hands together and squeezed. Her knuckles were white. "I just don't want to hurt you any more than I already have," she said, finishing.

Evelyn stood there, her feet rooted in place. When she realized she was staring, she forced herself to look away. It wasn't easy. She didn't know how to respond to that, and, of course, a response was necessary. A normal person, a *feeling* person, would say something to acknowledge how difficult this was for Poppy. Would try to alleviate the discomfort as much as possible. But Evelyn had spent so much time with her anger, stoking it into a proper inferno, that she found she couldn't open her mouth. And she probably wouldn't have been able to get her tongue to cooperate if she had. So she simply stood there, feeling so out of place that she wanted to cry because of it. She didn't belong here. But at the same time, she knew she was in the presence of one of the only other people who shared the unique trauma of losing Danny. If she didn't belong here, where *did* she belong?

Poppy shifted on her feet. "Anyway. I just wanted to tell you that."

From somewhere deep inside, Evelyn finally found the presence of mind to at least nod, until she could think of something appropriate to say.

And then, miraculously, she didn't have to. From behind her, the bell above the shop door tinkled, and she and Poppy turned to see Mary and Cora walk in, looking chilled and windblown.

"Evelyn!" Mary said with a wide, gap-toothed smile. "Hey!"

Evelyn smiled back. Nobody was ever this happy to see her. It was probably why people had dogs, to be greeted so enthusiastically when they came home. She suspected that Paul sometimes retreated into the next room when he heard the garage door open. It wasn't his fault. She could be a difficult person to live with. Her husband loved her, but she wasn't sure he liked her half the time.

"Hi, Evelyn," Cora said hesitantly. This was what Evelyn was used to getting from all the Sawyers. They didn't trust that she wasn't going to come unglued when she saw them, so they had to be on guard at all times. Understandable.

"Did you come to shop?" Mary asked. Her lips and tongue were bright blue, and she held a bag from the candy shop down the street.

"Actually, I came to bring you something."

Mary's eyes widened. She had pretty eyes. Her mother's eyes.

"You did?"

"I did," Evelyn said.

"What is it?"

"Remember when we talked about roller-skating?"

"Sure. The skating angels?"

Cora and Poppy exchanged a confused look. That was okay. They'd find out soon enough, but for now this was still something special between her and Mary.

"Well, I came across a pair of my son's old roller skates," Evelyn said. "And I thought you might like to have them. Have you skated before?"

Mary beamed. "A couple of times. I liked it. It was fun."

"I hope they fit. If they don't, I bet you can find someone else who can wear them."

"Can I try them on?"

"Of course."

"Don't forget to say thank you," Cora said.

"Thank you, Evelyn! You're the coolest!"

Evelyn watched her swipe them off the counter and run to the back of the shop. That was a first. She'd never been called the coolest before. Or even remotely cool, for that matter.

Her face warmed as she stood between the two other women, who seemed to be stunned into silence. Clearly, they hadn't expected this. Neither had Evelyn. But here they were, in the same room, being civil to one another. Of course, Poppy had never been anything but civil. It was Evelyn who'd had the civility problem.

She felt some of the nervous tension drain from her shoulders. She didn't feel anxious anymore, just tired. Tired, as if she'd accomplished something. Like she might feel after a particularly long walk on the beach, or a challenging yoga class. She'd done a hard thing. She'd done a good thing. And now, she wanted some time to reflect on it, maybe even go home and tell Paul what she'd done. He'd be surprised. Actually, he'd be gobsmacked.

Putting her hands in her jacket pockets, she turned to go. But before she did, she smiled at Cora. And then, incredibly, at Poppy.

She'd done it before she could help herself.

And then, she walked out the door with a wave. Just like a neighbor who'd dropped by for a visit.

Chapter Twelve

Poppy stood in her little bedroom, and looked at herself in the full-length mirror. She'd thought all afternoon about what to wear, changing her mind roughly a million times. She'd finally decided on something simple, casual, but with a touch of femininity that she didn't usually get to indulge in. In Portland, she lived in a world of power suits and sensible pumps. Nobody wanted to break their neck running around a busy television set in stilettoes. Tonight, she'd settled on dark-washed jeans and a silk top with quarter-length sleeves and a delicate flower print. She'd pulled her hair into a ponytail, and fished out her mother's diamond studs that her father had given her on one of their anniversaries before the divorce. Her mom hadn't wanted them anymore, and had given them to Poppy with nothing more than a shrug of her shoulders.

Poppy looked at the way they sparkled in the mirror now. She guessed they should probably make her sad, reminding her of all the things that weren't around anymore. But they always did the opposite. Brought her back to a time when she'd felt whole. When her family had felt whole. The earrings made her happy, and she always wore them on special occasions. She swallowed hard. Was this a special occasion? Her first date with Justin?

She knew the answer to that. It was incredibly special. Especially since she had no idea if there would be a second date. There were too many questions that needed to be answered, too many unknowns for her to feel like anything between them, even friendship, would ever work.

She knew after he dropped her off tonight she'd have to face all those questions, all those unknowns. But right now, looking at her reflection in the mirror, she didn't want to face anything but the way her eyes seemed to sparkle like the diamonds in her earlobes. She looked happy. And she wanted to *feel* happy for a few precious hours.

There was a knock on her open door, and she turned to see Cora standing there, smiling softly.

"Wow," her cousin said. "You look amazing."

Poppy stepped away from the mirror and leaned down to put on her favorite pair of strappy sandals. It would probably be chilly tonight, with the wind coming in off the ocean, but she'd painted her toenails, and at this point, looking cute was her first priority.

"Thanks, Cora," she said. "I'm not sure about *amazing,* but I guess I clean up okay."

Cora laughed, stepping inside. "You've gotta be kidding me. You know you're gorgeous. Always have been."

"I look good on camera, and that's all that matters."

Her cousin sat on the bed with a sigh. "You're a lot more than just a pretty face, Poppy. Besides, you're going to have to start seeing yourself as something other than a news anchor if you stay here for the long haul."

Turning, Poppy put her hands on her hips. "Is that really what I'm going to do? Stay for the long haul?"

Cora's expression was drawn. It was the question they'd all been asking themselves since losing their grandfather.

Since opening the shop again. They'd agreed to stay the year. But would they end up staying past that? With every day that passed, they were sinking back into their lives in Christmas Bay. There was no denying that. When this place grabbed hold, it didn't let go easily.

"What are you going to do about KTVL?" Cora asked.

At the mention of her station, Poppy's chest tightened. She'd managed to negotiate a leave of absence, with the understanding that she might not be able to come back to her same position. Her boss, never one to pull any punches, had made it clear that it was far from guaranteed, but they'd try and find something for her, and she could work her way back to the anchor desk if that's what she wanted. Not a perfect scenario, but one that would give her the time she needed to figure out what else she could do with her life, if it wasn't reporting on the news. In the meantime, she'd already gone back to Portland, and in one frantic weekend, had managed to clean out her apartment and sublet it in one fell swoop.

"I guess I'm stalling," she said. "It's hard to imagine staying. But the longer I'm here…"

"I know. The harder it is to imagine leaving."

Poppy gave her a small, knowing smile. "Yes. That."

There was a faint rumbling sound on the first floor. And then, a crash.

"I'm okay!" a voice at the base of the stairs called.

Cora put her face in her hands. "She's going to break something on those skates. But I can't get her out of them. She loves them. Like, *loves* them so much I'm surprised she doesn't sleep in them."

"I mean, it's a pretty epic gift," Poppy said. "And from Evelyn, too. Can you believe it?"

"I honestly can't. She seemed so *different* the other day. Like she might even…"

She didn't finish that thought. But it wasn't hard to fill in the blanks.

Poppy walked over and sat down beside her. "Like she might be starting to forgive me?"

Cora nodded.

"I don't know," Poppy said. "She hasn't said so. But she was definitely different. Mary might have something to do with that."

"Right? It's the strangest thing. Mary adores her."

Cora might think it was strange, given Evelyn's surliness over the years. But Poppy remembered how she used to be—bright, sunny, cheerful. And *funny*. She was always cracking a joke, prompting Danny and Justin to roll their eyes good-naturedly. It was cliché to say that someone lit up a room when they walked into it, but Evelyn really had. She'd been a force of nature back then. Poppy had envied her—had even aspired to be like her. But then, the accident happened, and the entire world had changed. And Evelyn had changed right along with it.

"Do you think she knows about your date?" Cora asked.

Poppy ran a nervous hand through her hair. "I'm not sure."

Cora nodded again.

"I mean, it's just a date," Poppy said. "Nothing more."

"Right."

"It *is*."

"Are you trying to convince me?" Cora asked. "Or yourself?"

Poppy took a deep breath. Cora was one of the only people in her life, besides Beau, who didn't let her lie to herself. Something she'd gotten very good at.

"Maybe both," she said evenly.

"What did he say? When he asked you?"

"He said he's always wanted to take me out." She shrugged. "There's nothing more to it than that."

But, of course, there was. There was intricate layer after intricate layer. And Cora knew that better than anyone. She sat there, looking at Poppy skeptically.

"What?" Poppy asked.

"I just think you'd better be prepared, that's all."

"For?"

"For this to escalate. For it to go somewhere you might not expect."

"There's nowhere for it to go," Poppy said. "This is one date, just to get it out of our system, and that's it."

"But what if it *does* go somewhere? Then what?"

Poppy shook her head. "It won't."

"Why? Because you don't deserve it?"

"I didn't say that." But she didn't have to. There was a reason why she never let herself fall for anyone. She was too suspicious of anything good coming her way.

"You're a grown woman, Poppy," Cora said. "You deserve to be happy. And if you and Justin make each other happy, that's not for anyone else to judge. Not even Evelyn."

But that's where her cousin was wrong. Evelyn would be the first to judge.

Reaching over, she took Cora's hand in hers. She loved her for sticking up for her like this. She loved her for believing in her. When the accident first happened, if felt like nobody would ever believe in her again. Her parents had sometimes faltered, blaming her without coming right out and saying it, but her cousins' support had been unwavering. It had sustained her in the months that followed. Their love, along with the love from her grandfather, had gotten her through.

But what nobody had been able to prepare her for back then was the fact that she'd carry that feeling of inadequacy her entire life, until it eventually became a part of who she was. She felt undeserving, because she *was* undeserving.

But since coming home to Christmas Bay, and since she'd begun talking to Justin again, she'd felt that numb part of her heart begin to warm for the first time since Danny died. She felt herself coming back to life, just the slightest bit, and with that awakening heat was the glimmer of hope that maybe she did deserve some good things. Because if Justin, of all people, could kiss her and hold her face in his hands, then what did that mean? Deep down, she hoped it meant forgiveness. And if he could forgive her, then maybe, just maybe, she might be able to forgive herself.

She squeezed Cora's hand. "Thank you for always having my back."

"You know I do. Whatever happens tonight, I'm just happy you're taking a step forward. I'm proud of you, Poppy. I know it isn't easy. Being back here, with all the memories, with all the people who remember. It must be so hard, but you're doing it."

There was a knock on the open bedroom door, and they both looked over to see Beau standing there, his baseball cap pushed high on his forehead. "What are ya'll doing in here?"

"Poppy's getting ready for her date," Cora said.

"For her *date*?"

"It's not a date, really," Poppy said quickly. "Well, I guess it is, but it's not a big deal."

"With who?"

"With Justin," Cora said.

"Why am I just now hearing about this?" Beau asked.

"Because you were out fishing."

There was a loud clomping sound coming from the staircase, and then a low rumbling over the hardwood floor before Mary rolled in on her skates. "What's everyone doing in here?"

"Your Aunt Poppy apparently has a date," Beau said.

"With *who*?" Mary asked, flopping down on the bed.

"Did you climb the stairs in those things?" Cora asked.

Mary laughed at the look on her mother's face.

The room felt noisy. Full of life. It had been a long time since Poppy had anyone asking her questions about her personal life that she was embarrassed to answer. Nobody had cared enough to be interested.

But sitting on the bed, with Mary's skates hanging over the edge, and Cora brushing her daughter's hair back, and Beau standing with his arms crossed over his chest like a big brother might, she found she was in love with this moment. Even if tonight went completely awry, she was grateful for the tenderness she felt for her family right now.

They were hers, and she was theirs, and she knew she'd be protective of their relationship from this point on. Coming home had reawakened their bond. And deepened it for the long haul.

Justin sat across from Poppy, watching her read the menu with her brow furrowed. He'd thought about driving her into Eugene for a fancier dinner, something they wouldn't be able to get in Christmas Bay, but he didn't want her to think he was running away from the locals, or anyone else who might have an opinion about them having dinner together. There would always be someone with an opinion, but this was his home. And her home. At least it was for the next year. He wasn't going to run away from anything.

She looked up and smiled at him in the candlelight. The restaurant was small, intimate. A cozy Italian place that he'd only been to once before, but he hadn't been able to forget how amazing the calzone was. He also remembered that Poppy liked Italian, so here they were.

"I have no idea what to order," she said, taking a sip of her wine.

She looked beautiful tonight, but she always looked beautiful. She was wearing less makeup than usual, and her hair was pulled into a ponytail, making him think of her high-school cross-country days. Looking back, it was hard to pinpoint exactly when he'd fallen in love with her, but he remembered those Saturday mornings well. He'd go with Danny to her meets, and watch her fly by. He'd been mesmerized by her back then. And he was mesmerized by her now.

He closed his menu and set it at the edge of the table. "I think I'm gonna have the chicken Parmesan."

"That sounds good. Maybe I'll have the same."

He smiled. It was surreal that they were sitting here together. It was like their kiss had broken down some kind of barrier between them, and they'd started fresh. It was a strange feeling for Justin not to be sad or resentful when he looked at Poppy. But at the moment, he was just enjoying getting to know her again.

She set aside her menu and looked at him. Shadows from the candlelight flickered across her face. Her eyes were dark, her lashes long and sweeping as she took him in. She tucked her hands in her lap and leaned forward.

"I still can't believe I'm on a date with you," she said.

"I know. I can't believe it, either."

He reached for his beer and took a long swallow, the alcohol warming his throat on the way down. She watched him intently as he licked the tanginess from his lips.

"What?" he asked.

"Nothing."

"That's not true."

"I was just thinking."

"About?"

"It'll make you sad," she said.

"I can handle it."

"I was just thinking how handsome you are."

He felt the corners of his mouth tilt. "So far not the worst thing in the world. Why would that make me sad?"

"Because I was also thinking about how much you look like Danny."

Hearing his little brother's name pricked his heart, like it always did. But he found the pain was different lately. A little less sharp. Was it because he'd finally found some peace where Poppy was concerned? He thought that might be exactly it. Maybe spending time with her was not only helping him move forward, but was also keeping Danny's memory alive.

"He loved you," he said evenly. "Danny really loved you, you know."

She looked away at that. Across the room filled with flickering candles, past the couples sitting around them, and out the window, toward the darkly churning water. It was hard talking about Danny. But this was a place to start. And that felt good.

"He never would've wanted you to carry the weight of this forever," he said.

"I know. Because he was a good person, and he wouldn't want me to suffer. But I'm not sure how to let it go. It feels wrong to."

"You think it's wrong to forgive yourself. But keeping his memory with you and letting the guilt eat you alive are two different things, Poppy."

She stared down at her hands, splayed out on the tabletop now. Her fingers were long and delicate, her nails painted an understated pink. He could see that they were trembling.

"That's the problem," she said. "It's really hard to separate the guilt from the memory of him."

He nodded. After a second, he took a deep breath. "Have you talked to someone about this?"

She looked up.

"It might help," he said. "Talking to a professional."

"I've been in therapy off and on since the accident. I've had some good therapists, and some not-so-good ones. But they gave me the tools I need to live with this in a healthy way. In the end though, I'm the one who has to use them."

"I hear that. Same."

"You've had therapy?"

"Yeah. One of the best things I've ever done."

"I'm glad. It's not easy asking for help."

"Grief is heavy. When I was struggling the most, it was scary as hell. I didn't want to spiral."

She nodded, taking a sip of her wine. Her eyes were averted, her lashes lowered. Had she been in danger of spiraling, too? He wondered whom she'd leaned on all these years. If she'd had someone, anyone, to confide in. The thought of her being alone made him sad. But surely, her family had been there for her. Surely...

"Poppy."

"Mmm?"

"What happened afterward?" His voice was low. The words were significant. He knew he didn't have to elaborate—she'd know exactly what he meant.

For a minute, he wasn't sure if she was going to answer. Or if she did, how open she would be. She wore an anguished expression that made him feel bad for asking. But at the same time, he wanted to know. It was a part of her story that he didn't know yet. But more than that, it was part of *her* that he didn't know yet.

"I was lost," she finally said. "So lost that sometimes I wasn't even sure if I deserved to live."

He waited, watching her.

"The kids at school were pretty vicious," she continued. "I dropped out for a while."

He'd known that. But at the time, he'd been too mired in his own grief to acknowledge it. He was ashamed of that now. She must've gone through hell.

"My friends didn't want to talk to me anymore. And I couldn't blame them. After a while, the only kids I felt like I fit in with were the ones who were alienated themselves, for whatever reasons. Sometimes really bad ones."

He'd known that, too. He'd heard that she'd gotten involved with some questionable kids. He'd thought about her nearly every day, but by that point, he was so overcome with anger that he couldn't see straight. And he'd stayed that way for a long time. The longer he went without seeing her, without talking to her, the more entrenched in anger he'd become.

"My parents started fighting, blaming each other for what happened," she said. "People in town treated them differently. Like the accident was their fault. Like maybe they should've kept me home that night, or they should've driven us to the dance, or...something. Our house was the saddest place. And it got to the point where I didn't want to be there at all. I'd stay out all night, sometimes not even coming home the next day. And that's when my grandpa stepped in. He saved me, I think."

Justin swallowed down an uncomfortably tight feeling in his throat. Poppy was gazing at him, but her eyes had a distant look in them, like she might not be seeing him. She was lost in her memories, he could tell. She'd fallen back to a place she must not let herself visit often. He understood the feeling of being transported back in time. Sometimes he fought it. Other times he didn't, and he'd stay gone for a long time, lost in the dark memories. It would take days to fight his way out again.

"He refused to lose me to whatever was happening to me," she said quietly. "He wouldn't give up. Eventually I came to work at the shop, and we spent a lot of time together, just him and me. Sometimes we'd talk all night long. About the accident, but also about my parents. And the rest of the family, and how we'd never be the same again. I knew that, deep down, but it was Grandpa who helped me come to terms with it. I went back to school and finished with honors. Then I went off to college, and left Christmas Bay behind."

But that wasn't the end of her story. She made it sound like it was, but in so many ways, he knew it was only the beginning. Because those were the years she'd grown up. The problem was that she still couldn't fully embrace the woman she'd become—it was obvious to anyone paying attention.

"I tried to outrun everything," she continued, "but it caught up to me, anyway. And now, here I am. Feeling seventeen again."

He reached for her hand across the table. "I'm glad you came back, Poppy."

Her eyes filled with tears. "I don't understand how you can be glad."

"I am."

"But why?"

"You know why."

"Because we're attracted to each other? That's not a good enough reason, Justin."

"I agree," he said. "That wouldn't be. But luckily, it doesn't have anything to do with the fact that I'm attracted to you. I'm just glad, that's all."

She shook her head.

"You don't get to dispute it," he said. "Sorry."

"I just don't understand it."

"Because you still haven't forgiven yourself."

"It hurts too much," she said, her chin trembling.

"I know it does."

"And when I think about how sweet you're being, it only makes it hurt more."

He frowned as he squeezed her hand. "You deserve kindness," he said. "You deserve forgiveness."

"I want to believe that."

That was the hardest part. Getting her to believe it.

He ran his thumb over the backs of her knuckles. Felt how warm her skin was against his. How delicate. It made his pulse quicken.

"Danny would've been the first to forgive you," he said. "You know that."

"I know."

"Then the judgment you might feel from anyone else doesn't matter. Right?"

"In a perfect world it wouldn't."

He waited. Watched the way the candlelight flickered across her face.

"Your mom came in to the shop the other day," she said. "Did you know that?"

"No. I didn't."

"She brought in a pair of Danny's old roller skates for Mary. And there was a moment there. It felt... I don't know. It felt different to me."

He realized that he was staring at her, and he cleared his throat. Danny's old skates? What had prompted that? All of a sudden, he had the unsettling feeling that he didn't know his mother at all anymore. When had he talked to her last, *really* talked to her? Not just in passing, not just to get her to ease up on him.

The rush of sadness he felt right then was pure and absolute.

She frowned. "What's wrong?"

"Nothing. Go on. Why did you feel like it was different?"

"For one thing, she didn't seem angry with me."

He listened, unmoving.

"And I thought she'd be furious," she said. "Especially after she saw us together at the hardware store."

The back of his neck warmed at the memory. He'd been expecting that, too. But this? This was almost unheard of for his mother. A huge step for someone who'd been mired in place for so long. It made Justin wonder if she was inching closer to forgiving Poppy. And if she was, what that would mean for their family? His mom had been dictating the pace of their healing, whether she wanted to admit it or not.

"What did she say?" he asked, suddenly overcome with a need to know. Wishing he'd been there to see this for himself.

"It wasn't what she said, really. But some of her sharpness was gone. And there was a softness there instead."

A softness... Justin liked that. It was nice to think of the sharpness receding.

They sat there for a minute, the restaurant humming quietly around them. Their waiter walked up to the table and took their order, and then they were alone again. Poppy smiled at him, and he smiled back, wondering if she had any idea how lovely she was. He knew she had to have been told it often enough, but did she really hear it? Like she had a hard time hearing him when he talked about forgiveness? He guessed she probably didn't.

"What about you, Justin?" she asked.

"What about me?"

"What happened to you after the accident?"

He took a gulp of his beer, and then another, before setting it down again.

"I was messed up for a long time," he finally said. "A really long time."

She gazed at him from across the table. For the first time since walking through the door, he was aware of someone they'd gone to high school with, sitting a few tables over. A friend of Danny's—which wasn't that much of a coincidence, since the entire town was full of Danny's friends. But since Poppy had come back, he'd noticed these old classmates more often. They were everywhere, and every time he ran into one of them, he was forced to confront the memories all over again.

Justin felt the guy staring over at them. *Mason*, he thought. Mason Detwiler. He'd been on the football team.

"Go on," Poppy said, jerking him back to the present.

"Well. I fumbled my way through the rest of high school. I'm not sure how I managed that. My parents weren't around much, and one day I noticed that none of us were talking anymore. We'd just gone our separate ways. I moved out, went to college for a year, then dropped out to travel. It was therapeutic for me. I went a lot of places, met a lot of people, but in the end, I decided there wasn't anywhere else I wanted to be but Christmas Bay. I came home, worked for a while and then opened the shop. It was something Danny and I always wanted to do together."

"I remember."

"He talked about it enough. I never thought we'd actually do it. But never say never, right?"

From the corner of his eye, Justin saw someone walk up to the table. He turned, expecting to see the waiter.

But it wasn't the waiter. It was Mason Detwiler.

Poppy stared up at the man looking down at her. It was obvious she recognized him. Christmas Bay High hadn't been that big, after all. Most of the kids had known each other, or at least known *of* each other.

Mason smiled, but it wasn't a kind smile. It was more of a sneer, and Justin braced himself. The man was swaying on his feet, clearly drunk. His date walked up and tugged on his shirt.

"Mason," she whispered. "Let's go."

He yanked his arm away. "No, I just want to say hi. I haven't seen these two since junior year. How are you, Justin?"

"Fine. How are you?"

"I'm great. I couldn't help but notice you're having dinner with Poppy Sawyer. Honey, do you know who this is?"

His date shook her head, looking embarrassed. She gave Poppy an apologetic look.

"She killed my friend."

Justin felt his muscles tense with a quick flash of fury.

"Leave," he said, his voice dangerously low. "Now."

"That was your *brother*," Mason continued.

The other patrons in the restaurant turned to look.

"Mason," his date said again. "Let's go."

He ignored her, glaring at Justin with clear disdain. "I heard she was back in town. I also heard there was something going on between you two, but I didn't want to believe it. I mean, who'd mess around with the bitch who killed their little brother? But I guess it's true. I mean, *obviously*." He waved his hand in a wide, sloppy arc toward Poppy.

Justin's pulse hammered in his ears. He pushed back his chair, ready to grab the guy by his collar and toss him out.

"He was let go from his job today," his date said quickly.

"And his cousin passed away last week. Car wreck. He's not himself, I'm so sorry. We'll go. I promise."

"I'm *fine*," Mason growled. "You don't have to *handle* me."

She didn't answer. Just hooked her arm in his, and pulled. Hard.

This time, he obliged, and let himself be led away. But not before turning to glare at Poppy one last time. A parting gift from one classmate to another.

She stared after him, white as a ghost.

Justin tried reaching for her hand, but she moved it away.

"No," she said.

"You can't let it get to you."

"He didn't say anything that wasn't true."

"Are you kidding me?"

"Why aren't you more bothered by this?"

"I *am* bothered by it. I'm pissed."

"But not at the truth."

"That was an extremely skewed version of the truth."

She took a sip of her wine, but her face remained pale, her expression strained.

"If you're ever going to move forward," he said, "you're going to have to be able to compartmentalize this kind of thing. It's going to happen. It doesn't mean it's fair or it *should* happen. But life isn't fair."

She ran her index finger around the rim of her glass. "I know it's not."

"You're a good person, Poppy. And he was drunk."

"Yeah."

"Look at me."

Slowly, she did. Her eyes were red-rimmed, but there were no tears. Maybe she was all out of tears.

"Forgive yourself," he said evenly.

She nodded. But didn't say another word until their dinner arrived.

Chapter Thirteen

Justin held the door open for her, and Poppy walked out into the cool night air. It was cloudy, so there were no stars overhead. Just blackness. The ocean breeze smelled tangy, like rain might be coming, although none was in the forecast. That was the thing about Christmas Bay, though. The weather could surprise you. Other things could surprise you, too.

She dug her compact out of her purse as Justin stood there talking to a few acquaintances who were coming into the restaurant. She'd taken a few steps to the side, so he wouldn't feel pressured to introduce her. She'd had enough interaction with the locals for one night, and wanted to make herself as inconspicuous as possible.

Opening the compact, she looked at herself in the mirror, and cringed. She'd managed not to cry at dinner, but her eyes had started watering a little when Justin had been paying the bill, and again when she'd excused herself to use the bathroom. In fact, she'd been fighting tears constantly since the encounter with Mason Detwiler an hour before.

It wasn't like she didn't expect this kind of thing to happen. It had happened with Justin's own mother, after all.

But she'd been having such a good conversation with Justin over their drinks. They'd been opening up to each other for the first time ever. She'd been feeling better about herself since Evelyn had come into the shop, and that was a good thing.

And then Mason had appeared beside their table, and that delicate peace had been shattered. Gone was the gentleness that Poppy had extended herself, and in its place was that horrible judgment again. From others, and even worse, from herself. She was used to living with it, so it wasn't that hard to welcome it back with open arms. But it still stung. It stung a lot.

She stood on the sidewalk now, listening to Justin tell the couple what his store hours were, because they needed to come in to buy some fencing supplies. Apparently, their boxer puppy kept getting out and wandering the neighborhood. Justin laughed and told them a quick anecdote about Roo.

Poppy snuck a look at him. He might not want to realize it, but he was in love with that dog. He'd bonded with her, it was obvious. Which was going to make Poppy's decision of whether or not to keep her that much harder. Didn't Roo, Justin, her grandfather and *everyone* deserve better than Poppy's inability to make good decisions? She rubbed her temple. The wine had given her a slight headache. Or maybe that had been Mason Detwiler.

After a minute, Justin said good-night to the couple, and walked back over.

"You okay?" he asked. "You kind of disappeared."

"I wasn't in a talkative mood. Sorry."

"You don't have to apologize, I get it." He put his hands in his pockets. "Sometimes living in a small town is exhausting."

She began walking slowly down the sidewalk, pulling

her sweater around her shoulders, and he fell in step beside her.

"Yes," she said. "But it can be wonderful, too. At least, I remember it could be." Her voice had taken on a slightly dreamy tone, and she cleared her throat, embarrassed.

Justin looked over at her. "You don't want to think of the good stuff too much, do you?"

"What makes you say that?"

"It's pretty obvious."

"It is?" She sighed. "I never want to get too sentimental, because you never know what might happen."

"Yeah. Don't get too attached because nice things don't last."

It was a jaded way of looking at it, but it was exactly how she felt. What kind of person didn't let themselves get attached? *The damaged kind*, she thought to herself. *Justin and I are damaged goods.*

The words ran through her head like a scratched record. She didn't like how it made her feel, although she'd known for a long time that she had issues. Baggage. Things that were going to keep her alone indefinitely. There was no denying it anymore. As much as she tried to appear otherwise on camera, to her KTVL audience, she wasn't perfect, not by a long shot, and neither was Justin. And at the end of the day, that didn't make them bad people. It just made them imperfect people.

"They *could* last, though," Justin said, slowing until he came to a stop beside her.

She came to a stop, too, and turned to look up at him.

He was darkly sexy with his shadow of a beard, and strong, angular jaw. She was transfixed, forgetting for a second what they'd been talking about.

"I'm sorry?" she asked.

"Good things could last. If you work at keeping them."

She let that settle as a car passed by, its headlights slicing through the gritty darkness. The old-fashioned streetlamps had winked on a few minutes ago, illuminating the sidewalk in soft light.

"Yes," she said. "I guess if you have enough invested. And you work hard enough…"

"The question is, is it worth it?"

She watched him.

"To put that time and effort in," he continued. "To open yourself up. To have something worth risking. I used to think it wasn't. But now…"

He reached up and touched her face.

"Now, what?" she asked. He had a way of making her feel important. Like she mattered. That was something she was still coming to terms with in her heart.

"Now, I'm seeing that it is," he said, leaning toward her just the slightest bit.

She let her gaze drop to his mouth, her heart pounding almost unbearably. She'd thought about him so many times over the years. Wondered what he was doing, how he was. How he was coping. And now, incredibly, she knew. She knew he was going to extend her grace. Possibly even forgiveness for the worst thing she'd ever done. The question was, was she going to let him? Would she accept that grace with some of her own?

She was still pondering that thought when his lips met hers. Then she forgot everything except how he made her feel.

"I'm sorry…what?"

Paul looked up from his crossword puzzle, his reading

glasses slipping down his nose. He was dressed for the office, since it was Monday morning. Looking sharp and handsome as always, in a dusty blue suit and a red print tie.

Evelyn walked over and pulled the chair out beside him, taking a piece of his bacon from his plate and popping it in her mouth.

He stared at her. She supposed it was because she hadn't eaten bacon since the boys had been little. Too greasy. Too hard on the thighs. But this morning, she found that she didn't care as much about her thighs as she had last week. She was too preoccupied to care. She'd been awake since three in the morning, unable to sleep. Her mind had raced with possibilities. It was a new feeling for her. She'd finally gotten up, made a pot of tea and sat on the sofa to write in her journal, the ocean wind whistling against the living-room windows.

She hadn't opened her journal in years, and had had to dig around a little to find it. Once upon a time, writing her thoughts and feelings down had been as much a part of her life as soccer games and school plays. But since Danny had passed, she hadn't written a word. It had simply been too painful. Until this morning.

Once she'd gotten going, she found that she couldn't stop. Writing so many things down, that before she'd known it, dawn was lighting the sky outside and her hand was cramping in that distinctive, writerly way. A sign that she'd been productive. A sign that she'd explored her emotions, and taken a closer look at her life. Even if it was only on paper.

Paul watched her hesitantly now. She smiled, patting his hand, wanting to put him at ease, but knowing that was a big ask. They'd been tiptoeing around each other for a very long time.

"Should I be worried?" he asked.

"Why? Because I want to enjoy the morning with you?"

He pushed away his crossword. "Well, yes. That…and other things."

"Am I that bad? No. Don't answer that."

That got him to smile a little. Nothing big, just the gentlest tug on the corners of his mouth. Paul had always had a wonderful smile. It was one of the first things she'd fallen in love with. But it had faded over the years, stolen by circumstances.

"What's going on, Evelyn?" he said. "Really?"

"I woke up early this morning, and I couldn't stop thinking."

"About?"

"About Danny, mostly."

Paul stiffened at that. The subject of their youngest son wasn't a place they visited often. Mostly because Evelyn had never been able to visit it without that old fury raising its ugly head.

"Oh?" he said carefully.

"It's okay, you know. I'm not going to have an episode or anything. I actually feel…good. If you can believe that."

He leaned back in his chair, watching her. His hair was threaded with silver, making him look gentlemanly and distinguished. He had crinkles radiating from the corners of his hazel eyes—deepened by his weekends spent golfing. From his weekends spent away from Evelyn. She'd never really minded that they'd grown apart. She didn't mind being alone. In fact, spending too much time together had only complicated things in the beginning. Instead of drawing comfort from each other, it had only made them grumpier.

"I'm listening," he said.

She shrugged. "I just feel good. Different."

"Different how?"

Taking a sip of her tea, she leaned back in her chair, too. She let her gaze shift from Paul to the window, where raindrops were beginning to tap against the glass.

"I gave Danny's skates away," she said. "I hope that's okay."

"Danny's skates… His roller skates?"

She nodded. Poor Paul. He looked so perplexed.

"No," he said. "I don't mind. But why'd you do that?"

"I ran across them in the garage, and they were just sitting there gathering dust. I remembered how much he loved skating, and that it would probably make him happy if another child could use them."

Paul rubbed the back of his neck, and was quiet for a minute.

"Yes," he finally said. "You're right, he would've liked that."

It felt good that they were in agreement. Although she'd known he'd be okay with it. He'd been trying to get her to clean out Danny's closet for a long time. To go through his things and sort out what they wanted to keep and what they wanted to donate, but she'd refused. Danny's room was exactly the way he'd left it that night. She'd turned it into a shrine, even knowing that wasn't healthy. Paul found it too hard to go in there, so he just avoided that part of the house altogether.

"Why, though, honey?" he asked. "Why now?"

The answer was complex. She didn't want to tell Paul

that it had to do with Poppy, someone he wouldn't really believe would have any positive influence in her world at all. Or Poppy's niece, a girl Evelyn barely knew. But the truth was, there *had* been a shift inside her since the Sawyer family had come back to Christmas Bay. And maybe that shift had been on the verge of happening for a while now, and Poppy's arrival had been a little shove, pushing Evelyn toward something she'd been heading to on her own. She wasn't sure. She only knew that it had happened, and she was still trying to make sense of it herself.

She tapped her mug with her fingernail. "Well... I met someone recently. And she was so sweet. She just lost her dad, she's only ten, and I thought she might like the skates."

Paul frowned. "How'd you meet her?"

"At the grocery store."

He looked confused.

"Well, *technically* at the grocery store."

"The grocery store?"

"But I'd seen her before that, so I knew who she was."

He shook his head. "I'm sorry, Ev. I have no idea what you're talking about."

He seemed so bewildered, she had to work not to laugh. It was a moment of levity that she hadn't known she'd needed. What would he say about her softening toward the Sawyers? And not just them, but toward Poppy, in particular? He might think she'd lost every marble she'd ever had. She wasn't sure she could say it out loud. She wasn't quite there yet. But that was okay. She'd take baby steps—there was nothing wrong with that.

"She was on Main Street with Poppy Sawyer a few weeks ago. Poppy is her aunt." Her cheeks heated as she remembered the details of that day. The horror in Poppy's eyes. The sorrow. Evelyn was ashamed that she'd made another human being feel that way.

"Poppy?" Paul asked.

"Yes. Poppy."

"You talked to her?"

"I confronted her."

The look on Paul's face made her feel even more ashamed. Because he wasn't surprised. Hearing that she wanted to be a decent person and give away a pair of their son's old skates surprised him. The fact that she'd ripped into Poppy didn't.

"You never told me," he said.

"I didn't want to talk about it. It wasn't a good day."

Paul knew about Justin and Poppy reconnecting. But Evelyn had no idea how he felt about it, because she never wanted to talk about anything. Especially when it came to Poppy.

"Mary," she said. "That's the girl's name—Mary. She was with Poppy that day, and I recognized her at the grocery store. She broke a jar of pickles and I helped her, and that was it, I guess. We made friends." She watched him for any sign that he thought she was losing it.

"You made friends."

"Yes."

"So you wanted to give her the skates."

"Yes."

"But what about…?" It was obvious he didn't want to finish that sentence, for fear of setting her off. *She's a Sawyer, hon. Aren't we supposed to hate her by association?*

Evelyn couldn't blame him. She'd felt the way she felt, and she'd made it very clear that if he loved her, he would follow suit. She didn't know how he *truly* felt. She hadn't cared enough to ask.

"What about Poppy?" she asked evenly.

He nodded.

"I don't know. I mean, I *thought* I knew. For the longest time, I thought I knew how I felt about her. But now… I just don't know."

"Does this have anything to do with Justin?"

What he clearly meant was, does this have anything to do with Justin *and* Poppy? Together.

Looking down, she tapped her teacup with her fingernail again. Thought on that question long and hard. Finally, she sighed, and looked back up at Paul, who was watching her just as hard.

"I think Justin has been ready to forgive her for a while now."

"I think so, too," Paul said.

"And he's angry with me, because every time he's mentioned trying to move forward, I attack him for it. Because I haven't been ready. But now…"

"Now?"

"Maybe I'm getting closer. And maybe that *does* have something to do with Justin. I feel like he might be showing me how. Does that make sense?"

He smiled at her. Put his hand on her knee. "It makes perfect sense."

She sat there for a minute, so overcome with emotion that she couldn't speak. So she didn't force herself to. And Paul didn't push. They just sat there together, listening to the rain tapping against the kitchen window.

She took a deep breath. Felt it saturate her lungs, giving her clarity where she'd been foggy before. Was it possible that she'd had an epiphany this morning? It wasn't easy to snap your fingers and just *change*. But Evelyn thought she wanted to try.

She was tired of being angry all the time. She was tired of being angry at the world. That kind of anger took a lot of energy, and she was too old to have energy to spare. She just wanted peace. That's what she wanted more than anything.

"I couldn't go back to sleep this morning," she said, "because I kept thinking about Danny."

Paul watched her, waiting. Listening for the first time in what seemed like months. It felt good that they were talking.

"We had a celebration of life for him," she said. "And that was good. We go someplace special on his birthday every year, and I really love that. But I'd like to do more."

"Like what?"

"I'd like to honor his memory by doing something for other kids."

Evelyn couldn't be sure, but she thought Paul looked proud. Proud of Danny, or proud of her, she didn't know. But at this point, it didn't matter. The only thing that mattered was the fact that they were talking about Danny. *Finally*, they were talking about their son.

"What are you thinking of?"

"A scholarship."

Paul's eyes grew misty. "I like that idea, Ev. I like it a lot."

She smiled. "You do?"

"I really do."

"I thought it could be a yearly scholarship for a senior who wants to go to a vocational school. Danny was so good at carpentry. At fixing things, like Justin is. We always thought he'd go to a trade school, remember?"

"I remember."

"So many families can't afford an education for their children. Danny was so generous, always giving kids lunch money, or rides to school when they had to walk. I feel like it would be a natural extension of his spirit. A way to keep it alive."

She took a breath. It turned out that raising the subject of Danny was like a floodgate. Emotions were rushing out and saturating her with love and hope and excitement for the future. For the first time, she could see herself busy with something other than yoga and grocery shopping. Who knew? Maybe the scholarship could turn into something even bigger. Maybe even a foundation in Danny's name. He would've loved that.

"So," she said softly. She knew that her cheeks were probably flushed because they felt hot. She was letting her guard down a little. Even if it was only with her husband, it felt profound. "What do you think?"

Paul didn't say anything. He simply pushed back his chair and stood, then held out his hand to her.

She let him help her to her feet. And then, let herself be wrapped in his arms. Against his chest, where his heart beat next to her cheek. She felt his breath against her hair. And the unmistakable shaking of his quiet sobs. His arms trembled with them, but still, he held her tight. As if their lives depended on it.

Her husband. Her sweet love. He'd tried to hold her like this so many times over the years, but she'd always pushed him away. Because she hadn't wanted to need him. She hadn't wanted to take comfort in his love, because it could be snatched away without warning. Just like Danny had been snatched away.

But now, she closed her eyes and relaxed into him. Breathed in his scent of a freshly laundered shirt and Irish Spring soap. And when her own tears came, they were pure and absolute. They weren't tears of frustration or anger, or even sorrow. They were cleansing tears.

Together, she and Paul cried. And as the rain fell outside, it felt like heaven was crying, too.

Chapter Fourteen

Poppy watched Mary skate back and forth between the aisles of the antique shop, her skinny arms pumping, her elbows sticking out at her sides like arrows. Turns out she was born to skate, something that irked Cora to no end. Her cousin had lectured Mary before leaving to run errands that morning—she was absolutely *not* allowed to skate with customers in the shop. Poppy was supposed to enforce this rule when she was gone, but she'd been a little lax. It was adorable, and honestly, most of the tourists got a kick out of it.

But now, as she watched her niece, there was an unmistakable weight lodged in her lower belly. She was dreading the talk she was about to have with her, but felt like it was the right thing to do. Never mind that she'd been fighting a general feeling of sadness since getting off the phone.

Honestly, she'd been considering keeping Roo. At least on a trial basis. If Justin could make it work at his shop, then she could make it work at hers, too. Especially if Beau and Cora agreed to help out.

But then a woman, an Irish-wolfhound lover, had walked into Brothers' Hardware a couple of days ago, and had seen Roo in her crate. She'd fallen in love instantly, and she and Justin had ended up talking for half an hour.

Her elderly Lab had passed away last fall. She had a little cottage on the beach, worked from home and had no other pets. And when Justin told her that Roo might be up for adoption, she'd said she'd love to give her a forever home.

Justin had told Poppy about this with a drawn look on his face. It was obvious that he wanted Poppy to keep Roo. And so did Mary. But he had to admit what a wonderful home this would be. A dream come true, really—a perfect situation that probably wouldn't come along again anytime soon, if ever. Plus, there was an element of fate to it. At least that's how Poppy felt. What were the odds that this woman would come into the hardware store and see Roo at the exact time that she was looking for another dog?

Poppy knew this might be a way of her subconscious easing the guilt a little, but she'd chosen to lean into it. Roo was a wonderful dog, but she was also a complication at a time when Poppy and her cousins were still trying to get their heads on straight. They were grieving their grandpa, and trying to readjust to being back into town. Plus, who knew what would happen a year from now? Where they would be?

She watched Mary turn the corner and head back up the aisle full of old musical instruments, her roller skates thundering on the century-old hardwood floor. The shop was empty at the moment—Cora would be glad about that. It was also the perfect time to tell Mary about the appointment she'd made to see this lady's house and her yard, and to get a feel about her in general. Basically, it was an interview. An interview to see if she was good dog-mom material.

Poppy swallowed hard, not liking that ever-present weight in her stomach, and cleared her throat as Mary got ready to make another pass.

"Honey," she said. "Can you come over here for a minute?"

Mary slowed, then turned in a showy circle. The planks that made up the floor were thick and scarred. Otherwise, Mary wouldn't have been allowed to skate on them period, even with no customers around. She tapped the toe of one of her skates on the floor and came to a stop with her thin arms in the air, grinning wide. She looked like an ice skater. All she needed was the sparkly costume.

"Sure, Aunt Poppy," she said, skating over to the front counter. She put her hands out and stopped herself in front of the cash register.

"You're getting pretty good on those," Poppy said.

"Yeah. I really like them. Mom had me send a thank-you note to Evelyn. Next time she comes in, I'm going to have her watch me skate. I know how to turn in a circle now, and I can even go backward a little."

Poppy smiled, wondering if Evelyn would be back. For some reason, she thought she might be. Maybe just to say hi to Mary. Maybe for something else, but either way, her coming back to the shop didn't seem like nearly as remote a possibility as it had before.

"Backward, huh?"

"Just a little."

"Maybe we can go to the park later, and you can show me. I know it's harder to get around in here with everything in the way."

Mary shrugged. "It's not too bad. I kind of like it. It's like an obstinkal course."

Poppy bit her lip so she wouldn't laugh.

"An obstacle course?" she asked.

"Yeah, that."

"I'm not sure your mom loves you skating inside."

"I know she doesn't, but she's not here. You are."

Poppy couldn't argue with that, and again had to work to keep a straight face. Ever since Mary had gotten these roller skates, she'd seemed lighter, happier, than when she'd arrived in Christmas Bay several weeks ago. It was an outlet—something she could practice and get better at. It was helping her take her mind off losing her father, even if it was only for a few minutes at a time. Poppy wondered if there might be other kids skating or Rollerblading at the park, too. Maybe Mary could make some friends before starting school in the fall.

She was still pondering this when Mary leaned against the counter and tapped her skate against the floor.

"Aunt Poppy?"

"Mmm."

"What did you want to talk to me about?"

"Oh…um. Well, it's about Roo, sweetheart."

Mary's face lit up, and Poppy realized too late that she should've started that sentence differently. *Stupid.*

"Justin said he met a really nice lady who wants to take Roo home with her," she continued quickly. Might as well just rip off the Band-Aid. "And I wanted to talk to you about that."

Mary's expression, which had been so hopeful a second before, fell. "I thought you were going to think about keeping her."

"I was."

"But now you're not?"

"There are a lot of reasons why having a dog right now isn't a good idea for me," she said, trying to ignore that persistent bricklike feeling in her stomach. The reasons to keep Roo actually outweighed the reasons for rehoming her, but it *would* be easier this way. And Poppy and the easy way out had always gone hand in hand.

"But we would help you with her," Mary said, begging with her eyes.

"I know you would, honey, but I'm not sure if your Uncle Beau or your mom want the responsibility, either. And this would be a good home. A really, *really* good home. This lady, her name is Lisa, she lives right on the beach. She'd take Roo for walks every day, and she said she could even sleep on the bed with her."

Mary watched her, her eyes glassy.

Please don't cry, Poppy thought. If Mary started crying, there was no way Poppy would be able to resist. No way in hell. She'd be putty in the girl's hands, and then what? She'd be a dog owner. But at the same time there was a little voice in the back of her head that whispered, *Would that be so bad?*

"She could sleep in bed with me," Mary said. "I'd take her out for walks and stuff. I'd even pick up her poop!"

This was no small promise, because they both knew Roo required an extra large poop bag.

"Mary, she's so big. She's too big for you to handle."

"But she's gentle—great-grandpa handled her and he was old."

This was true, so Poppy couldn't let herself get sucked into that argument. Instead, she pivoted to a safer place, which was this potential home and how perfect it would be.

"I know you would help take care of her, honey," she said. "And I know you'd be great at it. And it's hard for me to explain this in a way that makes sense, but I just don't feel up to having a dog right now." The little voice in the back of her head took exception to that. *Excuses, excuses. You could do it if you really wanted to. You're just afraid.*

She forced herself to go on. "This would be such a good home for Roo. She'd be spoiled rotten, just like she was with Grandpa."

"But I could spoil her, too."

Poppy sighed. "I know."

"But I understand, Aunt Poppy."

It was almost too much. The look on Mary's face, and the guilt in Poppy's belly.

"You do?"

"Yeah. When Dad was sick, I wanted a hamster, and Mom told me the same thing. It was too hard with everything going on."

Poppy gazed down at her. Nobody was sick right now. Poppy was only being Poppy.

"It's okay," Mary said. "I know you feel bad. I don't want to make you sad about not keeping her."

Poppy didn't trust herself to speak for a few seconds. She balled her hands into fists so tightly that her nails bit into her palms. She focused on the sharp feeling, the little bite of pain, to keep herself on track.

"I was going to take a drive over to Lisa's house," she said after a long moment. "Do you want to come? Help me decide if it's the right place for Roo?"

Mary's expression lightened at this. She was probably happy to be asked. That was something Poppy was doing right at least.

"Yeah," Mary said. "I'll go."

"Okay, we have to wait until your Uncle Beau gets back. He went out to the river to…well, I'm not sure what he's doing. Trying out a new fly or something. But then, we can head out. Maybe we can stop for something to eat afterward? Just you and me?"

Mary smiled gamely, and nodded.

"Okay, kiddo. It's a date."

Mary pushed away from the counter and skated down the nearest aisle. But she looked a little deflated now. A little sad. And why wouldn't she be? Life had been hard for her lately.

Poppy watched her, feeling sad herself. Wondering again if this was the right thing to do.

The road out to Lisa Anderson's house was twisty and narrow. Exactly the kind of road Poppy liked to avoid. If there was a safer route, she usually took it, even if it made the trip longer or more inconvenient. But Lisa lived out of town, off the main highway, on an access road that led through the mountains to the beach, and then wound south alongside it. There was no easier way to get there. This was it.

It was dusk, the sun having gone down a few minutes ago. The sky was gritty and purple, the mountains jagged and dark in the distance. Towering evergreens stood sentry on either side of the road, and beyond that, the forest, black with its nighttime secrets.

Mary sat in the passenger seat playing her Nintendo. Poppy had her turn off the sound a few minutes ago. She didn't like this road, and she especially didn't like this road at dusk. She wouldn't have come out this late, but hadn't realized how far out Lisa's place really was. Not mapping it ahead of time had been her first mistake.

"You all buckled up?" she asked.

"You already asked me that."

"Sorry."

"I thought you said she lived on the beach."

"She does."

"This is the mountains."

"Well, it's the mountains and the beach," Poppy said. "You'll see when we get there."

"It'll be too dark to see anything."

Poppy resisted the urge to sigh. Mary had been sullen since getting in the car. Apparently, the excitement of getting asked to come had faded now that they were actually on their way. She wanted to keep Roo so badly that it was hard for her to be anything but morose about it. Poppy understood that. But if they could just get to Lisa's house, and it was as nice as she hoped it was, maybe Mary would start feeling better about the whole thing. It was a long shot, but maybe.

Mary looked back down at her Nintendo, pushing the buttons with expert ten-year-old dexterity.

Narrowing her eyes, Poppy saw a glowing set of eyes through the darkness, just at the edge of the headlight beams. The woods out here were alive with animals, and Poppy could feel them watching the car as they passed. It was eerie, unsettling. She'd always loved the forest, but she had a healthy respect for it, too. Growing up in the Pacific Northwest in a town that teetered on the edge of the ocean meant that nature had to be respected, period. People who didn't usually ended up regretting it.

"Aunt Poppy?"

"Mmm?"

"What do you think happens to us when we die?"

Poppy glanced over at her niece, then quickly looked back at the road.

"I'm sorry…what?"

"What do you think happens? Do you think we go to heaven? Or do you think it's something else? Like we come back as a dog or a cat or something?"

"I…" If anyone else had asked her this, she would've been able to give a quick, honest answer. *Yes, I think there's some kind of afterlife.* And leave it at that. But this wasn't just anyone. This was Mary. Mary, who'd just lost her father to cancer. Poppy's answer needed to be thoughtful and nuanced. Not just thrown out there to satisfy her for the moment.

"Evelyn believes in heaven," Mary said. "She believes in angels. Well, she said she likes the idea of it, and that's almost the same thing."

Poppy tightened her grip on the steering wheel and shifted in the Mercedes's soft leather seat. "She said that?"

Mary nodded.

"What do you think?"

Mary looked out the window. "I think there's a heaven. It makes me feel better to think that."

"I'm sure it does. And the thing is, heaven is probably a little different for everyone. My idea of it might be different than yours, and yours might be different from Evelyn's. And that's okay."

Mary continued looking out the window as Poppy eased the car around a particularly tight curve. There were no guardrails up here, which made her nervous.

"I miss my dad," Mary said.

Poppy glanced over at her niece again. She couldn't be sure, because the car was fairly dark now, but she thought she might be crying. Her face was turned away, her hair falling next to it in fine waves.

"Mary…"

She didn't answer. Just continued looking out the window.

Slowing at another curve, Poppy cursed herself again for coming out here in the dark. Of course, it hadn't been dark when they'd left the shop, but she'd known it would be dark when they got back, and who the heck didn't map addresses in advance these days? Maybe it was the fact that Mary was definitely crying now, and there was no place to pull over safely, but Poppy had a feeling of mild foreboding in her stomach.

She maneuvered the Mercedes around another sharp curve, and wondered again if this whole thing with Roo was a mistake that she wouldn't be able to fix once the wheels were set in motion. And hadn't she made enough mistakes to last a lifetime? Hadn't her grandpa known a thing or two about his granddaughter? Even if she couldn't see how this might be good for her, *he* obviously had. He'd known enough about Poppy to write down his wishes in his will. And what was she doing? Looking for the easy way out. As usual.

Beside her, Mary was sniffling softly. Missing her father. Trying to be brave about saying goodbye to a dog, and a potential companion and friendship that had never been realized.

Poppy felt the sting of tears at the backs of her own eyes. She missed her grandpa. She missed the safety and warmth of the little antique shop on Main Street. And she missed Justin—the beginning of something special that had taken her by surprise. She felt small and unanchored now, navigating this decision about Roo alone, and she hated that feeling. It was true that Mary would survive this latest disappointment. In the grand scheme of things, it wasn't life or death. But why should she *have* to survive anything else? Why should Poppy? And what was she doing out here in the middle of the woods, in the dark, looking for the easiest road, when she knew damn well that nothing in life was easy? At least nothing worth holding on to. It seemed so obvious now, that her head felt dizzy with the sudden clarity.

She reached for Mary's hand. When she found it, she squeezed the girl's fingers. And Mary squeezed back. She may have been sullen a few minutes ago, but it was clear she trusted Poppy. She trusted that whatever decisions she made would be the right ones, simply because she was the adult, and Mary was the kid.

It made Poppy want to hug her close, and tell her how sorry she was. About her dad, and so many other things. She was just sorry, that was all. But here, in the darkness of the car, for the first time, it felt like some of those things could be fixed. And if they couldn't be fixed, at least she might be able to learn from them. To grow from them.

Grazing her bottom lip with her teeth, she wondered if this was how Evelyn was starting to feel. Maybe it was why she'd come into the shop with the skates. Maybe it was a step toward finding some of that goodness, and grabbing on to it with both hands. Poppy realized right then how much courage it must've taken for Evelyn to have done that. How gutsy it had been.

"Mary…"

The girl turned. She could feel her gaze on her.

"What if we decided to keep Roo?" she asked.

Mary sucked in a breath. Bolted up in her seat, making the Nintendo slide off her lap and onto the floor with a thump.

"Just on a trial basis," Poppy said quickly. "Just to see if it could work."

"Aunt Poppy! Are you serious?"

Poppy smiled at the dark, winding road ahead. "No promises. I still worry it could be too much. But maybe we could give it a shot. Would you still be willing to help out? Give her walks and feed her? Pick up her poop?"

"*Yes!* Yes, yes, yes. Anything!"

"A trial basis, okay?" Poppy said. But it was obvious there was no unringing this bell. Mary was about to lose her ever-loving mind. And that made Poppy very, very happy. Whatever happened with Roo, they could tackle it as a family, because that's what families did. Her grandfather had known that from the beginning.

Mary bounced up and down in her seat, making the leather squeak. "Yes, a trial basis! And I promise to help out. She won't be any trouble, Aunt Poppy, I promise."

Poppy knew better than that, but it was sweet, nonetheless. "I haven't talked to your mom or Uncle Beau about this yet…"

"I think they'll be excited, too. Don't you think?"

"I'm not sure." This reminded her of bringing stray pets home when she was a kid. If one parent agreed, the other wouldn't. And there were always tons of reasons why *it wasn't a good idea right now*.

"I think they'll *love* having a dog," Mary said, unfazed.

"I hope so."

"Oh, I know they will. She's so cute! Don't you think she's *so* cute?"

Poppy smiled. There were a lot more things that went

into having a dog besides it being cute, but Mary was right. Roo *was* cute. And she had the potential to be therapeutic for them all. Of course, it would take a while for her to get used to being with Poppy and her cousins over Justin, where she was obviously so happy, but deep down, for the first time in days, Poppy felt at peace with this decision. A decision made with her heart. And that felt right.

"Lisa will be disappointed," she said. "But I know she'll understand."

"Maybe she can adopt a dog from the shelter. We could even help her find one."

"Well, maybe."

"And we can always bring Roo out to visit her. Do you think she might like that?"

"I'm not sure I want to tackle this drive again anytime soon."

"Aunt Poppy?"

Poppy glanced at her niece. Just for a second. Her eyes were big and dark, the expression on her face unmistakably happy. Again, she knew she'd done the right thing.

And then, Mary screamed.

Poppy looked back at the road, and time came to a stop. But it didn't quite stop, that wasn't the right word. It slowed. It slowed to a drip of molasses on the coldest day of the year. It crawled like a dying man toward water. And Poppy felt every single movement that her body made. Her eyes widening, when she saw the deer jump in front of the car. Her foot stomping on the brake pedal. Her ears acknowledging the screech of the tires. Her arm shooting out to hold Mary against the seat. And her heart, slamming against her rib cage. Pounding out every second of every minute of every day and month and year that had passed since that first accident that had changed everything.

She was aware of the single question flickering across her brain as the car narrowly missed the deer, and careened toward the edge of the road... *Will this be another accident that changes everything?*

She knew in that split second, in that lightning bolt of time, that there would be no recovering from another one. There would be no forgiveness. There would be no redemption. There would be no grace. She would never be able to extend any of those things to herself, and she wouldn't want to, anyway. The only thing that mattered was Mary. Just like the only thing that mattered before was Danny.

But accidents didn't care who mattered or who didn't. They happened to everyone. No matter how much anyone didn't want them to, or how much people thought they were prepared for them. No matter how many walls someone built up around themself, life had a way of crashing through them, anyway.

Poppy was vaguely aware of those thoughts, those brief snippets of brain activity and feeling and emotion, as the tires skidded on the pavement, and then onto the gravel at the shoulder of the road. She wrestled with the steering wheel, turning into the skid, like she'd been taught. But she'd learned that lesson too late, hadn't she?

The screeching of the tires pierced her ears. So familiar. So terribly familiar.

Mary screamed again. Danny had never made a sound. There hadn't been time. The car had flipped and metal had crunched, and that had been the end.

This time though, this car—this dark, shiny, expensive car—skidded instead of flipping. It skidded on the gravel and down an embankment, and Poppy sent up a prayer that there wasn't a cliff at the edge of this embankment. That they wouldn't fly off the edge into the cold, dark ocean.

And then, like the hand of a giant reaching down, the car slammed into a tree, and came to a merciful stop.

Poppy sat there as the world came to a stop along with the car. Sound stopped, movement outside the windows stopped. Her heart was the only thing that seemed to keep going, pounding in her ears, in her throat.

She turned to Mary, petrified of what she might see. She wanted to close her eyes, to squeeze them shut like a little kid, and pretend this was all a dream. But it wasn't, and she was the grown-up here. So she did look. And miraculously, so very miraculously, Mary sat there looking back at her. She was the same beautiful girl who'd climbed in the car with Poppy a half hour before.

"Aunt Poppy?"

It was only then that Poppy was aware of the tears streaming down her face. She was scaring Mary, and she was already scared enough. Her niece was also holding her arm, cradling it next to her chest. But other than that, she looked okay. Unhurt, untouched. Miraculously. Poppy kept thinking of that word over and over and over again. *Miraculously.* They could've been killed. But the tree had stopped them.

She glanced past her niece at the gaping darkness beyond. No other trees, just darkness. It was a cliff she was looking at. Just like she'd been afraid of.

"Aunt Poppy..."

Mary's face contorted. The shock was beginning to wear off, and it was obvious she was in pain now.

"Sweetheart," Poppy said. "Try not to move, okay? I'm going to call nine-one-one. I'm sorry. I'm so, so sorry."

"It wasn't your fault."

Poppy absorbed the words that, just like the screeching tires, were so familiar. *It wasn't your fault.*

Mary seemed to be alright, at least as far as serious injuries went, but she'd still be traumatized because of this. And for Poppy, it was the opening of a wound that had just begun to heal. It was wide-open now, and bleeding freely. She wasn't sure if she'd be able to get past this. And maybe she *shouldn't* get past it. It was as simple as that.

"Please don't cry, Aunt Poppy. Please."

Poppy took her niece's face gingerly in her hands, and kissed her cheek. Mary would never know how much she loved her. Or how much her sweetness meant in this moment. But Poppy would never forget it as long as she lived.

And then, she dug her phone out of her purse and called for help.

Chapter Fifteen

Justin climbed into his truck and shut the door behind him, the rain drumming steadily on the roof.

He looked out over the cemetery, which was a subdued kind of beautiful this morning, with the mist and the wet spring grass that was the exact color of the Irish countryside. He'd never been to Ireland, but he'd seen pictures, and it was on his bucket list. A bucket list that seemed to be growing by leaps and bounds lately.

He knew why. Over the years, he'd decided that if Danny couldn't live his life, Justin would live it for him. So he'd begun to add things to his list—places to go, things to see, accomplishments to be completed. The hardware store had been one. Forgiving Poppy had been another. Because Danny would've been the first to hug her and tell her it was okay. Danny had been an exceptional hugger.

He looked up the hill at his little brother's grave, where there were now two bouquets of fresh flowers. The one Justin had brought this morning, and another that had already been there. He wasn't positive who'd brought it, but he could guess. He knew Poppy came up here often. She always had, even right after the accident, when visiting the cemetery had been the hardest for everyone. At least it had been for him. As angry as he was at her back then, a part of him liked knowing Danny was in someone else's heart, too. That he wasn't forgotten.

He sat there thinking about how things had evolved these last few weeks. How they'd moved from something turbulent, into something calm. He no longer blamed Poppy for anything. He no longer felt anything but love for her, and that was why he was up here this morning. It was silly, really, because he knew that Danny, wherever he was, would be okay with whatever direction Justin's life took. Even if it was in the direction of Danny's one true love. But Justin still felt like he needed to talk it over with his brother. He felt like he needed his blessing, however strange that might seem to anyone else.

As the late spring rain streamed down the windshield, Justin felt nothing but peace. Nothing but gratitude, because he'd finally entered a new phase of his life. He'd discovered the man he'd always wanted to be, but had been too afraid of embracing until just recently. A man who could forgive wholly, and love without reservation. And he'd been shown the way by the unlikeliest of people. The woman who'd been driving the car the night his brother had passed from this world.

He sat there, lost in his thoughts, in the memories, until his cell phone buzzed, jarring him back to the present. He picked it up, and saw Poppy's name on the screen. His chest filled with a long-forgotten anticipation. She was back in his life, and calling him on an ordinary spring day.

He cleared his throat and answered. "I was just thinking about you," he said.

There was a moment of silence on the other end of the line. A beat or two where he wasn't sure she'd heard him.

"You were?"

He could hear background noises. People talking, some beeps and buzzes. He wasn't sure where she was, but she wasn't in the antique shop. He switched the phone to his other ear and frowned, watching the raindrops make their way down the windshield.

"I need to talk to you," she said. "Are you going to be at the store today?"

His pulse tapped in his neck. He didn't like the sound of her voice. Something was wrong—he could feel it.

"I am. But if you need to talk, let's do it now. What's wrong?"

More silence. He could hear someone over an intercom in the background… *Please report to patient services…*

The tiny hairs on the back of his neck stood on end. She was at the hospital.

"I didn't want to do this over the phone," she said.

"Are you okay?"

"I'm okay. I'm fine."

"Then what the hell is going on?"

Anyone sitting next to him would assume he was angry. But he wasn't. He was scared. Ever since the accident, he lived in a perpetual state of fear that someone else would be taken from him. That fear came across as biting sometimes, hard to read. But it wasn't anger. It was never anger.

"I'm at the hospital—"

"I know."

"Mary and I had an accident last night. We're fine, we're okay. But a deer ran out in front of us, and we went off the road. She's getting an X-ray of her arm, they had to wait until the swelling went down, but other than that, we're okay."

Her words were coming in a rush. She was desperate to

let him know that it wasn't more serious than it was. She'd know, of course, that this would be triggering for him, and it wasn't an easy phone call to make. And she could say she was alright until the cows came home, but he knew better. This was triggering for her, too.

Justin put his head in his hand. Feeling so emotional that he couldn't say anything right away.

He could hear her sniffing on the other end of the line. She was probably crying.

"Poppy," he said quietly.

"No. Let me say this now, or I won't be able to."

He waited, staring at the rain coming down. In his gut, he knew what she was about to say. Because Poppy wasn't used to sticking when things got hard. At least, she hadn't all those years ago. He realized, even as he thought it, that that wasn't fair. His own mother had basically run her out of town. She'd been a kid then who was struggling. But she wasn't a kid now.

"I thought I was getting to a point where I could let myself need someone again," she said. "I was actually letting myself fall—"

She stopped short. He could hear her breathing hard on the other end of the line, and he ground his teeth. He wasn't going to tell her it was okay. He wasn't going to make this easier for her, even though every instinct he had was screaming to do just that. Protect her. Wrap her in his arms and keep all the bad things away. But that wasn't life. That wasn't reality. Bad things happened. People just had to push through to get to the other side, and so far, Poppy hadn't pushed hard enough to get anywhere.

"Letting yourself fall," he said. "Letting yourself fall... what?"

She paused, and the silence nearly broke him in half. His heart, which had been pounding before, slowed to a dull thump inside his chest. He hated this. He hated everything about it, but he was too old to play games.

"I was letting myself fall in love with you," she finally said, her voice hitching. "And that's not going to lead anywhere good, Justin."

He clenched his teeth. He sure as hell didn't want her telling him where this would or wouldn't lead. He wanted to take her in his arms and kiss her long and hard, and find out on his own. Now, he might never know.

"Say something," she said. "Please."

"What do you want me to say? That you're right? That we're doomed? I can't say that, Poppy, because I have no idea what would happen between us, what we'd become. That would take a leap of faith. And that's something we'd *both* have to take. Not just one of us."

She laughed, but it was bitter-sounding. "You're saying you'd want to take a leap of faith with me?"

"I'm saying I already have."

The words settled between them. He couldn't blame her for wondering how he'd taken that leap of faith, he couldn't help but wonder himself. Not because Poppy wasn't worth it, but because he was supposed to be the angry one. The one who couldn't get past his brother's accident. The one who couldn't forgive and move forward. But somehow, he was here. At this place where he was holding out his hand to her, and she didn't trust him enough to take it.

"I can't do this, Justin," she said quietly.

"You mean you *won't* do it."

More sounds in the background. More doctors being paged, more machines buzzing. He knew he was probably fighting a losing battle. In order to move forward, Poppy was going to have to *want* to move forward. She was going to have to trust him, and that might be too much to ask of someone who didn't trust anyone at all. Least of all herself.

"Do you want me to say I'm scared?" she asked. "Okay. I'm terrified."

"I am too."

"You only make it worse when you do that, you know."

"Do what?"

"When you're so nice to me," she said, biting out the words. "When you're so *understanding*."

"I'm sorry that I understand how you might feel."

"Stop it. Just stop it, Justin. When I thought you hated me, it made sense. I was comfortable with it because I hated myself, too. But this doesn't make any sense."

"You don't want it to make sense, Poppy."

"I *can't*."

"So you're going to leave again? Is that it? Is that what you're getting at?"

"I'm not leaving." She sounded farther away now. More accepting. Probably because she'd made up her mind that whatever he said, she wasn't going to let him sway her.

"I'm going to stay," she continued, "because Cora and Beau need me here. And so does Mary. And I'm going to take Roo, because that's what Grandpa wanted, and I owe him that. But as far as you and I go, I'm just not there yet. I meant what I said. I'm not the same person I used to be."

He rested his head back against the seat and closed his eyes for a second. When he opened them again, he focused on the mountains in the distance. On the mist shrouding them. It seemed like a safer place than looking at anything in his truck, which felt too small all of a sudden. Too claustrophobic.

"You don't think the person you are now is worthy of love," he said evenly.

"Well, no. Maybe not."

"I'm here to tell you that you are. And I'm sorry you can't see that. I'm sorry for you, because it's all I *can* see."

He heard her exhale a long breath, and then sob. He thought of his mother then, and how she'd been so consumed with anger and grief all these years. How she hadn't been able to move forward, either. They'd all been stuck because of Danny's death, and there was no way to get unstuck, except to claw their way out. He thought he'd be able to help Poppy with that, but he'd been naive to think that just because he loved her, she'd be able to love him back.

It was a realization that made him swallow hard and grip the phone tighter. He stared out the window, numb except for the tingling in his fingers. He didn't know what to say. Or if there was anything *to* say.

"I have to go, Justin," she said. "The doctor just came in."

He forced himself to relax. To breathe in and out again. In...out.

"Take care of yourself, Poppy," he said.

And hung up.

Finally back home, Poppy sat on the edge of Mary's bed, watching her sleep. She'd dozed off a few minutes ago. A few minutes after Poppy had turned the last page of her favorite book, *The Giving Tree*. It had been Poppy's favorite as a kid, too, and she'd savored reading it to her niece. Slowly, so as not to come to the end too soon.

She sat there now, the book warm in her hands, and stared down at Mary's arm that had a bright purple cast on it. Beau had already broken out the Sharpie and had drawn a cartoon fish jumping out of the water toward a cartoon man holding a fishing pole. It was pretty impressive, really. If his fishing career didn't pan out, he could always fall back on art.

Mary looked cozy all wrapped up in the flannel quilt that Poppy's grandpa had sent her last Christmas. He'd been so sweet like that. Always thinking ahead, never forgetting a birthday or holiday.

Poppy's chin trembled as she tucked the quilt carefully around Mary's arm. She missed her grandfather now more than ever. He would've been the first to offer words of wisdom last night. And this morning, when she'd told Justin that she couldn't see him anymore. Her grandfather would've been there, giving advice, giving hugs, helping her put things into perspective. Poppy had always been rotten with perspective. To her, any mistakes she made were monumental, and nothing anyone could say would change that. But her grandfather had still tried his best, and helped where he could. And when he couldn't help, he'd offered a shoulder to cry on.

Mary sighed and turned her head into the quilt. She was okay. She had a broken arm, but it wouldn't require surgery, and she'd actually been excited to get the cast and pick out the color. Kids were so resilient. That's what Beau had said when he'd pulled Poppy into a very grandpa-like hug. *She's fine*, he'd said. *Just look at her!* She'd been eating ice cream at the time, giggling at something Cora said. She *had* looked fine. But Poppy still felt horrible.

Her cousins, her niece and the police who'd shown up

last night, had all said this was an accident that could've happened to anyone. Poppy wasn't speeding, she hadn't been intoxicated or looking at her phone. She hadn't done anything wrong. Accidents happened, end of story.

Except for Poppy it wasn't the end of the story. It was just a continuation of a long, drawn-out tale. A nightmare, really. A dark place where she kept having accidents, she kept hurting people and she was never going to be happy again. Not really. And anyone who wanted to love her, like Justin, never stood a chance.

Biting her bottom lip, she eased herself off the bed, and with one more look at Mary, tiptoed out of the bedroom.

She walked into the kitchen and set the book down on the counter, where Cora was making a couple of cocktails. Espresso martinis, Poppy's favorite. She might have trouble sleeping tonight, but that wasn't anything new. Since coming back to Christmas Bay, her mind usually raced the minute her head hit the pillow. Thoughts of Justin, her grandfather, Danny, Evelyn—they all dipped and bobbed behind her eyes like birds in flight.

"*The Giving Tree*, huh?" Cora said, handing her a martini. "Mary's favorite."

"I know. Mine too."

Cora wiggled onto one of the barstools at the counter. Poppy eased herself on one too, and took a sip of her drink. It was strong, but that was okay. She needed something strong tonight.

She and Cora were quiet for a minute, with the clock ticking above the stove. Beau had gone out to pick up some Thai food, and would be back any minute. It was late for dinner, but it had been a long, tiring day. When he'd offered to go get takeout, Poppy had practically cried with relief, realizing that she hadn't eaten in almost twenty-four hours.

She looked over at her cousin now, and licked the sweetness of the martini from her lips. She'd lost track of the amount of times she'd apologized at the hospital, but another one teetered on her tongue, anyway.

Cora watched her over the rim of her glass, and held up a finger. "Don't say it."

"Don't say what?"

"You know what. It could've happened to me, or Beau, or anyone."

"But it didn't."

"No, it didn't. It happened to you, because you were sweet enough to take Mary with you last night. She was so happy you asked."

Poppy sniffed. "Yeah. And now she has a broken arm."

"We can thank the deer for that."

"Right."

Cora ran her finger over the rim of her glass, her eyebrows furrowing. "I'm just so grateful to you and Beau right now, Poppy. You have no idea."

Her cousin's eyes grew misty, and Poppy frowned. "Hey. I'm supposed to be the one crying here. What's wrong?"

Cora stared at the countertop, and it was clear she was trying to compose herself. She hadn't mentioned Travis since moving in, and Poppy had assumed it was still too fresh, too painful. But now, she wondered what else might be going on.

"Being here," her cousin said, "it's brought up a lot of things for Mary. Since losing her dad, she's been asking questions. She's been curious about Neil."

Poppy exhaled. That was a name she hadn't heard in

a long time. Neil Prescott had been Cora's high-school sweetheart. He was also Mary's biological father, something Mary had always known. Cora had wanted to be honest, telling her daughter about Neil from the time she was in Pull-Ups. But Mary had such a wonderful father in Travis, that she'd never wanted to know anything more about Neil. Until now, apparently. It made sense. Mary was a preteen, and she'd just been through an enormous trauma. Something that would change her fundamentally. And, of course, with the grief would come questions. Curiosity.

"What are you going to do?" Poppy asked.

"I'm not sure. I've been expecting this. But you know, I thought it would be when she was a bit older. And I always thought Travis would be here to help me with it."

"Beau and I are here for you. You know that."

"I know. And I don't know what I'd do without you. But I'm not telling you this because of Mary."

Poppy bit the inside of her cheek, waiting. Cora had dark shadows underneath her eyes. She probably hadn't slept last night, courtesy of another accident that could have changed their lives forever.

"I'm telling you," Cora continued, "because I overheard you talking to Justin at the hospital."

"Oh…"

"I was getting some coffee and I heard you on the phone. I'm sorry. I didn't mean to eavesdrop."

"Are you kidding? You have nothing to be sorry for." Poppy was aware of the irony here. It was refreshing to say this to someone else for once, instead of someone saying it to her.

"Anyway," Cora said. "I heard you. And I know you've

decided not to see him anymore. Poppy, that's a mistake. Believe me. I've been there."

Poppy watched her closely. They'd been nearly inseparable as kids. As adults they'd gone their separate ways, and hadn't confided in each other often. Still, she thought she knew Cora pretty well. Like a sister. And this caught her off-guard.

"What do you mean?" she asked. "Are you talking about Neil?"

Cora nodded.

"But you loved Travis."

"I did love him," Cora said. "I *do* love him. Of course, I do. He was a perfect husband and father, and we had a wonderful marriage. All of that is true. But Neil..."

A boat sounded its horn in the harbor, a reminder that life was moving forward outside the four walls of the little apartment. Even though to Poppy, it felt like she and her cousin had stepped back in time.

"Neil was different," Cora said quietly. "We were so young, and so in love. We had this connection that..." She shook her head. "It's hard to explain. But I loved him very much. And I let our circumstances, our families, drive us apart."

"You can't take all the blame for that, Cora. I was there. I saw what happened. Neil let you go."

Cora shook her head. "It doesn't matter anymore. What happened, happened. But in the end, we lost each other. He was my first love. If I could go back and change things between us... I don't know. I'm just saying that I might."

Poppy wasn't sure what to say. She'd never seen Cora, who was always so stoic, seem this unsettled. Sad? Yes, of course. But this was different. Poppy knew, because she'd been living in a permanent state of unsettled since high school. It wasn't a nice place to be.

"Just give him a chance," Cora said. "Give whatever is happening between you a chance, Poppy. After all this time, you deserve it. And so does he."

Poppy took a breath to answer, but before she could, the door opened behind them. Beau came in holding two plastic bags full of takeout, and the apartment immediately smelled warm and spicy.

He stopped in his tracks. "Uh-oh."

"What?" Cora asked.

"You two are having one of your talks."

Of course, he'd be able to tell they were in the middle of something heavy. Their heart-to-hearts used to be legendary. He'd learned as a teenager to leave them alone when they got to talking.

Without waiting for an answer, he walked over and started unpacking their dinner.

Poppy licked her lips and took another sip of her drink. Thinking about what Cora said just now, so matter-of-factly. *After all this time, you deserve it.*

That was the problem. She still wasn't sure she did.

Chapter Sixteen

Poppy stood outside the hardware-store door—off to the side, where Justin wouldn't be able to see her if he glanced outside. She just needed a minute. Time to gather her wits, time to settle her thoughts. The same ones that had been churning so chaotically over the last few days.

She'd made up her mind. She'd gone over and over this, and still wasn't able to come up with any other way forward. At least not with Justin. Not right now. She had too many things to work through. She thought she'd been close, but the accident with Mary had taken the gains she'd made since coming home and dissolved them like sugar in a cup of coffee.

She stood there on the sidewalk, thinking about that very first day when she'd been on her way to see Roo with Mary, and Evelyn had stopped her. It felt like a hundred years ago now.

A woman walked past and muttered an *excuse me* as she reached for the front door and pulled it open. The hardware store scent wafted out—that woodsy, leathery smell that reminded Poppy so much of Justin. It gave her butterflies, even as she was getting ready to go in there, gather up Roo and tell him this was it. It would be easier on everyone if they didn't see each other for a while. At least not outside of normal, merchant business on Main Street.

But what she really wanted to do was to run the other way. Because she knew she loved someone that she wasn't going to give a chance to love her back. No matter what Cora had said, no matter what her heart was begging for. Her brain *knew* this was the smartest thing. And maybe later, much later, when she was alone, she'd let herself cry. Grieve this loss. This chance to be loved. But right now, she'd just have to soldier on the best way she knew how.

Taking a deep breath, she reached for the door and pulled it open. Again, she took in the scent of the shop, of Justin himself, and let it permeate her senses. No use fighting it.

Her belly tightened as she looked over at the front counter, expecting to see him there. Expecting him to make this hard for her right off the bat. But he was nowhere to be seen. Neither was Roo, whose empty crate was visible from where she stood.

Something nudged her hand, and she startled. Looking down, she saw Roo standing there, looking back. The dog gazed up at her with those liquid caramel eyes, and before Poppy realized what was happening, she'd licked her hand again.

"Roo, come."

The dog turned and meandered obediently back to Justin with a wag of her long tail.

Poppy let her gaze settle on him. On his tall, muscular frame. On his handsome face, where a new beard was coming in nicely. On the way he was watching her, with such obvious affection in his eyes.

She smiled, unable to help it. And he smiled back. The

shop wasn't quite empty, but the two or three browsing customers were several aisles away. There was also a teenage boy stocking paintbrushes next to the counter. Technically, she could ask Justin to step outside with her, but if she waited to say this, even a minute or two, she knew she was going to lose her nerve. It needed to be now. Before he reached for her. Before she went to him. Customers watching be damned.

"I got your message," he said. "I have all her things ready. Her food and toys. Her favorite blanket."

Poppy's heart squeezed at this.

"You'll probably want her crate. I can bring that over later," he continued. "But honestly, she doesn't really need it anymore. She might be a little homesick for me at first, but she'll get over it. I'm sure Mary will help with that."

Poppy nodded. Mary was over-the-moon excited for her aunt's new dog. But everyone knew she was really going to be Mary's.

She and Justin stood there for a minute, watching each other. And then Poppy looked down at her feet, at her new tennis shoes that she'd bought the other day. They were more practical for standing around the antique shop than the cute little ballet flats she usually wore. She was finding she was starting to care less and less about how she looked, and more and more about how she felt.

"Justin…"

"If this is about us," he said. "I don't really want to hear it."

He couldn't have known what she'd been about to say. But then again, maybe he did. Maybe he knew, and he was going to be nice about it, like he'd been nice about everything else so far.

"I have to say this," she said.

"You did. You said it over the phone the other day."

"I feel like I have to explain things better."

"You already explained them," he said. "But it doesn't matter, anyway. Because I'm choosing to hold out hope that you're going to snap out of this. That you're going to find a way to love yourself again."

She stared up at him, and he took a step forward. He smelled so good that her stomach dipped. How she longed to step into his arms, to let him hold her and kiss her, and tell her all the things she wanted to hear. But she was simply too scared. She'd already had so much loss in her life. The loss of Danny, her innocence, her family. She didn't think she could take the loss of Justin, too.

So she stood very still, trying to ignore the way he smelled, and the flecks of green in his eyes. How kind he was, and especially how kind he was to *her*. She pushed away all of those things by sheer force of will, and raised her chin just the slightest bit. Enough to fool herself into thinking she was strong enough to resist him. Even though the energy between them was like an electrical storm—snapping and popping and driving her over the edge with longing.

"I'm doing you a favor, Justin," she said. "Believe me."

"No. You *want* that to be true, because it'd be the easiest thing. But the truth is, we're very much alike, Poppy. We always have been."

"I can't do this."

"You've said that, too."

He stood there looking down at her. But to his credit, he didn't reach for her. She didn't think she would've been able to stand it if he had.

Maybe this was it. Maybe he was finally going to let her go.

"Poppy—"

She held up a hand, tears threatening at the backs of her eyes. She didn't want to cry. She didn't want to let him see how tempted she was to believe everything he'd told her these last few weeks. She just wanted to take Roo home to Mary, and start nursing what was left of her heart. She wanted to get as far away from Justin and his magnetism as she could, before the waterworks started in earnest.

"Don't," she said. "Please. I really want to be strong. But if you say anything…"

He nodded, seeming to understand where she was coming from on a primitive level. He might want to argue with her decision, but he wasn't going to. At least not right now.

"Let me just get Roo's leash," he said evenly. "I'll bring the rest of her things this afternoon."

Poppy swallowed down the lump in her throat as he disappeared in the back room, and then reappeared holding a long leather lead.

He walked over to the dog and kneeled down beside her. She immediately leaned into him, and he put an arm around her, holding her head next to his face.

Poppy watched this through blurry eyes. She was trying her best to hold it together. But all she could think about were the circumstances that had brought her here. To this moment in time. She missed her grandfather. She missed Justin, even though he hadn't gone anywhere. She was the one going. She'd always been the one who left.

Justin gave Roo a good pat, and then stood. He handed Poppy the leash, and to her surprise, the dog came with a slight tug on the lead. She trusted Poppy to take her where she needed to go. That kind of trust, that kind of acceptance, was humbling.

Without another word, Poppy took a step toward the door. Roo stood there for a second, and watched Justin, obviously confused. But in the end, she followed Poppy out the door with the gentlest of whines.

Poppy knew how she felt. Her heart was breaking, too.

Justin watched them go. His stomach was upside down, and there was a dull throbbing at his temples.

He didn't know how he'd let this happen. He'd planned on not letting her out the door without saying how he felt first. Without all the other crap in the mix—without all of his bitterness from before. He wanted her to know how he felt *now*. Right now, right this minute. And somehow, he'd let her leave without uttering a single word.

He scraped a hand through his hair, frustrated at how easy it had been to slip back into that old fear that had kept him from reaching out to her all these years. Even though he'd had a lot to say for a while now. She'd stood there just now looking at him with those clear blue eyes, and he'd given in to his fear. But he'd also given in to hers as well.

"Tyler," he said.

"Yeah, boss?"

The teenage boy turned from the display of paintbrushes with a questioning look on his baby face. He was the best help Justin had ever hired—smart, hard-working, good with customers. He was a senior in high school and had been applying to colleges, so he'd be leaving in the fall. But Justin had convinced him to come back and work for him over the summers. He was a good kid, and he also reminded him of Danny. So, truthfully, he'd have a job here until the end of time, if he wanted it.

"Watch the counter for me, okay?" he asked. "I'll be right back."

He didn't wait for Tyler to answer. He was out the door before he could think twice about it.

He jogged down the sidewalk, the ocean air cool against his skin. Tourists stepped aside, giving him room to pass, holding their bags close as if he'd snatch them on his way past. It was comical, really. It felt like a scene out of a rom-com, him running down the street to declare his love. But he guessed that's why so many movies ended this way. So many books, so many songs. It was because standing by and letting love slip through your fingers wasn't an acceptable ending. Nobody wanted a story to end that way.

He passed a large group of people coming out of the café a few shops down. They parted to let him by, and then he saw her. Standing at the crosswalk, waiting for the light to change. Roo standing obediently by her side. She had her hand on the dog's head, and was rubbing her ears.

Justin slowed, taking in the image. The woman he'd loved for so long now. But it hadn't been acceptable to love her, had it? Society said he couldn't, his family wouldn't have been able to comprehend it. And the people in town? The ones whose memories were so long? Forget about it.

But that was the thing—he didn't care who approved of this and who didn't. Even his parents, whom he loved fiercely, would just have to learn to live with it. For the first time in Justin's life, he was going to do what felt right for him, not what was right for anyone else. And if it was a mistake, a monumental lapse in judgment, he'd learn to live with that, too. Because life was short, and he was done walking through it so damn gingerly.

"Poppy," he said, his voice carrying over the group of people on the sidewalk.

She turned.

"Wait," he said.

"Justin, no."

"Just wait a minute."

He felt no less than a dozen people watching curiously. He hadn't meant for there to be an audience, but it was what it was.

Roo wagged her tail.

He walked up and held his hand out, and she licked it eagerly. "Good girl," he said. "Good girl, Roo."

"What are you doing?" Poppy asked.

"I need to say something. I should've said it a long time ago. I should've said it just now, but was too much of a coward apparently."

She glanced at the small crowd behind him. "Here?" she asked. "Now?"

"Right here. Right now."

His heart was beating in his throat. She was so beautiful, inside and out, but she'd had a hard time believing that. So much had happened since that rainy homecoming night. Life had been bumpy since then, hard. Sometimes it had been so hard, he wasn't sure how he'd get through it. But he had. And he was standing here now on the cusp of something that he knew might be hard, too. But it would also be worth it. Good things always were.

"I love you, Poppy Sawyer," he said.

The look in her eyes was one of such disbelief that he stepped forward and took her face in his hands. The fa-

miliar ocean breeze blew against the back of his neck, reminding him of everything he'd always loved about this
town. Of everything he'd always loved about Poppy. She'd
been gone for years, but somehow that feeling had been
resurrected inside of him, stronger than ever.

He ran his thumbs along her cheekbones, vaguely aware
that the little crowd surrounding them had grown.

"I love you," he repeated, quieter this time. "You don't
have to love me back. That's okay. I just wanted you to
know. You're a good person, Poppy, and you deserve to
be happy again."

She took a shaky breath. He wasn't fooling himself that
his feelings for her would magically fix what was wrong.
But maybe, just maybe, they were a place to start.

She opened her mouth to say something, but before she
could argue and tell him that she wasn't ready, or she didn't
deserve this, or whatever else she could come up with, he
leaned down and kissed her.

Her lips were soft and warm. She tasted impossibly
sweet. *And she kissed him back.*

The crowd around them erupted into applause. There
were some whistles and cheers. They thought they were
witnessing a happily-ever-after.

Justin still wasn't sure what this was. But before he
could question it, he wrapped his arms around her and
pulled her close. Where he'd always wanted her to be.

Chapter Seventeen

Poppy picked up the antique picture frame and wiped it down with the worn rag that she'd found in the back. Her grandpa had cut up one of his old robes years ago, and used the flannel squares to clean all the silver and glass pieces that came into the shop.

Her throat squeezed as she held the rag in her hand, so soft against her fingertips. She knew the pattern well—little blue stars against a white background. She remembered the robe from when she was little. She could almost smell her grandpa in its fibers, but, of course, she knew that was impossible. His scent was long gone from it now, but her heart still remembered.

"Aunt Poppy, look!"

Poppy glanced over at her niece, pulled from the comfort of the memory. She found that her memories were more and more like that lately. More comforting than sad. More soft than sharp.

Mary had Roo sitting politely in front of her, waiting for her next treat.

"Shake!" Mary said.

Roo stuck out one of her ginormous paws, and Mary grabbed it.

"Nice to meet you," Mary said, and gave Roo the treat.

They were special salmon-flavored training treats that Beau had picked out himself. He'd gone to great lengths to get the healthiest, tastiest treats he could find at a specialty pet store in Eugene. Which Poppy thought was going a little overboard, but nothing was too good for Roo, who'd become their official shop mascot. Everyone loved her. The customers were charmed by her, of course. But her new family adored her most of all. Turns out, the Sawyer cousins had needed a dog, they just hadn't known it until one had been left to them in a will. Just like magic, their grandpa had waved a wand, knowing exactly what would bring them all back together again. A dusty antique shop on Main Street. And a big, wiry-haired dog who slept underneath the covers. Mary's covers, to be exact.

Poppy grinned. "Well done, honey!"

Mary draped her cast-covered arm over the dog's shoulders and leaned in for a kiss. Roo was never short on kisses.

"I'm going to teach her to speak next," she said proudly. "The book says that one's pretty easy."

Poppy set the picture frame down on a lovely vintage coffee table that Beau had picked up from a dealer last week. "She's so smart, and has such a good trainer, I know it'll be a breeze."

"I'm gonna go show Mom," Mary said. "Be right back."

The girl jumped up and jogged to the back of the shop with the dog at her heels. They disappeared into her great-grandfather's office, which Cora now used to do the books. It was a comfortable space, a cozy spot to get work done. Mary had done her homework back there during her last few weeks of homeschooling. Next year, she'd be enrolled at Christmas Bay Middle School, but for now, she was enjoying the beginning of her first summer vacation on the coast.

Poppy turned toward the counter, where the roses she'd gotten that morning were sitting in a pretty glass vase. Their fragrance filled the space, reminding her of the flowers in her grandmother's garden. She'd been very little when her grandma died, and her memories of her were foggy, but she clearly remembered her roses.

And these roses were special, too. Because these were from Justin.

Taking a deep breath, she pulled her phone from her back pocket and brought up the text thread that she'd had going with him for the last few months. Since she'd come home to Christmas Bay. Over the last several weeks, since their kiss on the sidewalk, their texts had grown longer, more intimate. More personal.

It had been a slow process, but one day Poppy realized she was texting Justin first thing in the morning, and the last thing before going to bed at night. She was telling him things about herself that she'd never told anyone before. And he was opening up to her, too. He'd told her he loved her, but there was so much more to say. And she found that she was here for it. She was here for all of it.

Thank you for the flowers, she typed out. I love them. But what's the occasion?

It only took a minute for her phone to ding with a response.

No reason. Just because.

She smiled down at the text, feeling her entire body warm at the words. They'd taken things slow since that kiss. He'd made it clear that if she wasn't ready for more, that was okay. And if she was never ready, that was okay, too. But he'd wait for her, just in case. He'd wait as long as it took for her to get to a place where she would be able to put her doubt, her fears aside.

She could feel herself getting there. It was like his love and patience were water for her very parched, very withered soul. And she could feel herself blossoming with that love. Slowly, slowly, slowly. He was bringing her back to life again.

The door to the antique shop opened with a tinkle of the bell above it. Poppy had learned to love the tinkling of that little bell. Every ring meant a new opportunity. A chance to talk to someone she hadn't met before, or to someone she'd met before and liked. A friend. A fellow shopkeeper. A tourist who kept coming back year after year to the antique shop that was beginning to gain a reputation along the coast for its unique treasures and its friendly atmosphere. Dogs were welcome, kids were welcome, everyone was welcome. That was their motto.

Poppy turned with a smile on her lips. Lately, she was a happier person. And she wasn't sure what had led to that. She guessed it was a lot of things. A lot of wonderful things.

But when she saw who had walked through the door in perfectly fitting yoga pants and a matching sky-blue pullover, her smile wilted a little.

Evelyn.

Poppy hadn't seen her since the day she'd come in to give Mary the skates. At least not up close. She'd seen her in town. She'd seen her drive by in her little Fiat, the top down and her hair blowing in the wind. Poppy had been struck by that, because the word that had automatically come to mind had been *carefree*. And that was not a word she associated with Evelyn Frost.

The older woman walked toward her now, taking off her sunglasses and looking around. Poppy thought of that first day on the sidewalk, when Evelyn had swiped off those same sunglasses and stalked up to her to draw blood.

Today was different. Poppy could see that now as the other woman's lips eased into a smile. As her eyes warmed, incredibly, as she got closer.

Poppy glanced behind her to see if anyone else was standing there. Cora maybe, or Beau. Or Mary, whom Evelyn obviously had a soft spot for. But there was nobody in the room but Poppy.

"Hello, Poppy," she said.

Poppy felt her pulse tapping in the hollow of her throat. "Hi, Evelyn."

There was a beat or two. A moment between them that was heavy with meaning, but Poppy wasn't quite sure where it was going.

"The shop looks nice," Evelyn said. "Really nice. I've been meaning to come in and look for an end table for our living room."

"Oh?"

"I've been collecting older pieces. Our house is kind of eclectic now. That's what Paul says, but I think he likes things with history. I got rid of all my old Pottery Barn stuff and started fresh."

Poppy smiled. She liked things with history, too. It came with the territory when you'd grown up in an antique shop.

"Anyway," Evelyn said, glancing around again. "I've been meaning to come in…"

After a few seconds, the other woman's gaze settled on Poppy again. And there was an expression on her face that Poppy hadn't seen before. It was a look of vulnerability.

"I've been meaning to come in," Evelyn continued, her voice thick. "But not because of the table."

Poppy exhaled. Bracing herself. She hadn't been sure when Evelyn would come back to finish the job she'd started that first day. But Poppy had been expecting it.

She felt her knees trembling. Felt her stomach quiver with nerves. Yes, she'd imagined this moment plenty. But somehow, the reality felt worse. Because she'd let herself begin to love Justin, despite everything. She'd begun to explore the possibility of forgiving herself. She'd begun to picture what that might look like, what that might feel like. She'd taken an important step, even after the setback from the accident with Mary.

And now, she knew there would be another setback. Another ripping open of that delicately closed wound. But the difference was, today she was prepared for it. It would hurt, but today there was a new hope that she'd be able to stand up again after that initial blow. That she'd be able to catch her breath after it had been knocked from her lungs. She was just beginning to find her strength. And her worthiness. It had taken a long time, and she still had a long way to go, but it was a start.

She forced her chin up, her shoulders back. Not in defiance of what the other woman was about to say, but as a reminder that she could take it.

Evelyn swallowed visibly and licked her lips. She really was a beautiful woman. She'd grown prettier in the weeks since Poppy had been home. There was a smoothness to her features that hadn't been there before.

"This has been a long time coming," Evelyn said. "And I'm ashamed of that. I'm ashamed of a lot of things, but I've been lost for a long time."

Poppy watched her, her heart barely beating at all now.

"Losing a child does something to you," she continued. "A part of me is gone forever, and that part will never come back. But there's a part of you that's gone, too. You've suffered, too, Poppy. You've suffered in a horrible way, and I'm so sorry that I wasn't able to see that until now."

Poppy blinked, and tears, sudden and hot, spilled down her cheeks. It was as if someone had turned on a faucet inside of her. They flowed freely, silently, like they'd been held behind a dam for the last ten years.

Evelyn gave her a small smile and stepped closer. "I should've hugged you that night. In the hospital. I should've held you close and told you that it wasn't your fault, and that I was so happy that you lived. I should've done that. I should've made sure that another child wasn't lost to that accident. I should've been there for you, and I wasn't. I don't think I'll ever forgive myself for that."

A sob escaped Poppy's throat. And then another. Until she felt her shoulders shake with them, one after the other.

Evelyn took another step forward. Until Poppy could smell her perfume. Until she could feel the warmth and softness she was radiating, when for so long she'd been nothing but cold.

And then, incredibly, she pulled Poppy into a hug. She cupped the back of her head and pulled it down to her shoulder, where Poppy cried like a girl.

"Can you forgive me, honey?" Evelyn asked.

Poppy blinked and focused on a spot across the room where her grandfather had kept the antique vanities. The really special pieces that had been in some families for generations. She saw the reflection of herself in Evelyn's arms. The other woman was holding her with such tenderness, that for a minute, she worried she wouldn't be able to speak at all. This was what she'd wanted her entire adult life. She hadn't always been able to put it into words, and she hadn't always been able to admit it to herself in her darkest moments. But this was what she'd wanted. This was what she'd *needed*.

"Of course, I forgive you," she whispered. "Do you forgive me?"

There was a moment where everything stood still. The earth. The ocean. And even the pounding of her heart.

"Sweet girl," Evelyn said. "There's nothing to forgive."

Justin leaned against his truck with his hands in his jean pockets. It was a warm summer day. He'd left his sweatshirt at home, and wore only a light T-shirt, liking the way the soft breeze felt against his arms.

He looked at his watch. She'd be here any minute. Poppy had called that morning asking to meet him here at noon. Tyler wasn't going to be in until later, so he'd had to close the hardware store, which was fine. He was finding that he'd go to just about any length to see her these days.

Running a hand through his hair, he looked over at the sound of a car coming up the dirt road to the cemetery. An electric blue Subaru that was bouncing over the ruts in the road like it had been made for this kind of thing. Which he guessed it had.

He smiled. He was still getting used to seeing her in anything other than the sleek black car that she'd arrived in all those weeks ago. But when she'd turned it in after the lease was up last week, she'd said she wanted something different to match her new life.

He watched her pull up next to his truck and cut the engine before she opened the door and climbed out, the breeze immediately catching her silky blond hair and whipping it around her face.

Reaching up to hold it back, she smiled. And like the color of her little car, it was electrifying. He felt the pulsing warmth of it in his chest, where his heart beat so heavily for her.

She held up a bouquet of flowers, a vibrant arrangement of different kinds of blooms that he wouldn't have been able to name if he'd tried, and walked toward him.

"I thought we could come here together for once," she said. "It's such a pretty day."

Justin let his gaze move past her to Danny's marker on the hill. It *was* a pretty day. A day that felt just about perfect in all the ways that mattered. Since his mother had come in to see Poppy at the antique shop, Justin's life had completed the shift it had begun that spring. Things that had been complicated for him before were now simpler. Things that had been painful were now bearable. He wasn't just existing from day to day, weighed down by sadness and regret. He was *living*. Something he was sure his little brother would be proud of.

Poppy stepped close and wrapped her arms around his waist. Tilting her head back, she looked up at him with such love that it shook him, even now. But the fear he'd felt in the beginning, the terror of letting himself feel the really heavy stuff, had receded to the point where the heavy stuff was what brought him the most happiness lately. Yes, there was always the chance that it wouldn't work between him and Poppy. But there was also the chance that it would.

"I had a dream about Danny last night," she said.

He moved her hair away from her face. The face that he'd once thought had been made for television. It had been perfect then, a little *too* perfect. Standing this close, he saw the imperfections in her skin—the freckles and feathery lines at the corners of her eyes. The imperfections were what made her beautiful. Now, she was just Poppy. And he loved her.

"You did?" he asked, cupping her cheek in his hand.

She closed her eyes. The cellophane that the flowers were wrapped up in crinkled. He felt her holding them tightly against his back. She held him tightly, too. As if she needed him to steady her. But he knew by now that she didn't *need* anyone. Poppy was a strong woman. So much stronger than she'd ever given herself credit for. In Christmas Bay, she was the truest version of herself, and he liked to think their journey together might have something to do with that.

"I did. He was laughing at something I'd said. I can't remember what it was now. But he was doing that belly-laugh thing he did sometimes. Remember that? How he'd get so breathless, and he'd make everyone else laugh, too?"

Justin's throat tightened, but the pain was fleeting. In its wake was only a peaceful feeling that moved through his entire body. He missed his brother. But he also knew his presence would guide him for the rest of his days, and that was a comfort.

"I remember," he said.

She bit the inside of her cheek. "I loved that laugh."

"Me too."

"Do you think he's okay, Justin?" she asked.

It was a question that had been asked since the beginning of time. By millions and millions of people who'd been left behind. This question was the same for everyone, no matter what religion, no matter what walk of life. Justin felt like it bonded humans everywhere. But the answer was what was most important. The answer that he couldn't prove—nobody could.

He leaned down and kissed her. She smelled good today, sweet, like sugar. He could smell the scent of the flowers moving in the breeze, the spring grass, tender and green up on the hill. He could hear the ocean waves crashing onto the beach in the distance, a marriage of water and sand. A love story for the ages.

He realized that despite the pain, he wouldn't trade this moment for the world. Life was pain. It was also healing and love and light. He was so glad that he and Poppy had found each other again.

"I think he's okay," he said quietly. "I think we're all going to be okay."

Epilogue

Poppy stood in the small auditorium at Christmas Bay High School, and shifted on her feet. She was wearing heels tonight, something she hadn't donned since her days in Portland. Working at the television studio seemed so hazy now, so far away.

These days, she was all about jeans and blouses. And the ever-present ballet flats that reminded her of her childhood.

But heels had seemed right tonight. She'd wanted to look her very best, and had even bought a new dress for the occasion. Something that was bright and floral, that also reminded her of her childhood. Of those roses in her grandmother's garden. Meaningful things were important to Poppy now. Things that brought her joy. She was getting better and better at embracing those feelings and moments. But she hadn't gone through this metamorphosis on her own. She'd had help from her family, and a few new friends.

She looked over at the front row, where Beau, Cora and Mary were sitting. Cora had been crying, dabbing at her eyes with a tissue that Beau had shoved into her hand.

And then there was Justin. He and Paul were sitting on the other side of Beau, looking handsome in their blazers and ties. Father and son, sitting amid an entire room full of people who'd come to see this. To support her, and to support Evelyn, whose brainchild this was. But mostly, to remember Danny, who would've been twenty-nine years old today.

The auditorium was dark and cool, the air-conditioning working overtime. Poppy felt goose bumps rise along her arms, but she thought that had more to do with what Evelyn was saying into the microphone than the temperature of the room.

The older woman smiled and glanced over at Poppy. She looked lovely tonight. Fit and polished, as usual. But happy and relaxed, too. Her eyes were bright, but she hadn't cried yet. She'd kept it together in order to say everything she'd needed to say, and that made her Poppy's hero.

The auditorium was full of the soft sounds of people shifting in their seats, coughing every now and then, rustling their programs. High-school seniors and their families who'd come to this awards night on the eve of their graduation. They were about to fly. And Poppy's heart was soaring with them.

"And with that," Evelyn said, "I'd like to announce the inaugural Daniel James Frost Memorial Scholarship. This is for a student who'd like to go to a trade school, like Danny would have."

The auditorium erupted with applause. Poppy felt the warmth of the stage lights against her skin, which was at odds with the chilly air-conditioning. Butterflies fluttered against her rib cage as her gaze settled on Justin. He was smiling at her. He mouthed *I love you*, and the tears she'd been holding back all night threatened at the backs of her eyes.

I love you, too, she mouthed back.

"It's my pleasure," Evelyn said, "to introduce to you, Poppy Sawyer, who was a dear friend to our son. And a dear friend to our family. It wasn't always that way, but that's what losing someone ultimately teaches you." Her voice broke and she softly cleared her throat before going on. "Danny taught us to love each other. To forgive each other. And to live life with intention. Poppy, will you come up here, please?"

Poppy stepped forward on wobbly legs. Evelyn wrapped her in a perfumed hug, kissing her on the cheek. Then she handed her an envelope, and Poppy gave her what she hoped wasn't too shaky of a smile. If Evelyn could do this without crying, she could, too. Would it be easy? No. But Poppy wasn't a stranger to hard things.

As Evelyn stepped aside, Poppy moved up to the microphone, and adjusted it a little. The feedback was loud, making her jump. Everyone laughed, and so did she. A welcome moment of levity. Something Danny would've appreciated for sure.

"I'm humbled to be standing here tonight," she said, "getting ready to award this scholarship to one very deserving senior at Christmas Bay High. Danny was a wonderful person, someone I'll carry with me always. He'll be with me in everything I do, and everything I'm able to accomplish. And I know he'll be with all of you, too. Not just the recipient of this scholarship, but with all of you."

She looked over at Evelyn, who was looking back with pride. Poppy didn't think she'd ever felt such peace in her entire life. It was a word that was used a lot, but it was the perfect one for this moment. *Peace.* It was a white dove, a vibrant sunset, the beat of a healing heart. It was all those things. And she was so grateful that she had found it at last.

Taking a deep breath, she let her gaze rest on Justin again. Sweet Justin, whom she'd also found at last. And then, she tore the envelope open.

"And the winner of the Daniel James Frost Memorial Scholarship is…"

She smiled, letting the joy in.

All of the wonderful joy.

* * * * *

Don't miss Beau's story,
the next installment in Hearts on Main Street
Kaylie Newell's new miniseries
for Harlequin Special Edition.
Coming soon!

HARLEQUIN
Reader Service

Enjoyed your book?

Try the perfect subscription for Romance readers and get more great books like this delivered right to your door.

See why over 10+ million readers have tried Harlequin Reader Service.

Start with a Free Welcome Collection with free books and a gift—valued over $20.

Choose any series in print or ebook. See website for details and order today:

TryReaderService.com/subscriptions